With

compliments

of the

publisher

HarperVia
An Imprint of HarperCollins*Publishers*

> UNCORRECTED PROOF
> – NOT FOR SALE –

The Dilemmas of Working Women

> This galley does not reflect the actual size or design of the final book. Reviewers are reminded that changes may be made in this proof copy before books are printed. If any material is to be quoted or referred to in a review, the quotations or reference must be checked against the final bound book. Dates, prices, and manufacturing details are subject to change or cancellation without notice.

The Dilemmas of Working Women

stories

Fumio Yamamoto

Translated from the Japanese by Brian Bergstrom

HarperVia
An Imprint of HarperCollinsPublishers

This is a work of fiction. Names, characters, places, and incidents are products of the author's imagination or are used fictitiously and are not to be construed as real. Any resemblance to actual events, locales, organizations, or persons, living or dead, is entirely coincidental.

THE DILEMMAS OF WORKING WOMEN. Copyright © 2000 by Omura Koji. English translation copyright © 2025 by Brian Bergstrom. All rights reserved. Printed in the United States of America. No part of this book may be used or reproduced in any manner whatsoever without written permission except in the case of brief quotations embodied in critical articles and reviews. For information, address HarperCollins Publishers, 195 Broadway, New York, NY 10007.

HarperCollins books may be purchased for educational, business, or sales promotional use. For information, please email the Special Markets Department at SPsales@harpercollins.com.

Originally published as *Planaria* in Japan by Bungeishunju Ltd., © 2000 Omura Koji. All rights reserved.

FIRST HARPERVIA EDITION PUBLISHED IN 2025

Designed by Yvonne Chan

Library of Congress Cataloging-in-Publication Data has been applied for.

ISBN 978-0-06-342358-9

$PrintCode

Contents

Naked
000

Planarian
000

Here, Which Is Nowhere
000

The Dilemmas of Working Women
000

A Tomorrow Full of Love
000

Naked

Lately I'd become obsessed with sewing stuffed animals.
　　I'd seen a bear in a store and thought it was cute, so I went to a hobby shop and saw they were selling kits that included the yarn, needles, and other little things you'd need to make any sort of animal. It seemed to be a thing. I bought a kit and went home and made a frog that very evening. I went back the next day and bought more kits: a dog, an elephant, a cat . . . every kind they had. I made one every night until I'd made them all; the next time I went back, I just bought yarn and felt and some buttons to use for eyes. I'd figured out the trick to it after about the fourth kit, so I wanted to start trying out my own designs. But apparently I'd lost any ounce of creativity I'd ever possessed, and the hippopotamus I made turned out not the slightest bit cute. So I went to a bookstore, bought a Pokémon handbook, and then made one Pocket Monster after another, starting with Pikachu. I was so into it that I forgot to sleep, forgot to eat, and out came Monster after Monster:

Jigglypuff, Togepi, Psyduck, Bulbasaur, Charmander, Squirtle, Eevee... but soon enough, I got bored with them too. So, thinking I'd try my hand at making a stuffed version of my PostPet, Momo, I turned on my computer for the first time in a while and saw that there were over twenty emails waiting in my inbox.

I had once been obsessed with PostPets too, these little animal characters who'd deliver your email; most of the messages were from "e-friends" I'd made on the PostPet site—I didn't know their real names or faces. Animals would appear—bears, turtles, hamsters—only to disappear, leaving letters behind in my inbox. The messages themselves were never anything of any importance, but the point of it was to make my little Pet deliver and receive messages, so while I was never particularly gratified, I was never particularly disappointed either. But today, waiting there in my inbox, was a bear named Momotaro from Asuka's House.

The content of the message was an invitation: *I'll be in Shinjuku next Saturday shopping for the Bon Festival, do you want to grab lunch?* Counting from the date on the email, "next Saturday" would be tomorrow. *Maybe I should call*, I thought, but then remembered how busy she was and decided to email a reply instead. *Whenever and wherever is fine by me.* The call from Asuka came before two hours had passed.

"It's been so *long*! How are you *doing*? I never got a reply, so I figured you were busy and decided not to bother you."

She seemed still unused to the idea that I had nothing but free time on my hands these days.

"I wasn't busy. How could I be? I don't do anything."

I'd meant to say it lightly, but Asuka grew silent on the other end of the line, seemingly at a loss. Worried that I'd said something wrong, I hurried to explain myself.

"The thing is, last week I got wrapped up in doing something and it started to interfere with my sleep, so I fell behind checking my email. It wasn't a job or anything, but still."

"What was it?"

"I'm sewing stuffed animals! Some of them have turned out really well, I'd love to show them to you."

There was no answer. It seemed I'd left her at a loss once again. I pretended not to notice and chattered on.

"What time should we meet tomorrow? I'll fit myself into your schedule."

A housewifely sigh escaped Asuka.

"I don't know whether to be happy or sad, hearing that from you of all people."

We decided on a time and place to meet and hung up. I found that I was neither particularly happy nor particularly sad. I just felt vacant, a white blank.

Soon it would be two years since I'd become unemployed. At first, the descriptor *Unemployed, Age 34* had sounded almost like a criminal charge, but I got used to it soon enough. Indeed, my ability to adjust so easily appalled me. Now I inhabited the identity—since revised to *Unemployed, Age 36*—body and soul.

It was two years ago that my husband told me he was divorcing me, which, since we had run his company together, meant I ended up losing my job too. Naturally, I reacted badly at first to this sequence of events, but the period of angry protests and crying jags was really quite short, and I acquiesced to receiving my settlement and removing my name from the family register with an ease that surprised even myself. What was this lack of attachment? It was as much a mystery to me as to anyone.

So this life of mine, this life of uncertainty, of not knowing if

I even wanted to do something with myself, simply continued, never dipping all the way into depression or desperation. Looking out the window from where I lay in bed, I could see the tall buildings outside shrouded by falling rain. It was July, but the long rains persisted.

About half a year ago, I was obsessed with making elaborate outfits for teddy bears, and I ended up giving all of them to Asuka for her kids. It occurred to me that I could do the same with these animals I was making, but the moment it did, I felt myself losing my will to create any more. I'd always had a personality that ran hot and cold, but now that my life had become one of infinite leisure, it was much worse. Giving yourself over to any old irresponsible urge feels good, though. It was even possible that, against all odds, I was happy.

The next day, I ate lunch with Asuka in a restaurant located among the rows of tall buildings I could see from my window. "This is for your little girl," I said, handing her a paper bag stuffed with a Monster I'd made, but she didn't seem as grateful as when I'd given her the teddy bear outfits.

"Oh! It's Pikachu, from Pokémon . . . uh, wow!"

Asuka seemed to be working hard to manufacture her enthusiasm.

"Does it look all right?"

"It looks great, just great! You know, now that I think about it, you've always been good at stuff like this, Izumi, arts and crafts and home ec. Are you sure it's all right for me to take it home?"

"Oh, I just made it because I wanted to make it. To kill time, you know."

"Thank you," said Asuka, and she indeed took it, but it was clear something was bothering her. I hadn't sewn the thing with anyone in particular in mind and had even been thinking of getting rid of it on the next garbage day myself, so if she covertly threw it out, it made no difference to me.

Asuka was a childhood friend since elementary school, the only one I still had. A working mother of two, she'd switched from part-time to full now that her youngest had started school. Busy with work and childcare, she still found room in her schedule to meet me from time to time. Before, I was the one who'd had trouble finding time to meet up, so it was quite the reversal now that she was no longer the one trying to accommodate another's schedule.

"You look thin, Izumi."

This was hospital-patient treatment. It was painfully clear how careful she was being, and I started to feel bad.

"Really? I don't weigh myself, so I don't know."

"Your color's not good."

"I'm not wearing any makeup, that's all."

Sitting there in this restaurant filled with tables draped in pure white cloth and decked out in cutlery of real silver, I knew how bedraggled I must've looked. Asuka wasn't dressed up, wearing just a summer-weight sweater set, but her hair was neatly done and her makeup exquisite; a pearl necklace shone from where her collar opened. By contrast, I was wearing a faded ringer tee and a pair of cargo pants that were all stretched out around the waist. I no longer bought clothes I couldn't just throw into the washing machine. Asuka should have been the one exhausted from the pressures of everyday life, but there I was, not even bothering to hide the dark circles under my eyes that clearly marked me as the one whose life was wearing her down.

"Are you still collecting unemployment?"

"Oh, no. That ended a while ago."

"Well, maybe it's time to look for something, if only to clear your head."

I could tell she was trying very hard, choosing her words carefully, and I laughed a bitter little laugh.

"I will, I will. Thanks for worrying about me. I have enough to get by for a while longer, it's okay."

"Money's an issue, of course, but it's not the only one..."

Muttering this to herself irritatedly, she brought her water glass to her lips. I knew what I could say to soothe her, but I decided to say something else.

"I've gotten tired of making the animals. I think I'll try my hand at sewing *yukata* this summer."

"I see. You might as well carve erasers into little shapes!"

She just said it, exasperated, and I dropped my eyes to my plate. When you say something cruel, it only makes sense you'll get something cruel in response. As we brought forkfuls of our respective fish dishes to our mouths in the suddenly tense atmosphere, Asuka got a look like she'd just thought of something.

"Why don't you make a website to sell them? If you've made all these nice things already."

"They're hardly 'nice things,' just silly knockoffs."

This time she didn't even try to hide her sigh. Perhaps deciding that no matter what note she struck nothing would resonate, a motherly smile spread across her face as she said, gently, "It's not easy getting back on your feet, is it? I'm sorry. I won't say anything more about it."

Before, I'd been the one to play the older sister, listening to Asuka's worries about her job and family, but at some point I'd become the unstable younger sister who needed to be handled with kid gloves. But if I never went back to being the suit-wearing hard driver so busy I'd cancel two or three times for every lunch date we scheduled, would she ever see me as truly "back on my feet"? It was depressing to imagine being compared with my previous self and subjected to disappointed sighs every time we got together.

I told her not to, but Asuka insisted on paying for lunch. Being unemployed means being treated to every meal you're invited to. It wounded my pride at first, but it was such a bother to put up a fuss that lately I just went with it. Asuka was hardly wealthy. She worked full-time because there was no way they'd make their mortgage payments and pay for their kids' educations on her husband's salary alone. Yet she still went shopping for other people's Bon celebrations and treated her unemployed friend to fancy French lunches. Even though that friend was jobless by choice. Even though that friend had ¥20 million yen in the bank. What would she have said if I'd told her that? Well, she was surely pure of heart enough to leave it at *You'll need that for your retirement, don't waste it now.*

We parted promising to email each other, and then, my desire to make things with my hands having cooled, I found myself with nothing in particular to do to pass the rest of the day and ended up going to a manga café.

There was one in particular I liked on the second floor of one of those buildings filled with all sorts of little businesses. It seemed like the businesses in those buildings changed all the time here in the heart of the city, what was once a lingerie bar becoming a massage parlor fifteen minutes later, but lately it seemed like every block had at least one manga café. For a while, I went around trying each new one as they sprang up here and there and everywhere, but in the end, it turned out to be this place, one of the first I tried, that had the deepest manga collection and the most courteous staff. Their all-you-can-drink coffee wasn't simmered into sludge, and since their prices were a little on the high side, the clientele tended to be a bit older than at other places; but what really decided it for me was the clean white sofa placed in a lovely, harmonious spot in the main room. Not being a smoker, I could ensconce myself there with no trouble in the comparatively underpopulated nonsmoking section.

Today I found a complete set of Osamu Tezuka's *Buddha*, which had always had its first few volumes already claimed by someone else whenever I'd looked for it before, and I checked out the whole thing, brought it to my table, and started reading. Soon I was so engrossed I even forgot to drink my coffee. After about the third volume, though, the thread of my concentration snapped, and I glanced out the window to find that it was already getting dark. I didn't wear a watch, so I didn't know what time it was. I went to the bathroom, refreshed my coffee, and as I passed by the counter to look at the clock on the wall behind it, I saw that it was already seven in the evening.

The napping salarymen around me had been replaced by a growing number of what appeared to be students. *Should I go home, or should I see* Buddha *to the end?* I mused as I sipped my coffee. I'd eaten a proper lunch for once, so I wasn't hungry, and it wasn't like I had any plans for tomorrow, or the next day, or the day after that, so what did it matter? Without a way to prioritize your activities it's almost impossible to decide on something to do. My eyes wandered over the shelves near me. I noticed that *Maison Ikkoku* was there, its volumes lined up in a neat little row, and I remembered that I'd started it once, back when I was a student myself, but never knew how it ended—*I'll read that next*, I decided. Suddenly filled with the desire to hurry up and finish *Buddha*, I stood up. When all was said and done, I ended up staying there late into the night finishing the whole set and then walking the twenty-minute walk back home. I found myself surrounded by drunks all the way there, and I ended the night drifting off to sleep thinking my usual self-pitying thoughts.

It occurred to me that I'd never really known the true meaning of having free time, what sort of state it really was or what it really felt like, until now. It was different from being bored. I'd been bored countless times before. In high school, sitting in class staring at the face of a teacher exponentially worse than the one in my cram school; in college, unwillingly brought along to a singles mixer; while working at the import-export company, trapped in a meeting that kept dragging on and on—I'd stifle my yawns and bear the boredom as I pretended to listen, making other, more meaningful plans in my head.

The meaningless and the meaningful. For a long time, I thought that these were the only two kinds of time there were in the world; it never occurred to me there might be others.

In high school, all I ever had time to do was worry about entrance exams, but once I got into college, things loosened up a bit and I began to have a little fun; still, I never forgot to focus on the tests and papers I had to write. Fellow students would come to me asking to borrow my notes, and even though I knew they muttered behind my back about how much of a grind I was, I'd let them copy them with a smile. To see those who'd mocked me suddenly humble themselves to win my favor became my secret joy.

Yamamoto Fumio

I applied to work at a midsize import-export company rather than a major one because I figured it would be the quickest way to become self-sufficient. And I was right—before long, I was given more and more responsibilities. If the plans I made succeeded, it was obvious, taking the form of maximized profits, and the pleasure this brought soon absorbed me completely. I'd get an idea, and it felt like no hardship at all to do whatever it took to realize it—however much research, however much schmoozing, however many sleepless nights. And none of this changed when I met my husband and quit my job to begin working with him. I loved working and hated being lazy. It was such a simple mode of being, it occurred to me now. I never wavered, not even once. Just before the divorce, my husband complained about my "empty, money-hungry" way of life, and at the time, I simply had no idea what he was talking about.

So all the way from childhood to my midthirties, this kind of life sustained me. And even now, I didn't see the satisfaction I felt as some sort of delusion, but it also never occurred to me that what I'd always taken to be solid ground beneath my feet could turn out to be so thin and fragile a layer of ice. When it broke, I thought I'd sink to a frozen death, but instead I found myself floating in this lukewarm water called *free time*. Lolling about in it was so much easier than I'd imagined, and at this point I'd lost sight of any motivation strong enough to make me drag myself back out.

I opened my eyes, once more unsure of how many hours I might have slept. It was hard to keep track of what day it was, as I didn't take a newspaper and my television had been broken since last month. I turned on the radio; a daytime program was playing. It was an AM station I never listened to. I was struck anew by the mysterious pleasure that comes with hearing the same voice at the same time every day.

I grabbed the watch lying next to my pillow and checked the date and day of the week. It was a name-brand chronograph my husband had bought me one Christmas. My name was engraved into its back, so even if I wanted to sell it, I couldn't; besides, it was a convenient enough thing to have around, so there I was, still using it.

My dilapidated one-bedroom in West Shinjuku was drenched in the humidity of the rainy season, and I could see where mold had begun to grow on the peeling wallpaper in the corner. Built twenty years ago, the concrete walls had cracks visible from the outside, and the kitchen furnishings and the window sash were shabby and cheap, but it wasn't a rental—it was mine, bought with my own money. My life here was so much more relaxed than the one I'd lived in the top-floor waterfront apartment I'd shared with my husband. When I left that apartment after the divorce, I found this place advertised in a newspaper insert; I could afford to buy it outright with my settlement, so I did. And I didn't regret it, but sometimes I did look back at myself then and wonder what I'd been so scared of. Was it that I couldn't be sure that I'd be able to keep up with rent or loan payments, so I needed to secure a roof over my head, no matter how rinky-dink? Surely I could have found something better for the same price in the suburbs, but leaving downtown hadn't even occurred to me. Living in a suburban apartment building surrounded left and right and up and down by happy, respectable families would surely have driven me crazy anyway. If I'd wanted a place where an unemployed, single woman in her late thirties would be inconspicuous, my impulsive choice turned out to have been a pretty good one.

Half of this broken-down building was office space and the other half was presumably places where people live; it was hard to say for sure. From time to time I would run into someone else wearing a T-shirt and jeans and waiting, like me, for the elevator, a plastic convenience store bag hanging from their grip. Whoever they were I'll never know, since we studiously avoided exchanging pleasantries or even glances; like two couples running into one another at a love hotel, we scurried to escape the other's sight as fast as we could.

A light rain was falling outside today as well. It was muggy, and, thinking I should maybe turn on the air-conditioning, I rose from my bed. I fished for the remote amid the drifts of dust bunnies and candy wrappers and manga weeklies, but as I went to activate the "dehumidify" mode, the numbers on the LCD screen faded before my eyes. Thinking the batteries must have run down, I took out the ones from my alarm clock and replaced the ones in the remote. But still, nothing appeared on the little screen. I let the thing fall from my hands back onto the floor. I pulled a chair over and stood on it so I could see if there was somewhere on the air conditioner itself to put batteries, but I couldn't figure it out. The television didn't work anymore either, and neither did the light in the kitchen. I imagined all the things in the apartment breaking down like this, one after another, until I was the only thing left and ended up breaking down too; it felt like someone else's problem, not mine. I also lacked the will to call a repairman—it all just seemed like too much bother.

I should have been so happy to have all this time to myself at last, and yet all I seemed able to do was waste it.

Ever since I'd left school, every day had been so busy, and I'd had a mountain of things I wanted to do if only I could get a moment to myself. The business I'd run with my husband sold traditional handicrafts and things of that sort, and I longed to tour the various places they were made. The main store was near Asakusa, so we had a lot of foreign tourists come in, and I'd wanted to get in touch with a tea master or flower-arrangement teacher to set up a little curriculum to give these tourists a taste of traditional Japanese arts. I'd always found myself refusing my friends' invitations to do things together, and I dreamed of going out to dinner or off to a hot spring with someone to whom I had no obligations. I wanted to go to the gym more than once a month, I wanted to go to the spa for a facial, I wanted to travel overseas more often, I wanted just to go shopping—if only I had the time to do it all!

But of course, as soon as I had the time, these things all lost their meaning. As soon as I was no longer in the position to give input into my husband's business or influence it in any way, the calls from everyone who'd been competing for my time and attention stopped, as if it hadn't been me, the individual, they'd wanted so badly to see, but rather me, the successful co-owner of a handicrafts store. It turned out I'd only felt the need to work out because my husband liked going to the gym, and I no longer desired designer clothes either, or the treatments meant to preserve some small portion of my youth. It turned out that the real me didn't really like going out at all, and preferred instead to stay at home sewing or whatever.

Or maybe it was just that having all this free time thrust upon me had left me in a state of confusion.

Since my teens, I'd always been striving to get ahead, to climb higher and higher, and this desire was real. I'd wanted to win. Just win, no matter what. But win at what? Was the old me who'd hated losing so much just exhausted now, asleep somewhere within me? Or had I been pushing myself too hard from the start, and this lazy me was my true self? Though even contemplating these questions seemed like too much trouble these days.

I ate a burger at a nearby fast-food joint and headed back to the manga café. It wasn't that I liked manga so very much, really; it was just that after losing my job and my ambitions, I lost my capacity to read regular books as well. I'd go to libraries, of course, but it takes effort to follow printed words and understand them, to transform them into pictures in your head. Truthfully, TV was the easiest thing, but ever since my set broke, it had been manga all the way for me. Though I found that even as reading them completely engrossed me, once I was done I was left with nothing, no memories or feelings or anything. Reading manga was just another way to kill time, no more, no less.

I poured myself a cup of coffee, piled the entire run of *Maison Ikkoku* on the table, and began reading it, volume after volume. During the reading process, I took one nap, went to the bathroom twice, and refilled my coffee three times. I lost all sense of time as I read, and when I finished, I looked up at the clock expecting it to be around ten at night only to find it was already past three in the morning. Looking around the café, I saw it had filled up with drunks who'd missed the last train home. I debated whether to walk back to my place. It had been unpleasant the night before when I'd had to make my way through crowds of drunks to get home, so perhaps it would be better to wait until morning here. It was only two more hours until the first trains would begin to clear the neighborhood of stranded partiers again anyway.

I left my seat on the sofa to get a collection of light gag comics to read, and when I returned, I found that the seat next to mine had been taken by a young, red-faced, cataclysmically inebriated salaryman. I stood looking down at his sleep-slackened features—something about them seemed familiar. From time to time his brow would furrow and he'd moan softly, as if having a bad dream. *Who is he?* As I stood there asking myself if I remembered him from my working days, his eyes popped open. The moment they met mine, he reflexively, and loudly, blurted an apology: "I . . . I'm sorry!" The other customers in the store looked over at us, at least the ones who were still awake. Seeing his face so flustered startled me into a reflex of my own: It came back to me all at once who he was.

"Hey, wait—are you . . . are you Izumi?" he asked.

I sat down beside him without answering.

"What are you doing in a place like this?"

"Shouldn't I be asking *you* that? What kind of person starts apologizing as soon as he sees your face?" I responded, vaguely irritated. He was a guy who'd worked under me briefly at the company where I'd first worked. He was about five years younger than me, if I recalled correctly. He was pretty incompetent, and I remembered having to get after him a lot. I remembered his face, but I couldn't remember his name.

"Well, it gave me quite a shock! I was having a dream where I was being yelled at by a supervisor, and I open my eyes and there's Izumi, looking at me!"

"Sorry about that."

"But still, what brings you to a place like this? Phew, I'm still a bit shocked. What are you doing here?"

I was at a loss for an answer. There wasn't any stock explanation to give for ending up whiling away an entire night at a manga café, and I didn't really want to get into the real reasons with some guy I barely knew.

"How many years has it been? Meeting you here like this, it seems like destiny or something, you know? Are you waiting for the first train out too, Izumi?"

Almost everyone who comes to a manga café does so alone, and as a result, they're usually quieter than libraries. This guy's drink-amplified voice was bouncing off the walls. Destiny, did he say? More like a curse. Embarrassed, I rose from my seat.

"Hey—are you leaving already?"

"Be *quiet!*"

He ended up following me as I went to the register to settle my tab.

"Well then, I'll go too!"

"*You'll* sit here and wait for the first train."

"It's dangerous for a woman alone out there in Kabukicho at this hour. Here, I'll get you a taxi."

I turned my back on him as he said this, hurriedly pushing open the door to leave. I'd meant to escape this nuisance by cutting him off and vanishing, but he hounded my heels as I descended the staircase to the street, and I ended up tumbling down it onto the sidewalk. I was dizzy. Something was wrong.

"Are you okay? Even the great Izumi can fall, it seems."

Rushing up behind me, he reached down to help me back onto my feet, and I found myself looking up into his face. It was youthful, a bit puppyish. I grabbed his hand, flushed with embarrassment, and let him pull me to my feet. I felt a queer feeling in my breast as I did—a little nostalgic, a little painful.

"I'm pretty hungry. Should we go for ramen?"

I realized two things as he asked me this. One was that the nostalgic pain I'd felt had been my pride, which seemed able to be wounded again after so long. The other was that the reason I'd fallen on the stairs was that I was famished.

The guy's name was Kenta Obara. *Oh, that's right*, I thought as I looked down at the business card he'd put on the counter beside me at the ramen place. There'd been a guy in his cohort at the company named Ken'ichi Ōbara, so everyone called Ken'ichi "Big Ken," while Kenta, who was shorter and slighter, became "Little Ken." The card indicated that he worked not at the company where we'd known each other, but rather at some subdivision of an appliance manufacturer, in customer service.

"You quit the old company?"

I asked this as I sucked noodles into my mouth, since I didn't really have anything else to talk about with him.

"Yeah, I left pretty soon after you did, Izumi. The supervisor after you was like a hundred times stricter than you ever were, and I got so stressed out I found a bald patch on my head the size of a five-hundred-yen coin. I thought if I didn't leave I'd die, so . . . I left."

You'd die, just from a strict supervisor? I thought, keeping my silence, and, as if sensing my thoughts, Little Ken pointed at me with his disposable chopsticks. "Ahhh—you're thinking, 'God, what a wuss,' aren't you?"

"I am."

I didn't feel any need to observe common courtesy with him at this point, so I answered truthfully.

"It's all right. I am, I admit it. I'm a loser, a whipped dog with his tail between his legs," he said with a surprising amount of joie de vivre. "And what about you, Izumi? What happened with you? Oh right, you got married, didn't you? So it's not Izumi anymore. I forgot your new name, I apologize. What was it again? Anyway, I remember your first name still. Ryōko. Ryōko Izumi, I always thought that was a pretty name, from the first time I heard it."

Little Ken kept talking instead of eating, and the amount of ramen in his bowl wasn't going down. I'd already finished mine, and I wiped my mouth with a tissue from my pocket.

"Hey, could I borrow one of those?"

I passed him a sheet, and he noisily blew his nose into it before stuffing it into the pocket of his suit and going back to his ramen. I rested my cheek on my hand and watched him. His suit was cheap, his tie loose. But his nails were impeccable. Taking a peek under the counter, I saw that his bag was beat-up and old looking, while his shoes were immaculately polished. His taste was bad but his detailing was good, it seemed.

"So, what kind of work do you do now?"

I ignored whatever he was saying to me and asked this instead.

"Customer service. Well, I spend most of my time listening to people complain, really, and dispatching guys to go out and fix things. Sometimes I have to go do the fixing myself. I get called up, yelled at, end up fixing the thing, bow my head, apologize. Just that, day in, day out."

"Really. I guess you must have a talent for it."

"It's no talent. Though my degree *is* in engineering."

He gave me another look that seemed less dispirited than his words and then poured the rest of the broth in his bowl down his throat. He looked back at me and seemed bashful for the first time that night. It appeared that his drunkenness had cleared up a bit now that he had some food in him, and he was confused as to what to do at this point, having gotten himself into this situation.

"Uh . . . is it okay if I ask you something?"

A bit sleepy myself after having eaten, I stifled a yawn as I nodded.

"Where exactly do you live? What are you doing in a place like this, at a time like this, eating ramen with the likes of me? Isn't your husband going to be upset?"

"I live in West Shinjuku, only about a twenty-minute walk away.

I'm eating ramen with you because you invited me, Obara. And I've been divorced since the year before last, so my husband no longer gets upset no matter what I do, or when I do it, or where."

I carefully removed any inflection from my voice as I answered, attempting to play it off as casually as possible. Still, Little Ken stiffened a bit as he listened. It might have been kinder of me to have provided a little more of an explanation, but on the other hand, I was sleepy and really couldn't be bothered.

"It's about time for the trains to start back up. You have to go to work today, right? You should go home."

I tried to say this as sweetly as I could, but Little Ken was still blinking blankly at me. Finally, he returned to himself a little and said:

"Izumi, what do you do now?"

"Nothing. I'm unemployed."

"No! How could you, the great Izumi . . . ?"

I felt a slight twinge as my self-respect took another blow. We thanked the guy behind the counter and rose to our feet, and as we did, Little Ken fumbled for his wallet. I told him it was okay, but to no avail: I ended up treated to yet another meal.

I felt the word *loser*, which Little Ken had used to describe himself, grow larger and larger in my thoughts. He was asleep next to me on my plain-Jane pipe bed, curled against my side, hugging me. I'd opened my eyes to find myself in this position, clutched tightly as if by a child, and, unable to get up without disturbing him, I resigned myself to lying back and staring at the ceiling.

After the ramen, I'd left for home, but Little Ken insisted on accompanying me. "I really don't want to go to work . . ." he said with a tone of resignation, and when I offered, "Well, it won't hurt to miss just one day," he eagerly nodded, happy again. "You know, I had a crush on you even back then, Izumi, you should know that, let it cheer you up", he said in a childish rush of flattery, and then he grabbed my hand. I'd never had one iota of romantic feeling for him as far as I recalled, yet as he put my hand in his, I found it didn't particularly bother me. It didn't particularly bother me, so I invited him up to my apartment. As soon as we arrived, Little Ken began throwing off his clothes, and I thought vaguely to myself, *Oh right, I guess this means we're going to do it*. We ended up going at it three times before we were through.

It had truly been a while since I'd last been touched. I couldn't remember when my husband and I had had sex for the last time, and not even counting sex, I struggled to recall how many years it had been since I was last kissed, or had my hand held or my back stroked or my shoulder rubbed by someone, anyone, man or woman.

So the simple truth was, it felt good. Also, as a side note, it gratified me to learn that I still had a sex drive at all. Little Ken nuzzled me along my collarbone, murmuring soft nonsense into the hollow. Stroking his head as if to hold it against my body was enough to quiet him. He really was like a dog.

What time is it? I thought, and I reached the hand that wasn't occupied with Little Ken to feel for my watch next to my pillow and turn its face toward me. It was just past ten in the morning. We'd hardly slept at all. *Well, it's not like I have anything pressing to do*, I thought, and closed my eyes to go back to sleep. Little Ken's head was heavy on my shoulder. I'd liked to sleep nestled in my husband's arms, but I hadn't realized how heavy a head could be.

He was such a nice guy, I thought, remembering my ex-husband.

The only son of a landlord in Shitamachi, he had a certain absent-minded way about him but was a quality person. He was optimistic to the core, considerate, and patient. Unlike me, he didn't hold grudges and never had a bad word to say about anyone. I'd loved these things about him at first, but after a while, they began to wear on me. Had his being so easygoing led to me becoming inconsiderate? I'd ended up assuming that the things that made me happy made him happy too.

Loser. The word danced back and forth before my closed eyes. Little Ken's hair felt good against me; he didn't use any product in it and it felt like he'd just washed it that morning. I burrowed my nose in it and breathed deeply. The scent of another was so refreshing.

Little Ken and I are perfect together, a perfect pair of losers, I thought, without a hint of malice or contempt. All it took was a bit of contact between my naked body and his to get me liking some guy I'd never given a second thought to before, it seemed—never underestimate the power of sheer skin-on-skin. I struck myself as a bit funny at that moment, as well as a bit stupid.

I began to hear a melody playing; it sounded like a ringtone. I didn't have a cell phone, so it must've been his. When I realized it was the theme from *A Dog of Flanders,* I couldn't help but laugh out loud. I was still debating whether to let my sleeping dog lie or wake him up, when he opened his eyes of his own accord, maybe hearing the ringtone himself. He sprang upright, his eyes alighting from time to time on my face as they swam around the room, searching it as he struggled to remember where he was and what he was doing, all the while bedeviled by his elusive, chiming phone. Finally, it ceased playing its little song, as if giving up.

"Um . . . um . . ."

"Good morning! Are you really planning to skip work?"

"Um . . . what day of the week is it again?"

The *Dog of Flanders* theme began playing again. Dressed only in his boxers, he gave a start and leaped from the bed to fish his phone from the pocket of his suit jacket where it hung from the back of the chair. He turned toward the wall and began apologizing earnestly to whoever was on the other end. I watched the bones of his skinny back as they twitched beneath his skin.

"They're pretty mad. I gotta go to work," said Little Ken, hangdog after he hung up, like an elementary school kid who'd just been scolded by his mother.

"It's my fault. I'm sorry."

"No, don't apologize, Izumi."

He clumsily pulled on his shirt and pants, then tied his tie. As soon as his suit was on, he was just another boring guy again. *He looks so much better naked,* I thought as I pulled on a T-shirt to walk over to the refrigerator to get a bottle of water; I poured a glass and offered it to him.

"Thanks. Were you always so nice, Izumi?"

Faced with such a question, I couldn't help but laugh again. Perhaps sleeping had rekindled my sense of resignation, but my pride no longer felt a whit of wounding at his words.

"Will I see you again?"

"Sure . . . Hey, do you know how to fix a TV? Or an air conditioner?"

"It depends on the model. Why, are yours broken?"

Little Ken flicked the television set on and off, peering at its distorted picture, and then took the batteries in and out of the air conditioner remote, his brow furrowed in thought. He scribbled the serial numbers into his notepad. Then he ripped a new page out, wrote his cell number on it, and held it out to me.

"You can call me at work, but I'm out a lot, so use this number, okay?"

I took the paper from his hand and nodded. Little Ken smiled happily, kissed me lightly on the lips, and bounced out the door.

The moment he was gone, everything that had happened since last night seemed to lose its reality completely, popping like a soap bubble. Though when I crawled back into bed, his doggy scent was still there. Enfolded within it, I indulged myself in a lovely, indolent sleep.

As it was getting toward evening, my phone rang, and, still blurry with sleep, I answered it thinking it would be Little Ken. It wasn't. It was a guy I'd known when I'd worked with my husband, and he was asking if I wanted to grab a bite to eat that night. I didn't have anything to do and had no reason to refuse, so I decided to go.

Look who's hot stuff all of a sudden, I thought to myself, tilting my head as I put on my makeup; I picked out a summer-weight suit from the ones I'd kept shut away since I'd moved here, but when I put it on, it somehow no longer looked right on me. *Maybe it's because my hair's all grown out, I haven't been to a salon in forever.* It wasn't like anything important was on the line, I figured, so I exchanged the suit for my usual cargo pants.

The place he'd picked was a fusion restaurant up in Aoyama North, and to get there I'd have to pass by one of our old stores. Surely that was on purpose. Yet, when I turned east onto Aoyama, admittedly with a bit of a flutter in my breast, I saw that where the store had been there was now one of those American coffee places that were popping up all over. I'd known it had closed, but still, it hurt to see it. The down payment needed to secure a place along this strip had been enough to make your eyes pop out if you were going to do it as an individual, but for an expanding enterprise, I'd thought it was no big deal. My husband and I had fought over whether to open a third store here. I'd been sure it would be an absolute success, but the sheer amount of the initial investment had scared him.

I arrived fifteen minutes late, but, as I expected, he'd still yet to arrive. I ordered a beer anyway, and as I was drinking it, he appeared, saying, "Sorry, sorry, sorry," with an expression on his face that wasn't sorry at all. This guy, Hyōdō, sold Asian-style goods wholesale on behalf of a handicrafts chain that was backed by a major apparel company. I was pretty sure we were around the same age, but sometime when I wasn't looking, he'd filled out quite a bit, gaining a certain presence.

"Hey, you've gotten skinny while I wasn't looking!" he said, voicing an opposite impression of me. He motormouthed through ordering drinks and food from the waiter. *Did I speak that fast back then too?* I wondered.

"So, Izumi, what are you up to these days?"

He cut to the chase, no pleasantries, no small talk.

"Nothing in particular."

"Sorry, I should have said. I'd heard you were banging around, and the truth is, I asked you here to see if you could do something for me."

Hyōdō produced a business card from the pocket of his expensive-looking suit jacket, recently remade, no doubt, to accommodate his newly filled-out frame. Unlike Little Ken's, it was pure white, its edges crisp enough to slice your finger. His company had been limited when we'd known each other, but sometime between then and now it had evidently gone public. His new title—managing director—ran proudly down the edge of the card.

"When I heard you were free, my first thought was: *Great!* You see, we're opening up a new location. We want to expand into traditional Japanese handicrafts and housewares. I want you to help us do that."

He spoke as if the possibility I might refuse had never occurred to him. The location he was talking about was scheduled to open next year at a major private railway terminus, and he wanted to hire me as the merchandiser. A merchandiser is like a buyer, but with an expanded purview: I'd help shape the company's concept directly, including the image the merchandise projected and how it was displayed. I'd control the timing of each item's introduction and the amount we'd order, and even have a hand in training the staff in how to work the floor. At the company where I'd first worked, I'd handled European goods, while at my husband's store I'd specialized in Japanese; in either area, I had the experience and knowledge to do the job right.

"I haven't worked for two whole years, though."

"I'm confident that you, of all people, can make up for lost time. And you don't have any obligations to your husband anymore, right? So it's payback time. Payback time, Izumi."

Payback time—the words brought me up short. I had no thirst for revenge anywhere in me. But I was reminded that from the outside, it looked like something terrible had indeed been done to me.

Now that I thought about it, I remembered that it had been at a trade show put on by Hyōdō that I'd first met my husband. I'd gone mostly just to go and have a look around, but I was struck by the figure of a man dressed in a kimono despite looking so young. I watched as he studied the catalogs and sample goods with utmost seriousness, and then took the first opportunity to strike up a conversation. He told me he wanted to convert the house he'd inherited from his grandmother, who'd passed away the previous year, into a store selling traditional Japanese crafts. Hearing that the house dated back to the Taisho era, I suggested that he not renovate it at all, but instead just hang a traditional indigo noren over the door and use it as is; his eyes shone at my suggestion. This encounter sparked the whirlwind romance that resulted in our marriage, after which we talked more and more concretely about opening the business together. I didn't have any particular attachment to the company where I'd worked for the previous six years. The prospect of marrying a nice guy and building a business together from the ground up appealed to me much more than playing the never-ending game of musical chairs that competing for titles at the company increasingly felt like.

"Remember those handmade little animals, and the traditional Japanese candles? Those were great. Your ex-husband doesn't sell those anymore, I don't think, and I'd love for you to handle them at our place."

Back when I'd commissioned a young artist to make stuffed animals for us and developed a line of Japanese-style candles to go with them, my husband hadn't been pleased; he thought they looked cheap. But I insisted, and when they debuted at the store, they ended up selling much better than either of us had imagined, even getting picked up and featured in a women's magazine, attracting customers from far and wide to our location, and some major department stores contacted us to see if they could sell them too. Thinking back on it, I wondered if it had been yet another thing I'd done to wound my husband's pride.

"Wait, hold up a moment. Let's not get ahead of ourselves."

Hyōdō reluctantly put his mug of beer back down at my words.

"Why not? I'm giving you a chance to get back in it, Izumi. You know, if you stay out of the game for much longer, everyone'll forget about you completely."

"The truth is, though, I never particularly cared much about handicrafts or housewares to begin with." The truth spilled from my lips before I quite knew what I was saying. Hyōdō leaned over the table toward me in response.

"But that's the point! Look, there're enough girls running around who love cute little things to hire and fire one every day. Loving the merchandise is more of a liability than an asset."

Faced with this unexpected response, I levelly returned his gaze.

"You must know what I mean, Izumi. A quality item and an item that sells are two completely different things. I mean, I'd love to handle only high-quality items made by master craftsmen. But your average customer has no eye for that kind of thing. The things that sell are cute at first glance and cheap enough to use for a season and then throw away once you get tired of them. I'm not saying you should sell anything that sells just because, but the thing is, if you don't sell anything like that, when the time comes that you do encounter something of true value, you won't have the capital to take advantage of it."

He told me this as if enlightening a bright child. *I said much the same thing to my husband*, I recalled. The things Hyōdō was saying were absolutely true, and I knew I couldn't make a living sewing silly Pikachu knockoffs all day, but still, his words left me unmoved.

My indifference must have been obvious, and he eventually

grew silent. Not bothering to hide his disappointment, he put a cigarette in his mouth and lit it.

"It was that much of a shock, then, huh? With your husband?"

"What?"

The group at the table next to us grew suddenly rowdy, drowning out his words.

"I thought you were wanting to get back on your feet, but it looks like I just brought up bad memories. I apologize."

Oh no, that's not true, I wanted to tell him, but the words refused to come out.

"When do I have to tell you by?" I asked finally, staring down at the food I'd barely touched.

"Well, let's see. We don't really have to move on this for a bit, so let's say the first of September? Think of it as homework for your summer vacation."

I should have been used to it by now, but still, when I saw Hyōdō produce a ¥10,000 note from his wallet and hand it to the server, it bummed me out. It also made me remember back when I'd been flush too and never split the bill with Asuka or my other friends, taking it upon myself to pick up the tab every time without asking. It had never occurred to me then what it might feel like to be paid for by others.

I'd fallen out of the habit, so the drinks from dinner started to make my head hurt; I hailed a taxi outside the restaurant and took it straight home. There I found a parcel waiting for me in front of my door. Wondering what it might be, I looked to see who'd sent it; reading Asuka's name, I got a bad feeling, and when I opened it, I found not only the Pikachu I'd just given her but seven teddy bears dressed in outfits I'd made.

I know I should keep these to spare your feelings, Izumi, but honestly, I just can't bring myself to. I'm sorry. I don't really know how to put it; all I can say is that taking a breather and running away are two different things. It's getting hard to watch. I'm truly sorry.

I read Asuka's frank words aloud to myself. *She could have just thrown them away without telling me,* I thought, rubbing my temples. *Friendship is a kind thing but also cruel.*

As I looked at the stuffed animals arrayed before me again like this, they indeed struck me as pretty nauseating. My mother used to tat doilies to use as coasters or put under vases, and I remember them striking me the same way. Nobody really wanted them, not even her, but still she went on making them. I should have pitied her, but instead I ended up becoming her.

I shed my clothes without washing off my makeup and crawled into bed. I could still faintly smell the smell of my doggy friend. But I had no wish to call him.

When I opened my eyes again, it was eight in the morning, a shockingly respectable hour. Not only that, but the sky was clear and sunny again after I don't know how many days, so I threw open all the windows and hung my futon and sleeping pad out on the veranda as I loaded up the washing machine. In the sunlight, my apartment's dirtiness stood out in stark relief, so I decided to do a little cleaning. I started filling a plastic garbage bag with all the stuff covering my floor. I popped the stuffed animals in it too, one after another, but when I went to close it up, my eyes met the perfectly round eyes of Pikachu. It did seem wasteful to throw them out. *Maybe I should at least take a picture before I get rid of them*, I thought, and then I remembered Asuka suggesting I make a website. *I'll go out and get a digital camera so I can take pictures for the site*, I thought, excited at the prospect of a brand-new project to waste my time on.

Leaving my cleaning half done, I walked to the electronics district and picked up a cheap digital camera. This emptied my wallet, so I stopped by a cash machine to replenish it. After receiving my customary hundred thousand yen, I glanced down at the receipt that accompanied it. The balance in my regular savings account was almost zero. I was living unbelievably frugally compared to my former lifestyle, but it shouldn't have come as a shock that spending money while earning nothing would drain my resources; nonetheless, I'd never really thought about it like that. I suddenly regretted my recent camera purchase and the taxi fare from the day before. No matter how much I reassured myself with "money in the bank," ¥20 million yen was ¥20 million yen. A considerable sum if you're saving up while working, but if you're trying just to live on it, after a few years it'll be gone. All that time studying harder than anyone else at school, working harder than anyone else at my job, and this was what I had to show for it. How hard would you have to work to make enough to never have to work again? It didn't look like I had a choice—I had to take Hyōdō up on his offer no matter how much I didn't feel like it, I told myself darkly. But I'd still wait until summer was over to tell him. *That's as much as I want to think about it*, I thought, shaking my head.

The first thing I did once I got back to my apartment was boot up my computer. It was just a run-of-the-mill desktop I'd gotten before the divorce, and I'd never used it for anything but email and casual web surfing, but now that I looked a bit closer I saw it was loaded with a rudimentary website builder. Not bothering to read the manual, I began to construct an index for my site.

From then on, aside from a few trips to the convenience store to get something to eat, I never left my apartment, absorbed as I was in my new time killer, until one night, after losing track of time almost completely, a heard a knock at my door. A deliveryman or newspaper carrier would ring the doorbell, so at first I thought I was just imagining it; still, I stopped my fingers from their tapping and listened, only to find that indeed, it really did seem to be the sound of someone knocking. Looking through the peephole, I saw Little Ken standing there stiffly in his suit.

"What's going on? You know, if you don't ring the bell, it's easy to miss you out there," I said, opening the door, to which he stiltedly responded, "Good evening."

"All right, come on in."

"Thank you very much."

His demeanor was hesitant, ultrapolite, a complete one-eighty from how he'd acted the last time I saw him. "I brought these," he said, offering me the plastic convenience store sack he was carrying. It held two chilled cans of beer and two containers of shaved ice.

"I didn't know which you'd like, so I got both."

"You could have called and asked."

"How could I? You never gave me your number."

Oh, that's right, I never did.

"Can you understand how I've been feeling, Izumi, waiting all this time for you to call?"

Little Ken, who'd been standing awkwardly all this time, finally sat down on the chair in front of the computer; I sank down onto my bed. Remembering the headache drinking beer the night before had given me, I chose the ice.

"You could have just come over..."

"How could I have known that? Imagine it from my side. When you didn't call me, I figured you must have wanted it to be a one-time thing, Izumi. How could I just come over if there was a distinct possibility I'd be turned away at the door?"

Little Ken was absolutely right, of course, but if I told him the truth, that I hadn't called him because it had simply slipped my mind, it would likely hurt him even more.

"I'm sorry. I've just been a bit busy lately."

"If I'm bothering you, I'll go."

"If you were a bother, wouldn't I have *turned you away at the door*?"

This finally got a smile out of Little Ken. He popped open his beer and drank it with gusto. Draining it in almost one gulp, Little Ken opened the second one and brought it to his mouth. I watched him, picking at my ice with the little spoon, and wondered if he didn't seem to be a bit of an incipient alcoholic. Finishing the second beer in no time, he rose to his feet, saying, "Well, then..." and reached into the large bag he'd brought, producing a small cardboard box. *What on earth...?* I thought, and then he opened it, revealing an air conditioner remote. He took some batteries out of the bag as well and loaded them into the device. Then he walked over to the air conditioner proper and flipped a switch on it, and the exhaust fan on the veranda shuddered noisily to life. A mold-scented breeze caressed my cheek.

"Oh—you fixed it!" I exclaimed, surprised, to which Little Ken shrugged, exultant.

"The battery case in the remote was rusty, so it didn't work, that's all. You need to take the batteries out to store it when the season changes again. And maybe clean your air filters."

"This is amazing!"

A cool breeze blew steadily throughout the space. I ran around the apartment, shutting all the windows I'd opened. When I returned, Little Ken had moved on to the television set, using a screwdriver to open up its back.

"You're fixing my TV too?"

"It's one of ours, it'll be easy. But it might take a second, so you'll have to be patient."

"Thank you so much! Oh, and can you replace the lightbulb in the kitchen? I can't reach it even when I stand on a chair, so . . ."

"Of course."

"Can I do anything to help?"

Sitting cross-legged in front of the television and fiddling with a part, Little Ken grew thoughtful as he considered my question.

"I could stand a little more beer, I guess."

"I'll go get it!"

I grabbed my wallet and went out the door. I broke into a little trot on the short way to the store. *What are you so excited about, you idiot?* I thought, but nonetheless, I felt a smile spread across my face. When I returned bearing four beers and a few snacks to go with, Little Ken was just returning the television to its previous position. The perfect, clean image of a sportscast filled the screen.

"Look at that! It's working!" I said in a loud voice, making Little Ken smile and blush.

"You don't need to be so grateful, it was nothing. The color balance was off, that's all. That, and it was pretty dusty, so I cleaned that up too. Dust can damage the set, you know. Can you tell me where the new bulbs are so I can change the light?"

"Of course, of course," I said, getting the bulbs I'd bought almost half a year ago out from where I'd stowed them in the closet. There was probably no more than five centimeters' difference between my height and Little Ken's, but it was enough to prevent me from reaching the socket on the ceiling no matter how I tried.

The kitchen filled with light. The empty instant ramen containers and dirty dishes filling the sink glowed in the brightness, and, embarrassed, I took Little Ken's hands in mine and led him to the bed, where I sat him down and kissed him on the cheek. He smiled happily and pulled the tab on another beer.

"Thank you so much, really. You saved the day."

"You're very welcome."

I'd always had the impression he was useless, but maybe he'd be pretty handy to have around?

"I'll pay you back, don't worry. New remotes don't grow on trees, I know."

"Don't worry about it. This guy I know at the electronics store gave it to me real cheap. Anyway, you said you were busy lately? What have you been doing? Did you get a job?"

"No, I've just been making a site."

"On the internet?"

"Yeah. You wanna see?"

I led Little Ken back over to the chair in front of the computer and showed him the site I'd been working on for the past week.

"Wow, it looks great! What's that, a Pikachu?"

"Yeah, I sewed him myself. I might get in trouble, actually, if I get caught selling it."

"Why not keep it?"

Sitting here talking like this, it felt like we were a real couple, Little Ken and I.

"Anyhow, you did a really good job. It looks great. And look at the number of visitors on the counter! You could do this as a real job."

Being praised so sincerely brought up complicated feelings. How hard was it to build a simple home page? I'd just looked around at a few sites made by professionals, gathered the basic building blocks, and thrown it together. I'd posted links to it here and there and let my PostPet friends know about it, and someone even posted a link to it on a forum somewhere without me asking. And that was it! I'd even received a few emails inquiring about how they might get the rights to sell my stuffed animals and teddy bear clothing; it was a bit unreal. But it also only really interested me at first, and I didn't have any new content to post or anything happening in my life compelling enough to write a blog about—in truth, I'd already started to tire of the whole thing.

I hugged Little Ken's head as he sat there in front of the computer. We pressed our lips together and giggled playfully. *I really am fond of this boy*, I thought. But it might be the same as with my handicrafts or my website—I'd get all wrapped up in him for a while and then just as quickly lose interest. My irresponsibility appalled me, yet I was helpless before the primitive impulses that gripped me. I stripped naked, *sans* shower, and we went at it yet again.

"If you'll forgive me for saying so, I think I like this Izumi better than the one I knew at work."

Little Ken said this as we lay tangled in the sheets, naked, bathed in the cool wind that blew from the newly repaired air conditioner. It startled me a little.

"Really? Everyone else seems to want me to get back on my feet, to be my old self again."

"Nah... I mean, when you announced that you were quitting to get married, you looked so happy and you were so, so pretty. But before that, the things you'd say and the way you'd say them were so nasty and abrasive, you struck me as being just a really unpleasant woman."

"You told me before that you'd always had a crush on me."

"Oh, I had a crush. You were a winner, unlike me."

Were a winner—the past tense caught my attention, but I decided not to think about it. Instead, I pressed Little Ken's head to me like a stuffed animal and petted his hair.

"Why'd you get divorced?" he asked, his voice muffled. I couldn't think of an answer, so he quickly added, "If you don't want to tell me, it's okay. I'm sorry."

"You know something, Obara? You're the kind of guy who really looks better naked."

As I evaded his question with a non sequitur, Little Ken gave a complicated little laugh.

"Is that supposed to be a compliment? I know the suits I wear are cheap. I have to buy a lot of them, I walk around in the heat all day for work. I can hardly go around naked, can I?"

I pressed my lips to Little Ken's indignantly furrowed forehead, quieting him.

After that, Little Ken started dropping by on his way back to work once or twice a week. He'd come by on Sundays sometimes too, dressed in a T-shirt and Bermuda shorts, and he'd fix the wallpaper where it was peeling off the wall or go with me to hang out at the manga café. It was easy being with him—he didn't tell me how much he liked me, or that he was in love with me, or ask how long I intended to stay unemployed, which freed me to stop thinking about anything at all.

Summer in the city meant asphalt hot as a frying pan, and I saw on the news that it would climb past forty degrees . I got woozy just walking to the convenience store. I was truly fortunate to have had Little Ken fix my television and air-conditioning before the heat wave. Going out while the sun was up was enough to make me almost pass out, and even after it set, the temperature didn't dip below thirty. I was bored of the internet, so I spent all my time staring blankly at the TV or sleeping, the air conditioner going full blast twenty-four seven. I had no appetite, but I'd eat a little of the cold Chinese noodles or ice cream Little Ken would bring me and somehow got by.

But by the time August rolled around, I was feverish with a summer cold. It was only to be expected after spending every day and every night beneath an air conditioner turned as low as it could go, and one night, Little Ken came by like usual and found me with a thirty-nine-degree temperature. Freaked out, he found a clinic open late and brought me there. The doctor told me that my immune system was weak due to anemia and borderline malnutrition, news that shocked Little Ken more than it did me. After the doctor warned me not to underestimate the problem and make sure I ate properly, Little Ken forced me into a taxi and brought me to his place.

His apartment turned out to be in a neighborhood about thirty minutes from downtown by train, and despite his apartment being on the second floor of a rundown two-story wooden building, the area was tree-filled and green, and a lovely breeze blew through when the windows were open. He tucked me into his bed and hid the air conditioner remote. *It's a good thing I had some summer vacation days saved up*, I recall he had said, and he ended up taking three days off, remaining faithfully by my side until my fever broke. He was no chef, but he cooked three meals a day for me and fanned my forehead when I'd get hot. His place was as shabby as mine, but the *tatami* floors felt nice against my bare feet. All this kindness made me grateful, but also suspicious. I couldn't figure out why he would be so nice to me. Sure, he said he was a "loser" in terms of his career, but he was handsome enough and amiable. Judging from what he told me, his supervisor seemed fond of him and his underlings adored him. It seemed impossible that he would have no luck with women. So what did he see in the likes of me that would make him be so kind?

My fever finally broken, I took a bath again instead of just a shower. The tub was old but he kept it immaculate, as was his way, and it felt good as I sat in it. There was a scale just inside the bathroom door, and when I weighed myself, I was surprised to see that I weighed thirty-nine kilos. *That can't be good*, I thought. *I'm 62 inches tall*. I told myself the scale must be broken.

That Sunday, I told Little Ken that I was feeling better and should be getting back to my own apartment. A forlorn look clouded his features momentarily, and then he offered to accompany me back to Shinjuku. "I feel bad imposing on you already—you can just see me to the station," I replied. I was filled to bursting with remorse for having cost him all his summer vacation time.

It was ten o'clock and the midsummer sun beat down as hard as ever, but partway through our trip to the station, Little Ken suggested we stop by a park he knew that was jungle-thick with trees, their shade offering cool comfort as we sat on a bench beneath them.

"I don't think that apartment in Shinjuku is very good for you."

Little Ken told me this as he drank from a can of iced tea he'd gotten from a vending machine.

"Good for me or not, I bought it. I can't very well move now."

"It feels cursed, that place."

"Don't be creepy!" I replied, meaning to make him laugh, but his profile remained serious.

"I couldn't think of a good way to say it, but . . ."

He spoke without looking at me, and then trailed off into silence. I braced myself, trying to think of what to say if he asked me to move in with him.

"When you first started staying at my place, Izumi, I couldn't stop worrying, and I ended up going to visit Big Ken, back where we used to work."

"You what?"

"He's a big boss now, you know. A real big deal, it's hard to believe we're the same age."

It took me a second to put it together that he was talking about Ken'ichi Ōbara, who'd been hired at the same he had; and as soon as I did, I had a sinking feeling I knew what he was going to say.

"It's not cool, I know, but I ended up asking him about you. He told me everything, every little detail. It's been pretty tough for you, hasn't it?"

It was a small world, the business I used to be in. I was sure rumors about my separation from my husband had circulated starting right after it happened. A certain amount of interpretation occurs as rumors get passed around, and the story had surely become festooned with unflattering embellishments before long.

After all, there was no linear, easy-to-trace progression that

Fumio Yamamoto

led to my husband asking me for a divorce. It all came down to my insistence on dominating every little thing having to do with the business. After the stunning success of the little animals and pop art–inspired Japanese candles I'd commissioned, we began stocking cheaper, mass-produced goods as well, and business started growing by leaps and bounds. Building on this, I pressed my husband to open two new locations, one in Sendagi and the other in Aoyama North, and he ended up acquiescing, though in truth, by the time he did it had been a nearly foregone conclusion anyway. My husband had been born and raised in Asakusa, so his heart lay in true handcrafted traditional goods; he soon started getting flak from old friends and members of his family: *I can't believe you're selling crap like that, what happened to your eye for quality?* I knew more or less what was going on, but I chose to pretend I didn't. I wanted to have children and knew I couldn't do it while working morning to night like I was; to prepare, I wanted to sell as much as possible as quickly as possible, and I did everything in my power to raise our yearly profits by every measly yen I could.

And indeed, the profits rose steadily, but things between my husband and me grew more and more strained, and the prospect of going back each night to the apartment my husband had bought with his parents' money started to depress me. I knew I shouldn't, but I spent more and more nights camped out at the store. And it was true, too, that I began to think of him as a spoiled little rich kid, as a man who didn't understand business, as not really much of a man at all.

Before long, he began seeing someone else. How fortunate for me that he ended up being the one to have an affair. His mother taught traditional Japanese dance; though she didn't advertise, she attracted a steady flow of young women to her classes through word of mouth. It was one of these students who ended up falling in love with my husband. She'd come to the store countless times, and despite her ultrashort, modern haircut, she looked great in a kimono—the effect was, in fact, not unlike the one that had so attracted me to my husband when I'd first laid eyes on him at that trade show.

So by the time he told me that he wanted to live with her, that he knew he could build a life with her that was rich and rewarding, unlike the profit-obsessed one he was living with me, he'd already made up his mind completely. He prostrated himself formally before me, promising that he'd do anything I wanted so long as I would agree to remove myself from the family registry. Even as I screamed and cried, vowing that I'd never give him the satisfaction, I knew in my heart as soon as he said the words that it was over. *I can't take the loneliness anymore*, he had said. And truly, the life we'd ended up leading had been lonely. Pushing harder and harder to get ahead, to climb higher and higher, I'd devised a way of life for us that had no room for distraction or even emotion—once he stopped believing in it, what else did I have to offer?

"Maybe I'm worrying too much, but you've changed so drastically—are you sure you don't want to rent a little room near here with me? I'd feel a lot better if you did."

I didn't know how much Big Ken knew or what he'd told Little Ken, but it was obvious that whatever he'd heard made him feel extremely sorry for me. Despite having recently gone back to its previous numbness, my pride smarted. My stupid, useless pride.

Both Little Ken and I grew silent. The buzz of the cicadas, the smell of the earth. The light, filtered through the leaves, moving across Little Ken's feet in their flip-flops. I was so confused. I had no idea what to say.

"You know, a guy I knew asked me recently to join the staff of a new store his company was opening up," I said, finally, the words coming out before I quite knew what they would be.

"Really? Is that so? That's great!"

He answered so happily, as if about his own good fortune.

"But I still don't know—part of me wants to do it, part of me doesn't."

"Well, with everything that's happened to you, it's natural to have mixed feelings..."

"You know what? That's not it," I said, more sharply than I'd meant to. Little Ken's eyes widened. I knew that sooner or later, I'd finally get back on my feet, rejoin society, and go back to work. I'd have my doubts, but even so, I'd start to strive again, push harder and harder, climb higher and higher. And yet, for some reason, it made me sad to contemplate it. It was the human condition to stumble and fall, to get hurt, and then to heal and get up again to fight another day. And I hated it. At some point, I'd begun to despise the very capacity of my heart and body to heal itself and move on.

"I mean, if I get busy again, I won't have all this free time to hang around with you like I've been doing." *Crap,* I thought, as soon as I said it.

"So you've only been with me to pass the time?" he said, staring down at the ground.

"That's not what I meant."

"It's all right. I get it. Once you get back on your feet and start working like before, what would a nothing guy like me have to offer you?"

"No," I said, but Little Ken got up and threw his empty iced-tea can away in the garbage can next to the bench. I found I lacked the voice to call after him as he fled down the path where we'd been walking together, hand in hand, just before.

I'd never spent as much time waiting for someone to call as I did then. But Little Ken never got back in touch, not after three days, or seven, or ten. The night I made up my mind to bite the bullet and call him myself, I couldn't find the slip of paper he'd written his number on no matter how hard I scoured my apartment, and finally I gave up. It was just like he said, I supposed. If it weren't, there'd be no way I'd have lost his number so easily.

The next day, my phone rang; I rushed to answer it, but it turned out to be Asuka. She kept apologizing, seeming really sorry for some reason. I was at a loss, unable to figure out what might have prompted this, until I finally remembered the stuffed animals she'd sent back to me.

"I sent you so many emails and you never replied, so I figured I must have really upset you."

"It's totally fine," I explained. "I even ended up making a website to showcase them." Hearing this seemed to finally calm her down. We'd had I don't know how many fights since we were kids, but none were ever bad enough that we couldn't make up afterward.

"I can't believe I'm saying this after doing something so mean to you, but I have a favor to ask," she said, hedging before she got to the point. "Do you mind helping my kids with their summer homework?"

According to Asuka, her husband usually helped the kids complete their projects for art class during the last two days of August, but this year, he'd been called away suddenly on business until September.

"You always got the worst grades in arts and crafts, didn't you, Asuka?"

"Exactly! He's so good with his hands, but I'm utterly useless. I have work all day too, so I just don't know what to do."

I hadn't seen Asuka's kids in over five years. Kids weren't exactly my strong suit, and I kind of felt that children should do their homework themselves without help, but on the other hand, it wouldn't be a lot of pressure with her husband not there, and besides, this seemed to be Asuka's way of extending the olive branch, so I agreed to do it. *It's got to beat languishing in this awful apartment all day, at least*, I thought.

The children, it seemed, wanted me to teach them how to make the animals their mother had mysteriously taken from them, but it seemed impossible to teach a couple of kids in elementary school something so complicated in only two days. Besides, I figured a teacher would respond better to something a bit more childish, so I looked up how to make papier-mâché on the internet and headed off to Asuka's place.

Asuka's apartment was located in one of a long row of high-rises about an hour by express train from the city. It was about the same size as the place I'd shared with my husband, but it housed a family of four, not two.

Her oldest was already in sixth grade and quite a little adult, greeting me formally as I walked through the door. The younger, a third grader named Rinko, was bashful and quiet, squirming nervously behind Asuka's skirt. As Asuka and I had some tea, her oldest showed no compunction coming up and talking to us, asking if he could play video games or if we could help him with his math homework. The younger, on the other hand, sat silently in the far corner of the room, sneaking peeks at us every once in a while. Kids, whether they're in your face or leaving you alone, are such a nuisance. But it was only two days, after all, and Asuka seemed so grateful.

You can buy papier-mâché premade at the store, but I figured the process was part of the fun, so I'd decided to show them how to make it from scratch with old newspapers. As I was starting to cut the paper into long strips, the younger one sidled up to me and said in a small voice, "Can I try too?"

"It's *your* homework! It wouldn't be right if you didn't help out."

I handed her the newspaper and scissors as I said this, and she started cutting it up right away. Then we put it in the water to soak, boiling it in a big pot. That was as far as we got that day, and I ate the dinner Asuka made along with the kids. I ran a bath before going to bed and saw on the changing room scale that I'd gotten my weight up to forty-one kilos.

The next morning, after Asuka left for work, we added flour and water to the newspaper that had transformed overnight into mush. This seemed to interest the boy more than the girl; "I'll do it," he informed me before stirring the mixture. Once it was ready, I decided to make a sample to show them how it worked and went about covering a bowl in plastic wrap and then carefully spreading papier-mâché across the surface. Later, when I removed the bowl, it kept the shape, and the kids responded with exaggerated glee.

The boy dove right in, making boy things like monsters and cars and fake poop, but his sister seemed to be at a loss as to what to do. I got out some other dishes so she could try using them as molds like I had, but she wasn't very good at it and they turned out pretty badly. Despite their clumsiness, though, I found their shapes somehow endearing, and I set them aside without trying to fix them. Before long, the boy had left to go play with a friend, leaving the girl and me alone to decorate the objects with acrylic paint. Little Rinko's color sense turned out to be excellent. She painted patterns on the bowls she'd made, and they turned out really nicely; she seemed like an old hand at holding a brush. I told her how good I thought she was doing, and she smiled bashfully in response.

"You're the one who made Pikachu for us, right?"

We were sitting in the living room, painting our creations atop newspapers laid down to protect the carpet, when she whispered this question to me. As I'd sat alone with the child, the room had grown hushed and still.

"I liked him very much, but Mom took him away. She said she only borrowed him and we had to give him back."

"If you want, I can give him to you," I said, and she looked thoughtful in response.

"Was he hard to make?"

"Pretty hard. Have you used a thread and needle before?"

"No."

"Well, next time I'll show you how."

Really? Her eyes shone at the thought.

"You really think I could do it?"

"Of course, of course."

We finished painting all her pieces, and when her brother got home, we grabbed him and made him paint his pieces too—his monsters, his cars, his fake poop. His color sense was pretty bad, as it turned out, but it was just an elementary-school vacation project; it was the nature of the beast, I supposed.

The girl seemed to have completely overcome her initial wariness and insisted that she accompany me in the bath and that we sleep together in the same bed. "Don't be a pest, Rinko," admonished Asuka, but I was delighted. It wasn't that I felt like I'd acquired a child of my own, however; it was more like I'd become another one of Asuka's.

So I found myself snuggled beneath a light blanket with little Rinko, in bed at the unbelievably responsible hour of nine o'clock. Turning off the bedside light, Rinko buried her face in the pillow and said, "I gotta go back to school tomorrow."

"You don't want to go?"

"I do! I do! I made all that stuff, I want to show everybody!"

I thought for a moment and then asked, as I stared up at the bedroom ceiling, "Why go to school at all?" *What elementary school kid's going to have an answer for that?* I wondered. But little Rinko did.

"It's fun. And I get to see my friends."

I couldn't think of any response to that, and as I pondered, she dropped off to sleep. She had both her arms wrapped around me, as well as one of her legs. It was awfully hot to be hugged so close by a child, but somehow it wasn't so bad. Her hair smelled faintly of the watermelon we'd eaten after dinner.

I closed my eyes, feeling the heat of the child's body against mine, and recalled spending summer vacations with Asuka. In elementary school, Asuka had been little and weak and boys had often picked on her and made her cry. I would grab these boys and start fights with them, beat them up for her. But in reality, I was the one who'd end up crying much more than she ever did during those summers, what with my parents, who never even so much as smiled at me if I wasn't showing them a report card. And Asuka had always been there to hold my hand, to comfort me.

Today was the last day of my summer vacation too. I still hadn't decided on how I'd answer Hyōdō. At my age, could it really be a simple matter of fun, of getting to see my friends? I wanted to talk it over with Little Ken. But he surely hated me now. I wanted to stop by his place unannounced, but I was afraid I'd be turned away at the door. Just like he'd been afraid once, I remembered.

I held my friend's child tight against me and began to cry. My initial tears begat more and more, until my weeping turned into wrenching sobs. I could sense that the child had woken up, startled by my outburst.

"Mama, Mama, she's crying!" The child called out in a voice that edged into a tearfulness matching mine. I listened to the sound of her steps as she fled to her mother for rescue.

Planarian

"I n my next life, I want to come back as a planarian."

I said this rather unthinkingly while we were all out drinking and joking around, but then everyone turned to look at me, unexpectedly fascinated by my pronouncement. I was out with three younger former coworkers from my old part-time job, as well as my boyfriend, who was sitting beside me.

"A planarian? What's that?"

"Oh, I know! It's a cute little animal, right? Looks like an angel? They swim in the ocean, beneath icebergs."

"Isn't that actually called a sea angel?"

Everyone started talking at once, debating the mystery, until I clinked the ice in my Four Roses to stop the chatter.

"No, no, not that. Though they're about the same size as a sea angel. Planaria live way up in the mountains, in quiet streams filled with clear water."

My former coworkers—two young women and a man—exclaimed in unison at my revelation: *"Reaaally?"* My boyfriend was already well-versed in what I was about to say, so he contented himself with silently stuffing his mouth with whatever snacks were left.

"I saw something about them on TV. They're like little brown leeches, about a centimeter long. They can be found beneath rocks in streams or in the irrigation ditches between fields where they don't use chemical fertilizer. If you look at them up close, you can see they have little triangle-shaped heads—a bit obscene-looking, to be honest!"

Everyone laughed at that. *Obscene? How?* I finished the whiskey in my glass and ordered another. We'd been drinking for close to three hours. The two girls and my boyfriend had already stopped and were nursing cups of oolong tea.

"Why would you want to be something like that, Haruka?"

The man in his twenties I used to work with—the only other one in the group who seemed still in the mood to keep drinking—posed the question. I was about to reply when I was cut off by one of the girls, who'd apparently decided to answer on my behalf.

"I think I get it! Think about it: If you were an animal like that, you could spend your time swimming around in clean, clear water and never have to think about anything else for as long as you lived."

"Ewww, I'd never want to come back as a little penis-headed leech or whatever! If I'm going to be reincarnated as anything, it's going to be as a supermodel!"

"Don't say 'penis-headed.' Be a lady!"

The banter was drifting off topic, so, irritated, I raised my voice to regain everyone's attention.

"The thing is, you can cut up a planarian all you want but it won't ever die."

Everyone turned to look at me, puzzled.

"Even if you, say, cut one up into three pieces, each piece will eventually grow back and you'll end up with three new planaria. And if you cut those three into, say, ten more pieces, they'll grow back again, like a lizard's tail, and you'll have fourteen planaria on your hands."

My strangely vehement yet childlike explanation left everyone momentarily speechless. The drinks we'd ordered arrived, and the girls took the opportunity to turn their attention to the menu. *I kind of feel like something sweet . . .*

"Is that true?"

Only the young man seemed still interested, and I continued my explanation with drunken fervor.

"It's true, it's true! Even a little guy who ends up as just a bit of tail, pretty soon a tiny dick head pops out and starts growing—he's come back to life!"

"Okay, Haruka, that's enough."

My boyfriend said this to me in a low voice. With the noise of the bar and the other three sitting on the other side of the table, though, it seemed I was the only one who heard him.

"Are planaria arthropods?"

"Arthropods? What are those?"

"I mean, are they basically bugs, like a butterfly or a worm?"

"No, more like a leech, I'd say."

"Like a single-cell organism, or . . . ?"

"I don't know exactly. But I don't think so; after all, if you leave it be, it gets bigger, and if you cut it in two, you get more of them, so . . ."

I leaned forward in my seat and raised my voice even louder.

"I don't really know the technical details, I just think it would be

- 51 -

really cool, you know, to have a body you could cut up all you want and it would grow back! Like, I had breast cancer, right? If I'd been born a planarian, I could have just cut off my breast and it would have grown back, no fuss, no surgery, no bother!"

I'd meant to make everyone laugh, but the young man just smiled weakly in response, while the two girls who'd been debating whether to get tapioca milk or strawberry sherbet for dessert fell into awkward silence, studying the floor.

"Well, maybe it's time to get going . . ." said my boyfriend, and then, without waiting for an answer, he rose to his feet. Clear relief flashed across everyone's faces.

"You need to stop."

Hyōsuke turned on the car's ignition as he said this, clearly appalled at my behavior.

"You saw how awkward everyone felt. You always do this, Roon-chan."

"It's no secret! Everyone knows."

"That's not the point. It's that everyone's drinking and having a good time and you decide to bring up something like that, it ruins the mood. You love showing everyone your worst side."

So breast cancer is *something like that*, something that *ruins the mood*? But I decided not to let my irritation show.

"You really need to stop bringing up your illness all the time, Roon-chan. If you don't, one day you'll wake up and you won't have any friends left. We have another get-together coming up, and I'm worried! They're my friends, so I'd appreciate it if you didn't act like you did tonight with them."

Roon-chan. That's what he called me, his nicknames evolving from Haruka to Haru-chan to Haroo-roon, and now to Roon-chan. We called each other by our proper names when other people were around, but when it was just the two of us, we became Roon-chan and Hyō-chi. That's what it meant to be lovers, I knew, to have little baby-talk nicknames for each other, but I still found myself increasingly put off every time I heard it: *Roon-chan*.

"I think I'm still feeling a bit sick . . ." I murmured.

Hyōsuke stopped at a light, and a wave of nausea washed over me.

"You drank too much again, is all. You say you still feel sick, but you drink several times a week anyway. What if you quit alcohol and tried going to the gym? You might slim down a little too."

He'd hardly spoken back at the bar, but now that it was just the two of us, he couldn't seem to shut up. His bashfulness in front of others stemmed perhaps from introversion, but also perhaps from his still being a third-year undergrad. He was about a hundred times more sensible than I was despite being four years my junior, but when we were in public, he always let me take the lead.

"You want to come to my place, Roon-chan?"

Hyōsuke's voice was suddenly gentle. "Didn't I just say I was feeling sick? Take me home, please. Straight home."

But I couldn't say such a thing aloud. I knew little Hyō-chi loved me. That was the reality I clung to, the only thing allowing me to keep things together. If I lost that support, I knew I'd start spiraling, that I'd cause even more trouble than I already did to my family and those around me. That I'd end up self-destructing entirely.

The year before last, I'd been diagnosed with cancer and had my right breast removed. It was about a month before my twenty-fourth birthday. It had felt at the time like a bolt from the blue, but thinking back on it now, I wasn't sure that was really the right expression. After all, it wasn't like the previous twenty-three years were exactly filled with clear blue skies either. It felt more like my bad fortune had reached its natural conclusion. Unlucky people live unlucky lives, simple as that.

Of course, I was hardly so philosophical at the time; my life had sustained deep impact, leaving me unable to do much else than cry and scream. The doctor told me that the cancer was already stage 4, so there were really no other options besides removing the breast as fast as possible.

The first surgery removed the cancer from the underside of my breast, as well as much of the fatty tissue around it, and then the following year, they took flesh from my back and used it to reconstruct my chest. It sounds simple enough when I put it that way, but I couldn't believe how painful the process really was, both physically and mentally. It's called *reconstruction*, but it's not like you get your breast back looking the way it did before. Even now, half a year later, the rise of my breast was completely surrounded by obvious scarring, and there was still a livid fifteen-centimeter slice across my back as if I'd been slashed by a samurai sword. On top of that, since the nipple couldn't be reconstructed until I'd healed more from the first surgery, my new false breast lacked any nipple at all. I'd initially wanted to go in and get my nipple back as fast as possible, but now the thought of having to go back into the hospital and be knocked out and undergo surgery all over again made me feel like I'd rather just leave it be and get on with my life.

I first got to know Hyōsuke right before the cancer was discovered. I had another, older lover at the time too—for the first time in my life, I, who had never had much luck with men, found myself juggling two lovers. I knew it was silly to think so, but sometimes it seemed to me that all this happened as a way to restore balance to the universe after someone as awkward and unappealing as me had let herself enjoy the attentions of two men at once.

Long story short, Hyōsuke was a short-term part-timer at the company where I worked. We would chat sometimes when everyone from work would go out drinking, and we took a bit of a liking to each other, until one night we got drunk enough to end up in bed together.

I remained thankful, though, for the one bit of luck I had left to me: that Hyōsuke and I first made love before the cancer was discovered—that he was young enough to unthinkingly gobble up whatever he was offered, and that, afterward, he turned out to be such a well-raised young man.

The older man, who'd been more properly my lover at that point, heard the words *breast cancer* and turned tail immediately, heading for the hills. I'd told him about the diagnosis over the phone, crying, and he'd replied, "Don't worry, I'll be there for you," but the next day his landline and cell phone were both disconnected, and when I called the company where he worked, I ended up getting yelled at by a total stranger despite having nothing to do with it (though didn't I?): *He took a week off work without warning and didn't even say why!* But Hyōsuke didn't run away. He blended into my family, crying along with us, meeting me every day even when I was upset and impossible to deal with, patiently consoling me. When I opened my eyes after surgery, there he was standing beside my parents, peering down at me with a concerned look on his face.

Ever since, Hyōsuke never left my side. When my emotional instability would lead me to break down and lash out, he would, in his youthful way, lash out in return, saying things like "You got cancer, there's nothing you can do about it! Accept it!" But even then, he never left me.

Once the car was parked in the pay-by-the-hour parking lot, we got out and walked, hand in hand, into his apartment. He'd grown up in the suburbs as the son of a prosperous family who owned a major shipping company, which allowed him to remain jobless and yet still afford a three-room apartment almost too spacious for a single person thanks to a generous allowance from his parents.

As always, he started heating up the bath as soon as we entered the apartment. A nearly pathological neat freak, he always made sure to take a shower as soon as he came back home. I, on the other hand, tended toward slovenliness but would nonetheless find myself half forced into taking a bath as well, a bothersome exercise I just wanted to get over with, which led more often than not to us bathing together.

Bath time had become a habit at this point, so there was nothing sexy about it as Hyōsuke scrubbed our bodies and hair with all the tenderness of someone washing a pile of dirty dishes. When we first started doing this, I found it hard not to get agitated, partly out of embarrassment, partly out of wonder that he would care for my body like this even in the sorry state it was in; but these days, I didn't think anything of it at all, and just sat there, allowing myself to be washed. Before, I'd thought of it as being loved, but now I didn't quite know what to think. Why would this man wash the body of another so diligently?

It wasn't just washing either—once out of the bath, he'd take a fluffy towel and dry my every nook and cranny with it. He'd even blow-dry my hair. He first started doing this after he saw me take a shower one day and then simply comb out my wet hair and allow it to air-dry. He had long hair too, and a professional hairdresser's skill with the blow-dryer. The icing on the cake, though, was that he had a pair of special scissors that he would use to trim my eyebrows. I didn't even own an eyebrow brush! I told him once that he should go to cosmetology school, but he just replied, as if no other alternative had ever occurred to him, that he planned to take over his father's business when the time came.

After bath time came sex, whether I felt like it or not. I'd been taking hormone shots ever since the surgery, so Aunt Flo never came around anymore. Which left me with no easy way to say, *Oh, it's not a good time right now*. I'd used other excuses before, saying I was tired or feeling dizzy, but when I did, I'd be met with a series of pitiful faces and a lingering bad mood that took forever to dissipate, so it seemed easier these days to go along and let it happen.

I let him do whatever he wanted with my body, just as I had in the bath. Before, I'd had such a strong sex drive I'd considered going into sex work, but now, maybe due to the hormone shots, I didn't seem to have any at all, making sex a rather arduous endeavor. Humans are so strange, though—I found that if I reminded myself that this was happening because I was loved, I could whip myself up and moan a bit and my body would end up responding more or less normally. I gave him what he wanted as a token of thanks, for loving me. His youthful inability to last very long was the situation's sole saving grace.

Once sex ended, it was finally time for tea. Not cold oolong from a plastic bottle either—this was properly made black or green tea, or sometimes even coffee, steeped in hot water and care. I'd been thankful at first for this as well, marveling that he would go to so much trouble just for me, but lately it had become obvious that he did it mostly for himself. The proof was in the way his gaze, which had been trained on me up till then, always ended up sliding over to the television he would inevitably turn on as we sat sipping. This is how it always went, about three or four times every week. It wasn't easy, being loved.

"Do you have school tomorrow, Hyō-chi?"

"Yeah, starting second period. Have you sobered up, Roon-chan?"

He said this while lying on the bed, absently staring at the TV. He seemed unaware of it himself, but asking "Have you sobered up?" was his way of saying "I think it's about time for you to go." He may have loved me, but he rarely seemed happy to have me stay over. It didn't seem like he was seeing someone else or anything; I think he simply preferred not to share his single bed with anyone while he slept.

"Tomorrow I have my hormone shot, so I should probably get going. I'll call you when I'm done. Do you want to have dinner together?"

I was already putting on my clothes as I asked him the question, but he didn't answer, as he was busy lying on the bed and pressing his fingertips to his temples instead.

"Are you okay?"

"Yeah, it's just that my head feels heavy. I might have a cold."

"Really? Maybe you should go see the doctor."

"No, I'm fine."

"You should go. Listen to your older cancer-patient lover, she knows what she's talking about."

Hyōsuke suddenly drove his fist into the pillow beside him. The case tore, sending feathers flying into the air. *I made him angry again?* I thought, and when he spoke, his voice was low.

"You need to stop."

Then he sighed, sounding completely exhausted.

"It's over. You're not a patient anymore, Roon-chan. You're

cured. How long are you going to keep milking this? Do you think you can just go on not working forever? That you'll end up marrying me and that will be that? Pull yourself together."

Over? I couldn't believe what I was hearing, and I opened my mouth to defend myself, but my mouth betrayed me, as I heard a small voice emerge from it saying, "I'm sorry, I won't say things like that again."

"I'm going to go home now," I continued as I stood up and got ready to go, and then, seeming to realize he'd gone too far, he followed me to the door and kissed me lightly on the mouth. But he also didn't seem to want to accompany me any farther, so I closed the door on him, smiling, and left.

After walking slowly to the parking lot, I paid the fee and pulled the car out. It was my parents' car, but during weekdays they didn't use it, leaving it free for me to take whenever I wanted.

Hyōsuke's parents had bought him a car before we met, but he'd apparently gotten in an accident right away and totaled it. Ever since, he didn't seem to want to drive if he could help it, only taking the wheel when I was too drunk to do so, like tonight. *You're a shipping company heir and you don't drive?* I once joked, but that had made him really angry too. *You just don't get it, Roon-chan.*

I felt heavy with fatigue as I drove. After my monthly hormone shot tomorrow, I would feel even heavier, to the point that it would be hard to get myself to walk. So depressing. Driving alone down the midnight highway, I wished again upon the stars above, though I knew it was no use: *In my next life, I want to come back as a planarian.*

Unemployed as I was, the only regular schedule I kept was my once-a-month trip to the number one hospital in the prefecture. It was too late to do anything about it now, but choosing this huge, hypermodern facility might have been a mistake. I always made sure to arrive right at nine in the morning, but I would always end up waiting at least four hours before I could meet my primary care physician anyway.

There were simply too many patients. People lined up to get their blood taken in assembly-line fashion, as if waiting to get into the hottest ramen shop in town. My veins were hard to find, and the nurse stabbed me again and again before finally drawing blood. I told myself not to let it get me down, but even as I did, I found I was pretty down already.

My head was filled with useless thoughts I couldn't help thinking even as I knew how useless they were. *I wish I'd never gotten cancer!* But it wasn't like I got cancer on purpose. So why should I be plagued with useless regret? I couldn't seem to make myself accept that it was just bad luck. Why was I the one with cancer, and not, say, this clumsy young nurse turning my arm into a pincushion? Though it wasn't true that I was the only one. Everyone waiting with me to see the doctor, all these people, male and female, young and old, each and every one of them might have it too, this great big seething mass of us. Passing together through the cancer assembly line.

So, I was kept waiting. It couldn't help but bring me down. Why couldn't there be appointments at set times? Why couldn't they keep to a schedule? I was unemployed, so it wasn't so bad for me, but what about working people? This service wasn't available on the weekends. What were they supposed to do? Besides, the examinations themselves never lasted more than five minutes. All he seemed to hear was when I said my period had stopped. *These hormones I've started taking, they make me dizzy as soon as I get the shot, my eyes pop open every couple of hours at night, I'm bathed in sweat, I can't sleep a wink, I'm so exhausted and drained I feel like throwing up (and do throw up!)* . . .

I'd say these things to my doctor and all he'd say in response was "Yes, that happens sometimes." Once, he said instead, "This regimen might suppress the breast cancer, but it might also cause uterine cancer." What was I supposed to do, then? How did that help? At a loss, I made my own appointment with a gynecologist, only to have her tell me, "People don't usually continue these injections for more than six months. You've been taking them for a year and a half, which seems odd to me." She was kind enough to confer directly with my doctor, but in the end, the only answer I ever received was that there was a danger that stopping now might cause the cancer to metastasize, so it might have been a good thing that we resumed the injections when we did.

I still worried, though. Could there be aftereffects from taking something meant to be taken for only six months for a period almost three times that long? Would I still be able to have children? But I didn't know where to find the answers to these questions. I went to the library and looked through a few books that seemed like they might help, but they turned out not to have much in the way of answers, and both my doctor and my gynecologist seemed so busy that I really didn't feel like pestering them with the same questions over and over. After all, it wasn't like they were being deliberately cruel, they just genuinely seemed not to know what to tell me.

Looking at it from the hospital's point of view, I'd grown a tumor nearly five centimeters in diameter and yet the severity of my condition was reduced to stage 1 just through surgery, no radiation or chemotherapy necessary, so in the grand scheme of things I was quite lucky. And I supposed that was true, but it was still hard to feel filled with gratitude to them for saving my life. For one thing, the money I was paying for all this was no joke.

In any case, today, after a four-hour-and-fifteen-minute wait, the nurse called me over and said, "The doctor has to go into surgery, so we have someone else here to see you. Of course, if you prefer, we can reschedule your appointment for a later date."

I'd arrived a bit anemic, and now, having had even more blood drawn, I lacked the strength to get angry, so I just nodded weakly. It wasn't like I had a strong, trusting relationship with my actual primary care physician anyway. Though I did wonder what I was going to say to a doctor I'd never seen before in my life.

Nevertheless, when I entered the exam room and was asked how I was feeling, I reeled off a list of my usual complaints: my nausea, my dizziness, my unease with continuing the hormone shots. The substitute doctor, who seemed to be still in his early thirties, replied to my concerns by saying, "I'm not your regular physician, so I'm not sure what to tell you. You might try going to Internal Care about the dizziness." *You vant to suck my blood too?* I thought, irritated, but kept it to myself and simply nodded meekly before leaving the exam room.

And then, finally, it was time to receive another ridiculously expensive, shockingly painful shot that for some reason wasn't covered by my insurance.

You can't let this kind of thing get you down! I told myself once again, but I started to get lightheaded as I walked to the parking lot, my eyes welling up with tears. Even as I found myself rather pathetic, my hand reached, as if by its own accord, for my phone and dialed Hyōsuke's number.

"Ahh, Roon-chan! Are you done at the hospital?"

His voice betrayed not a whit of concern. Hearing it, I found myself gripped with a complex mix of emotions, equal parts happiness and rage.

"Yeah. You're still at school? Should I come pick you up?"

"Oh, that would be great! I'll be in the McDonald's."

My mood was, in fact, somewhat improved as I hung up, and then I looked up to see a small-framed woman nodding at me as she walked across the parking lot. There was still some distance between us, but I recognized her right away, thinking, *Oh right, her*, as I returned her greeting with a nod of my own. She was a woman I'd often see in the smoking area when I'd been hospitalized, though this was the first time I'd seen her since then.

Maybe it was normal for a hospital, but it still seemed rather stingy for a facility consisting of three tall towers to have only one smoking area in the entire place, a single six-mat room with no windows, just a ventilation system; you could hardly call it comfortable. Even so, as soon as I was able to walk on my own, I would take the cigarettes my friends would slip me and make regular pilgrimages there to smoke. That's when I would see her, dressed in her hospital-issued pajamas. She was always alone, absently smoking her cigarettes, and so beautiful she drew the attention of everyone around, though she had a certain air of unapproachability. The fathers and aunties who also frequented the area were completely impervious to her standoffishness, though, and spent all their time trying to exchange even a few words with her, this glamorous woman who looked like she might be an actress. The woman would deflect them deftly enough, but it seemed as though all the attention indeed began to get to her, as, after a while, she stopped showing up. I heard someone repeat a rumor that she'd been seen smoking on the roof, and all I could think was *She's up there because you lot can't keep your mouths shut!* Even if we never exchanged words, seeing her pale profile and delicate fingers as she smoked her cigarettes always made me happy. Beautiful women frequently put me in a bad mood, as they stirred up baseless feelings of jealousy, but this woman somehow only stirred up feelings of attraction, making me think things like *How wonderful it would be if I'd been born so lovely!* After a while, it seemed she must have been discharged, as no one saw her around anywhere anymore.

Now that I was seeing her again after so long, she still gave an air of untouched purity, even dressed as she was in a simple T-shirt and jeans. Alone as always, she climbed into a shiny top-of-the-line Japanese car and pulled smoothly out of the parking lot with practiced ease. I couldn't help but stare the whole time. And then I laughed a little at myself, realizing that I'd memorized her license plate number like a proper stalker.

I ended up eating dinner with Hyōsuke at a family restaurant, and then, perhaps out of pity for me and my postshot paleness, he ended our evening early. I managed to drive home even as the edges of my vision grew dark and waves of nausea made it all I could do to keep the shrimp doria I'd eaten from coming back up. I arrived to find my mother home too. A rare occurrence.

"You're back early."

Sensing a certain hostility in her tone, I just said, "You too," and stretched out on the couch.

"You went to the hospital today?"

"Yeah."

"How did it go?"

"The usual."

The resignation in my tone prompted my mother to chew her lower lip, a concerned look on her face, as she stood there in her pantsuit.

"Did you see Hyōsuke today?"

Nausea washed over me again, along with an intense hot flash, and I felt sweat run unpleasantly down my forehead and under my arms. I was losing the energy to continue fielding my mother's questions.

"If you're feeling so poorly, you should stop running around every day and stay home and rest instead."

"It's just that I had my shot today. It's not usually so bad."

I braced myself for what was surely next: *If that's the case, then why don't you try going back to work?* But she abruptly turned her head and left the living room instead. My mother had worked at the city hall since she was young, and by now her salary well outstripped that of my father, who worked at a shoe wholesaler. My mother nearly always got home from work late, which bothered my father, and he would drown himself in liquor every evening and usually end up coming home in the dead of night.

Yet, perhaps because I was an only child, I'd always felt well loved by my parents. Perhaps too well loved—I was spoiled, always given exactly what I wanted to eat, until I came to a realization one day: I was fat.

Fat kids are bullied. That was what I learned in kindergarten. I was the one the boys would throw rocks at and the girls would shun. I also learned that it's no easy thing for a child who's given anything and everything she wants to eat her whole life to change her habits through sheer willpower.

So I spent elementary and middle school being called *pig* and worse, but it was when I turned fifteen that I truly, in my heart of hearts, began to feel that if I didn't go on a diet, I might very well be bullied to death. As soon as I began high school that spring, I found myself ganged up on by girls in higher grades just for being fat, calling me *eyesore*. I realized I might actually end up being killed if things continued like this, so I forced myself to lose forty kilos in under a year. I still felt a bit chubby, but it seemed I successfully fooled everyone into thinking I was a normal person, and the bullying stopped completely, as if it had never happened.

When I told my doctor about it, he responded by saying, "Overeating might have been a factor contributing to your condition." Later, I drunkenly lashed out at my mother, saying, "You let me stuff my face with anything I wanted as a kid, and it gave me cancer!" My mother tearfully apologized, but it was too late for tears and apologies. And besides, I knew I was just using this as an excuse to vent. But I also knew that if I was going to get through this alive, I needed to find a bad guy to blame.

But Hyōsuke was right—all that was over now. Even I realized that I needed to put a period on my struggle with cancer and move on.

And the truth was, it was my own slovenliness that led most directly to my condition.

About two years before my cancer was discovered, I started noticing some brownish bloodlike fluid leaking from my nipple. It didn't hurt or even itch, though, and I'd just started a new job and was preoccupied with my love life, so I put it out of my mind. Subsequently, my love life became quite busy indeed, and I noticed a bit of itchiness in my nether regions. Talking about it with a friend, she said it might be chlamydia, so I made an appointment with the gynecologist, and during the examination, when I mentioned in passing that I'd noticed some fluid leaking from my nipple, I watched as all the color drained from her face. She gave me a series of tests, and the next day I received a call at work from the hospital telling me I needed to come in immediately. "Right now?" I remember asking, to which I was told, "Yes, come right now, and have a family member accompany you if possible."

Once at the hospital, there was no hemming and hawing, just the bald announcement: "You have breast cancer. We have to cut it out as soon as possible."

I wasn't the only one to fall apart upon hearing the news—my parents were a mess as well. Things might have been different if it had been discovered earlier, but as it was, the tumor was so big there was no wiggle room to consider other options or debate the finer points of treatment. Besides, it was such a huge, hypermodern facility. People came from outside the prefecture just to be treated there, and the surgeon assigned to cut me open was said to be the best there was. Neither my family nor I really had any choice in the matter.

My mother cried and cried, asking why it couldn't have been her instead. My father, whom I never recalled ever touching me since I'd become old enough to be aware of such things, squeezed my hand, tears in his eyes. I am loved, I thought. Friends and acquaintances sympathized with me as well. But love and sympathy can't cure cancer. An old friend familiar with my perverse nature said, "If you make it through this, it might end up really changing you, Haruka."

But in the end, I didn't change one bit. I read my share of diaries and personal accounts written by others who'd battled cancer, but the renewed appreciation they spoke of for the miracle of health, the importance of family, the precious gift of life itself—I didn't feel that at all.

Both during the initial surgery and the reconstructive surgery the following year, my family and friends and boyfriend were all incredibly nice to me. When the anesthetic didn't agree with me and I would throw up all over the place, or when the tubes sticking into various places on my body became so itchy and uncomfortable I would lie in bed weeping, everyone did all they could to help me. I knew this was true.

Now that it was over, though, I couldn't help but wonder what all that kindness really amounted to. It was like the aftermath of a festival. My family and my boyfriend both kept telling me the same thing: *You're healthy now, there's no reason to keep mentioning cancer all the time!* But if it were really over, why was I still dizzy every day, why did I still feel like throwing up, why couldn't I sleep at night? To me, nothing was over at all.

But even as I felt this way, I did make an effort to rejoin society. After the first surgery, my right arm would hurt when I moved it, but after some physical therapy, I went back to my job after three months off. My boss said, "Look at you, back doing your best after such a serious illness! I admire that." I chalked it up to my native perversity that I couldn't accept his praise at face value.

I ended up quitting again for no other reason than that I didn't want to do it anymore. Everything seemed like too much bother. Just being alive seemed like too much bother, but it also seemed like too much bother to die. It would be logical, then, to stop going to the hospital and let the cancer come back and kill me, but the truth was, that was the thing that scared me most. It was a contradiction. A contradiction that exhausted me.

After quitting again, I spent all my time outside my monthly hospital visits loafing around; I met up almost every day with Hyōsuke, who had plenty of free time himself as a student, and occasionally picked up a temp job here and there to make a little spending money.

My parents seemed to have been quite shocked by my accusation that their letting me overeat as a child gave me cancer, so they never quite came out and said, *You need to get a proper job again*, but at the same time, they no longer walked on eggshells around me either. I could see *You need to stop* written across their faces as they dealt with me, but, like a tyrant, I pretended not to notice. Sometimes I thought I might even be exacting a form of revenge on them for spoiling me body and soul in the name of love. *I'm such an idiot. To act this way at this age.* Yet the fact remained that I simply couldn't face going back to work. I couldn't stand the thought of rejoining society and having some guy look at me like he knew me and say, *Look at you, back doing your best after such a serious illness! I admire that.*

That weekend, Hyōsuke had gone all the way back home just to celebrate his mother's birthday (!), so I was free to go out with a friend for once. It was the childhood friend who'd made the remark about my brush with cancer possibly changing me. She'd recently broken up with her boyfriend, leaving her with too much time on her hands, so she asked if I could pick her up in my parents' car and take her shopping to cheer her up. Finding the idea of hanging around doing nothing at home depressing, I readily took her up on her proposal.

As we pulled into the parking garage of a recently built department store that boasted the largest square footage of sales space in town, I noticed that the car in the space next to mine seemed familiar. I checked the license plate, and sure enough, it belonged to the woman I'd seen the other day in the hospital parking lot. It was a small town we lived in, so it wasn't so strange that we'd end up going shopping at the same department store on the weekend. Still, it would be fun to run into her—my heart beat a little faster at the thought.

"Does that belong to someone you know?"

My friend noticed me staring at the car and asked about it, her tone slightly mocking.

"Yeah . . . Well, sort of."

"Ooh, is it a guy? Let's leave a note!"

"No, no, it's just a woman I met back when I was in the hospital."

My friend snorted, clearly doubting my explanation, and then my phone began loudly playing its little song in my back pocket. I hurried to answer it; just as I suspected, it was Hyōsuke.

"Roon-chan, what are you doo-ing?"

He was stretching out the words at the ends of his sentences like a girl.

"I'm out shopping with Mii-tan. What're you up to, Hyō-chi?"

"I'm shopping too! I wanna have Mom cook me something go-od. I found a re-ally nice marbled steak, and bought a cake to go wi-ith!"

"Oooh, that sounds so-o-o go-od! I wanna have some to-o!"

"I'll make it for you sometime! All right, then, don't be out too late toni-ight!"

"I wo-on't!" I trilled, and then hung up, only to have my friend slap me lightly on the head.

"*Mii*-tan, *Roon*-chan . . . it makes me ill just listening to you! Aren't you ashamed to talk like that?"

"I'm well aware of how we sound."

My tone was a bit self-righteous, and my friend shrugged her shoulders, clearly put off. But back when she had a boyfriend, they'd called each other every day, and I'd have to listen to her answer the phone like *Hello-o-o, this is Mii-tan!* Isn't it more embarrassing to sound like that and not even realize it?

My friend and I walked from the parking garage into the department store and then split up, making plans to meet up again in two hours. The clothes she planned to peruse didn't interest me at all, and even if they did, I lacked the funds to buy any of the brands being sold, so I planned instead to waste time browsing in the bookstore.

But I'd come all this way to see this brand-new place, so I decided to take the elevator down to the basement level and look at the food vendors there first. It was the weekend and the weather was nice, so the place was filled with couples and parents with their children. Once I reached the basement, I wandered through the displays, eyeing the rows of confections and fancy prepared foods lining the aisles. Remembering what Hyōsuke had told me, I found myself wanting to buy something for my own mother. Would she like some little snacks, or would she prefer a cake?

Hating a person is a form of loving them, I knew. I would say the most horrible things to my mother and yet also pick up little presents to give her, or decide to give her a break at home and cook or clean for her. We often went on shopping trips together, or even little spa vacations at the nearby hot springs. From the outside, we must have seemed like the closest of mother-daughter pairs. But I knew what we really were: a mother and daughter who couldn't properly separate from each other and move on, as if still fused together at the womb.

It was still too early to be evening, but the prepared-food section was jammed with housewives, and as I tried to wade through them, I found myself getting lightheaded again. It looked less crowded over by the traditional Japanese sweets, so I decided to head in that direction, but as soon as I did, I felt a hard tug at my sleeve.

"Excuse me, young lady, do you know where the exit is?"

Startled, I turned in the direction of the voice at my elbow and saw an older woman about a head shorter than me speaking in a loud voice.

"Well, um..."

"Where's the exit? I've been trying my darndest to get out of here, but I can't figure out how!"

The old woman had my sleeve gripped tightly in her fist and wouldn't let go. At first I thought she was just very short, but looking closer, I saw that her back was painfully hunched. She wore pants and a cardigan of the same washed-out color, and she was clutching a cane in her other hand. Her huge eyes goggled up from the middle of her wrinkled face, peering into mine as if trying to climb into them. Their cloudy whites provoked a feeling of déjà vu, and my stomach rumbled as the yakisoba I'd eaten for lunch threatened to make a return appearance.

I brought my left hand to my mouth, thinking, *Oh no, I can't throw up here!* The old woman had my right arm in such a grip that I couldn't move it at all. My vision began to blur, and all the strength drained from my legs.

"Don't you know where the exit is?"

Unable to stand up any longer, I slid slowly to the floor, but even this failed to stop the woman from shouting her question at me again and again. The vendors around us finally seemed to notice something was wrong, and I sensed people beginning to gather around us. I heard a voice say, "Are you okay?"

Then: "Oh—it's you!"

Fighting to suppress my nausea, I looked up and saw her staring down at me—that woman again, dressed now in a white smock.

"... Uh, hello ... how are you ..."

"You're about to pass out from anemia, we can skip the small talk. Can you stand? I'm going to take you to the nurse's station. Um, excuse me, ma'am, you're going to have to let go of her now ..."

Here I am, rescued again, I thought, before grabbing the woman's shoulder and managing, somehow, to pull myself to my feet.

Being hospitalized twice taught me how much I lacked the skills necessary to live among others. It had never before occurred to me that even hospitalization was something that someone could be good or bad at.

After my surgery, I'd barely turned over in my bed before the nurses began to hate me. I never smiled or thanked them—all I did was complain, asking why I had to suffer so, going on about how much it hurt, how hard everything was. No wonder they became steadily colder to me. Beneath their uniforms, these angels in white were nothing more than middle-aged women, after all. I was likely also jealous of the good health emanating from their bodies, the well-adjustment emanating from their psyches. *You can do it!* they'd say. *Be strong!* But the more they encouraged me, the angrier I'd become, even as I knew my rage was misdirected. I was sullen and unpleasant to the very end, sometimes even refusing entirely to speak when they spoke to me.

Even so, the nurses were there to do a job, and they were never mean to me—I was a patient, after all—and they generally left me alone. The bigger problem I had was with fellow patients, especially the older ones.

I got goosebumps thinking about it even now. Both times I was hospitalized, I was stuck in a six-person room, and both times, the average age of the other patients must have been around seventy.

Why does everyone start to look so similar as they get old? Exacerbating the issue, every patient in that vast hospital wore the same striped gowns, making them look like monks in their work clothes, so it was nearly impossible to tell anyone apart; I spent the whole time unable to remember anyone's names or faces. Not that I was exactly trying, but still.

I especially hated mealtimes. We were given plastic plates filled with food made with care only for its calorie count, and its smell would blend with that of disinfectant and other people's piss, everything mixing together into the same disgusting stew. My appetite was already ruined by the sweets my visitors would bring me, so the sight of my toothless roommates gumming their food made me want to scream, *Do you really want to live so bad, even like this?* But then I'd remind myself that everyone would eventually end up like that, including me, and a great wave of listlessness would wash over me, leaving me with nothing else to do but joylessly clean my plate.

The fact was, the old people who were too weak to get out of bed never really bothered me—it was the lively ones who were the problem.

I had no interest whatsoever in any of my fellow patients apart from the beautiful woman from the smoking area, but I seemed to be unique in this. Once I was able to get out of bed on my own, whenever I would start making my way toward the bathroom, dragging my IV bag on its trolley behind me, everyone would rush over to try to make conversation.

Where do you live? What do you do for work? Where does your father work? Why are you in the hospital? If I failed to answer, they would just talk about themselves instead, boasting about their various illnesses with unseemly fervor. I felt like a new inmate entering a prison yard, and it made me even less inclined to talk to anyone. I tried my best to keep to myself, maintaining my silence no matter what was said to me or who said it, until one day a nurse took me aside and told me, "Uehara-san, everyone's complaining about your bad attitude, please try to be more careful of other people's feelings." My strength left me then completely. No diagnosis, no matter how dire, could free me from the prison of group life.

"How are you feeling?"

As I lay on the bed in the department store nurse's station, memories from my time in the hospital came up one after the other, making me weep softly to myself until the woman who'd brought me there stuck her head back into the room. I hurriedly wiped my eyes and sat up.

"Oh, I think I'm okay now. I just got a little dizzy is all."

"Are you really okay?"

"Yes. I'm totally fine now."

The woman smiled broadly, then pulled up a rolling chair to sit next to the bed.

"Do you work here?" I asked.

"Yes, at the candied bean shop right where you collapsed. I saw you and thought, *Oh, it's Uehara-san! Bothered by an old lady again!*—and then down you went! I mean, I know it's not really a laughing matter, but it was still kind of funny."

I laughed too, blushing. She was right, she'd rescued me in a similar way once before, back in the hospital. Tired of my room, I'd ventured out to loiter in the lobby, where I was accosted by an old woman with dementia. She all but forced me to sit down next to her and listen as she went on at great length, complaining about her illnesses and every member of her family. I didn't have anything else to do with my time, though, so I sat there listening to her, but as I watched her dentureless mouth working, I began to feel sicker and sicker to my stomach. When I decided to excuse myself and return to my room, she scolded me sharply, shouting, "Hey, where are you going? I'm talking to you!" I unthinkingly responded in kind, raising my voice, and it began to turn into an actual argument—onlookers began to gather. I felt so unwell, and the hospital staff began treating me like I'd been the one bullying this old woman, so I lost my grip on things completely and ended up collapsing onto a nearby sofa. That was when this woman intervened, saying, "It's not her fault, I assure you!" I fled to my room as fast as I could at that point, and I don't recall now if I ever thanked her for what she'd done.

"Well, thank you for now, but also for back then."

"Forget about it. I saw you recently, right? Back in the hospital parking lot? Are you still having to go regularly?"

"Yes, once a month."

"Once every three months for me. But they always make me wait, I hate it. Why isn't there a set schedule? I have to spend my whole day off there!"

"That's so true!"

I responded with unexpected verve. I felt like she was the rare person it was easy to talk to. She seemed to be around thirty years old, maybe a bit younger. She had a low, gentle voice, and despite wearing the white smock and headscarf that constituted the uniform at the Japanese sweetshop where she worked, it didn't seem dowdy on her at all. The modest earrings twinkling in each earlobe were very becoming. She wore a name tag on her chest: *Nagase*. I realized I'd never known her name, yet she'd called me *Uehara-san* just now.

"How did you know my name?"

"Well, back in the hospital, all the old biddies gossiped about you, so I learned it without even really trying."

Which meant she must've known what I'd been hospitalized for, I realized. I remembered how all those women would come up to me, saying, *Oh, breast cancer, that's tough*, even though I had no recollection of either me or anyone in my family talking to anyone about it. Hospital patients were people without privacy.

"Is today a day off for you?"

"Well, no . . . I mean—are you on your break right now?"

"Yes. Why?"

"I feel bad taking up your precious time like this."

My words made her burst out laughing.

"I was worried, so I came here to talk to you! But thank you for your concern. It's kind. You're a sensitive soul."

My face blushed deep red at being called *sensitive*—me, who'd given herself breast cancer out of sheer slovenliness! Not wanting to deceive such a lovely person any further, I opened my mouth and the truth came out.

"You should know, I don't have a job."

"Oh, really?"

"And I'm fine now, physically. I just can't make myself go back to work. So I spend my days loafing around instead."

Hearing this, the woman grew thoughtful. Anticipating her contempt, I looked down. I caught sight of my shirtsleeve, still bunched up where the old lady had grabbed me.

"Uehara-san, if it wouldn't be too much trouble . . ."

She spoke slowly, as if carefully weighing each word.

"Would you consider working part-time at the sweetshop? One of our most dependable employees just up and quit, so we could really use the help."

"Really? But—"

"You don't have to answer right now. But please think about it."

The sudden offer left me at a total loss.

"But, but, I—but . . ."

"But, what?"

The woman smiled at me as I kept repeating the word *but*.

"But . . . I'm unfit for society!"

The woman's eyes grew wide, and then she giggled. Despite having no evidence to back her up, she spoke with confidence. "Oh, you are not!"

So, that was how I came to work four days a week at a shop selling Japanese-style candied beans. My perverse nature made me react with irritation to the sheer joy displayed by my boyfriend and family as they congratulated me for "Getting back on your feet at last!" but it was nonetheless true that I was in the mood to give it a go. Even if the hourly wage was only two-thirds the going rate.

It was only after I started working there that I learned that the woman, Nagase-san, was actually the manager, and that our ages were, shockingly, only a year apart. Yet here she was, such an adult, while I was such a child.

I was hardly a connoisseur of candied beans, so I hadn't realized that the shop was a franchise, part of a chain that could be found in department stores and supermarkets all across the prefecture and was on its way to going national. The shop in the department store was small by design, though, with only three employees: the manager, Nagase-san; a middle-aged woman who worked part-time; and me. Nagase-san also managed a branch that had opened up in a nearby train-station building, so she split her time between the two locations and met frequently with people involved with the franchising, so she wasn't around all that much. The other part-timer and I exchanged greetings, of course, but she would leave when I arrived, so we never spent enough time together to get to know each other.

This may make it sound like I spent my time at the shop mostly alone, but this was not the case. Rather, since the shop shared a counter with vendors on both sides, I spent my days surrounded by fellow workers selling Japanese sweets—almost exclusively older women. In other words, my worst nightmare had come true.

Old women are all the same, whether at a Japanese sweetshop or a hospital. Indeed, the Japanese-sweets area wasn't ever all that crowded, so each of the frequent lulls became an opportunity to pepper me with questions.

Where do you live? How old are you? Are you single? Where did you go to school? What did you do for work before this? These were exactly the types of questions I'd hated answering in the hospital, but I hid my discomfort behind a smile and responded as cheerfully as I could, as I didn't want to damage Nagase-san's reputation. Once their questions were answered, the women would get a satisfied look on their faces and start going on and on about their own lives and problems as I made sympathetic noises and pretended to listen.

The job itself wasn't so difficult. It took about two weeks for me to master the trickiest tasks—ringing things up on the newfangled register, gift wrapping boxes of sweets—without having to ask the women around me for help. The actual challenges of the job were keeping up the conviviality necessary to deal with the ladies surrounding me and that the shop's clientele were, for the most part, old people as well.

Come to think of it, young people didn't really flock to purchase traditional sweets like candied beans. How many times was I brought to the brink of madness by an old man taking ten, even fifteen minutes to decide which beans to purchase, or by an old woman lingering interminably at the counter, trying to make conversation and giving no indication she ever intended to go home? The witchlike crone who'd grabbed my arm before, asking *Where's the exit?* turned out to be a regular visitor, wandering around the basement buttonholing workers and fellow customers alike nearly every day.

I've made a big mistake, I thought, but at the same time, Nagase-san had done me a kindness by offering me this job, and I knew I'd never find another boss who'd be so understanding of my condition, allowing me to take time off whenever I felt too under the weather to come in.

"Hey, I don't think I've ever asked—how do you and Nagase-san know each other?"

The woman to my right, who sold jellied bean paste, asked me this one day during a lull.

"We met when we were hospitalized."

I spoke without thinking, and the woman's face contorted with the keenness of her sudden interest.

"*Hospitalized?* What was wrong?"

"Breast cancer."

"Really? Nagase-san had *breast cancer*?"

The woman's braying voice filled me with contempt, but I kept it inside, smiling as I said, "No, I did. They cut my right breast off and then used flesh from my back to reconstruct it. I wasn't able to work at all for a long time."

I remembered what Hyōsuke had said: *You love showing everyone your worst side.* The woman knit her brow in a show of concern, but I could see what she was really thinking: *Oh, this is juicy!* The entire Japanese-sweets section would hear the news by tomorrow, I knew.

"Oh, that's a pity, you're so young. But here you are, doing your best! I admire that."

"I assure you, I'm hardly doing my best."

"In any case, do you happen to know why Nagase-san was in the hospital?"

There she is, I thought. Nothing in this world would stop her from asking her burning questions.

"I really have no idea. I feel like it's a bit indelicate to ask someone something like that straight to their face, you know?"

I'd meant to needle her, but she just nodded in response, smiling.

"Yeah, that makes sense!"

But I wondered—what *had* Nagase-san been in the hospital for? I couldn't deny I was curious, but the fact that she never brought it up herself made me think it was something she preferred not to talk about. Though now that I thought about it, I didn't know where she lived or if she was single either.

Right then, the PHS handy-phone in my pocket began to ring. The sweetshop was in the basement where a regular phone couldn't get a signal, so Hyōsuke, unable to stand not being able to reach me at all times, had bought me a handy-phone that would work down here.

"Roon-chan, is this a bad time?"

"No, it's fine. There're no customers."

"Come over tonight. I got that marbled steak I told you about, I'll cook it for you!"

"Wha-at? Amazing, I'll come over as soon as I'm off!"

I glanced over and saw the jellied-bean-paste seller, who'd been so friendly up till then, shoot me a cold look and walk away.

The next day, Nagase-san said, "Do you want to grab a bite to eat after work?" I thought she must have a family waiting at home, as she would always close out the register as fast as possible and leave the moment business hours were over; we'd never even had so much as a cup of tea together since I'd started. Her unexpected invitation thus made me inordinately happy, so I canceled a date with Hyōsuke at the last minute and walked with her into the city.

Nagase-san claimed to hardly ever eat out, so she left it to me to choose the place. I suspected she might be treating me to this meal, so I felt shy to pick a place that was too expensive and ended up choosing a Western-style gastropub that was on the chic side while still being cheap enough that Hyōsuke and I could afford to go there sometimes. As we sat down at the bar, the first thing out of her mouth was "Pretty lively, isn't it?" I was a little shocked, thinking that this was her way of complaining that the place was noisy. But we ended up ordering our beers and toasting without incident, making harmless conversation about various people in the department store.

"Tell me, Haruka. Are you getting used to the job?"

Nagase-san asked me this right after we ordered our second beers.

"Little by little, yes."

"And your health is improving?"

"Little by little too."

I'd meant to make her laugh, but she just lit her cigarette, her expression unchanged. It seemed like she wanted to say something else, and then, just as I suspected, she mustered up her courage and opened her mouth once more.

"You had breast cancer, right? The woman next to us told me."

I was a worker who talked with her boyfriend on her handy-phone all the time and had a bad habit of sneaking chestnut-flavored candied beans on the job, so I was a bit relieved that this is what she'd decided to bring up.

"You didn't know?"

"How could I have?"

Her tone was slightly reproachful.

"I'm sorry. Everyone seemed to know that's what I had when I was in the hospital, I'd just assumed you'd heard too."

I apologized, feeling rather abject.

"Don't apologize. But it would have been nice to have heard it from you, rather than from some old lady gossiping."

"I *am* sorry, though. Would you have offered me the job if you'd known?"

At this, she stubbed out her cigarette, still only half smoked, in the ashtray in front of her.

"What a thing to ask! Do I really seem like that kind of person?"

"*Sorry* . . ." I murmured once more, bowing my head. *Why must I be someone who always says things that make others feel bad?*

"What I was wondering, though, was why you told that woman. You must have known she'd spread it around the whole place."

Nagase-san asked this completely sincerely, no trace of enmity in her tone. *I love showing everyone my worst side*, I almost said, but decided to put it another way.

"It's my identity is why."

"Identity?" She seemed baffled. "You mean the cancer?"

"Exactly. Maybe *identity* is too grand a word for it, but it's the only special thing about me. I don't have anything else to define me, that belongs to me and no one else."

The beer arrived then, and she brought it to her lips with an expression that made her seem more baffled by me than ever. She was already getting red around the eyes, giving the impression that her tolerance was pretty low. It suddenly came to me, watching her, that she was surely the type of woman who's always been able to have any man she wanted.

"So, are you okay now?"

She seemed to be asking this as a way to draw the conversation back to safer ground. I was in the mood to talk now, though, and words came rushing out of my mouth all at once.

"People ask me that all the time. *Are you okay?* It's easy to say *Yes, I'm okay,* but it makes me wonder: *What's okay? Okay how?* I don't actually know. I had my breast removed and then reconstructed, and the danger of the cancer spreading seems low, but that's not a sure thing, you know? I still have to take hormone shots that make me dizzy and nauseous all the time, it's not like everything's fine now. But everybody wants it to be over, they tell me get over it, to forget about it. But it's not over for me at all!"

I stopped myself and took a breath, then a sip of my beer. Even though I knew drinking would only make me feel worse.

"I have a body that can work again. So I have to try and forget what happened, to act like nothing did. But, for example, right now it's actually very itchy inside my fake breast."

"What?"

"When they were reconstructing my breast, there's a part where the skin has to be folded and sewn together, like a dart in a blouse, and sometimes I get hot flashes that make that area really itchy. But it's actually *inside* my body, and it's not like I can reach in to scratch it, right? I can get through it—it's not like an itch is going to kill me—but it *is* really uncomfortable. So the question is, Is this okay? Am I okay?"

Nagase-san sat stock-still as I prattled on, seemingly rather taken back. But once I stopped talking, she exhaled, visibly relaxing, and then apologized. "I'm so sorry."

"Oh, no! I didn't say all that to make you feel bad!"

"It's all right. You know, I kind of know what you mean. I myself am allergic to mountain potatoes."

Her eyes were wet as she said this. *If I were a man, I'd be putty in her hands*, I thought as I listened to her allergy story.

"Of course I try to avoid eating them, but the other day, I was eating out somewhere and the dipping sauce for the meat had been thickened with some potato paste, so when I ate it, the whole inside of my mouth broke out in hives, and my throat too—it felt like my whole digestive system had hives! It was so itchy I sincerely thought I might die."

"And you can't reach in there and scratch it either!"

We both started laughing at that point. Nagase-san was finally letting her guard down with me; I was so happy.

"You know, I forgot to mention it, but I ended up telling that lady next to us that we first met in the hospital too, and she seemed really keen to know what you had. I'm sorry I let that slip."

"Oh I know, that part was being spread around along with the story about your cancer."

She laughed a little.

"Oh gosh, I apologize!"

"No need, it's fine. I'm not trying to hide anything. It was something so minor compared to your situation, I feel a little bad talking about it. An ovarian cyst. I had to have surgery, but it was really very easy, and I think I can even still have children. In my case, it really is something that's over and done with."

She was absently running a single delicate fingertip along the rim of her glass as she spoke. It was the kind of gesture that if, say, someone like me were to do it, it wouldn't seem like an expression of elegant ennui at all. Even if she were single, there was no way she didn't have a man in her life. And not some low-rent bozo like Hyōsuke.

"It's not really such an obscure condition, but at the last place I worked, someone told me that I must have gotten it from being too beautiful and playing around with men too much. They meant it as a joke, they said, but still. People say the cruelest things."

I'd always believed that beautiful people should never call themselves beautiful, so her story made me recoil a bit. I'd vowed not to be nosy anymore, but a cruel impulse of my own made me inquire further.

"Do you have a boyfriend, Nagase-san?"

"Not a boyfriend—a husband."

Of course she's married, I thought, slightly deflated. Though on second thought, being disappointed by finding this out was just a symptom of my own inferiority complex, wasn't it? As I sat silently thinking about all this, I looked over and realized that Nagase was sitting silently too, probably bored, so I racked my brain for something, anything, to talk about. I decided on my old favorite, the planarian.

"Nagase-san, in your next life, what would you want to come back as?"

"What's this all of a sudden? Hmmm, well . . . I wonder if there *is* a next life . . ."

"Just supposing there is."

She appeared to sink deep in thought, cocking her head and murmuring to herself as she considered her choices. *A bird? A dolphin? A cat?*

"I want to come back as a planarian."

"A planarian? That little sluglike thing that if you cut it in half, it grows back?"

"Yes, exactly! You're the first person I've ever met who knew what I was talking about!"

I was elated, filled with excitement. "Why do you want to be a planarian?" she asked, and I began my reply with the explanation my former coworker had given the last time I'd brought this up.

"I could spend my days swimming beneath a rock in a clean mountain stream, not cute enough for anyone to pay me any mind. I could live my whole life without thinking about anything at all! And since I would regenerate if I got cut up, I could live free from the fear of death. I wouldn't have to worry about sex either—I could just reproduce by splitting myself in two. So much simpler."

"But you know, they're not immortal. They get old and shrivel up eventually."

"What? They do?"

"I mean, I'm just remembering something I saw on TV, I don't know all the ins and outs of it."

I saw it on TV too! I was about to say, when she opened her mouth and finally answered the question.

"You know, in my next life, I wouldn't mind coming back as myself."

I felt all the joy drain from my body. *Has your life up till now really been that blessed? Or were you just saying the first pretty words that popped into your head? What bullshit*, I thought, and then was immediately appalled at myself for thinking that. Why did I insist on being so perverse? Couldn't I accept that there were people in the world who thought differently than I did?

Just as I'd anticipated, Nagase-san picked up the bill. "Thank you for treating me," I said, and she laughed. "We'll have to do this again sometime!"

Even if she made me uncomfortable sometimes, I knew she was a good person—in fact, she was the one person in my life I felt sincerely drawn to. As I walked alone through the night-darkened streets toward home, I thought: *Everyone in this world has something about them that, eventually, will make someone else feel uncomfortable. It's nothing that should get you down*, I told myself.

But my unease about the future came true even quicker than I'd thought, knocking me right back to square one.

The next week, I was enjoying my usual day off from work, a day when Hyōsuke was busy with a report due the next day and my parents were both at work, leaving me oddly relieved to be alone in the quiet apartment unsupervised, when a package arrived, addressed to me.

It was from Nagase-san: a cardboard box that wasn't all that big but was awfully heavy for its size. *We see each other four days out of every week*, I thought, as I started peeling the tape off. *Why is she taking the trouble to have this delivered to my home?*

Inside the package were six books. All about cancer. I stared at them in my hands, dumbfounded.

One of them was a memoir by a celebrity about her battle with cancer that I'd read before, but the others were thick medical tomes. I picked up one that focused specifically on breast cancer and leafed through it, only to be confronted with an explicit photo of a breast cut wide open, exposing the muscle. I immediately shut it, but before long, my curiosity got the better of me and I cautiously opened it again. Scanning through the pages with images, I saw that they were a rather gruesome collection of photos showing the results of various mastectomy procedures. There were also many photos showing the aftermath of breast-conservation and breast-reconstruction surgeries. Only one showed a procedure that resembled my own, reminding me again of how many different procedures there really were out there addressing this problem. But I reached my limit when I turned the page and saw the photo of a woman who'd allowed her breast cancer to progress unchecked for over ten years, an image that even a breast cancer survivor like me couldn't bear to look at directly. I shut the book again immediately.

Besides the books, there was also a manila envelope included in the package, and even though I was already dreading it, I couldn't keep myself from opening it just to see what might be waiting inside. In contrast to the books, it turned out to be a bundle of brightly colored printouts.

Glancing at the top page, I saw what they were: magnified

photos of planaria. Looking through them, I realized they must be photos she'd found on websites and printed out for me. A thin floral-printed envelope fell out from between the pages. A letter from Nagase-san.

It was a simple letter, no more than a single page, explaining that she had a relative who'd had breast cancer and who'd passed along these books to her, and that she'd done a little research on the internet about planaria and decided to send along what she'd found.

As a postscript, she added that I should refrain in the future from talking on the phone and snacking on the merchandise during work hours, and then there was a little drawing that looked like her own face, accompanied by a cartoon heart and the words, *Let's go grab a drink again soon!*

All the strength left my body. I sank to the floor, surrounded by books and printouts, at a total loss.

Was this just her way? *People have all sorts of methods for expressing their goodwill; perhaps I should simply understand this as one and thank her for it.* The seemingly incidental inclusion of her criticism of my comportment at work possibly indicated that she couldn't bear to say such a thing to my face, so she devised this elaborate diversion to allow her to pass the message along. Thinking of it that way, she cut an unexpectedly cowardly figure.

But the emotion bubbling up within me as I sat there was the exact opposite of gratitude. *I mustn't!* I thought, but no one can really make themselves feel differently than they actually feel.

Should I call her at the store right now? Or get in the car and drive there directly to tell her exactly how I felt, right to her face? But, in the end, I was able to suppress these urges. Hot blood was raging through my head right then, but by the next day, I may well have calmed down enough to feel the gratitude I knew she expected me to feel. To accept her attempt at kindness at face value.

In any case, though, I certainly didn't feel like reading the books and perusing the planarian printouts arrayed around me. I stuffed them back into the box they came in, and then shoved the box into the closet.

It wasn't yet evening, but I shut off my phone and went to bed anyway. Blessedly alone, I was free to cry like a child as loud as I wanted until I couldn't anymore, and then, exhausted, drift off into a deep, restful slumber.

After that, I missed work twice without calling in. I just couldn't make myself go, and though I knew I should have come up with a bogus illness or some other excuse, I couldn't even make myself do that. My head had cooled, but my will to force myself into action had deserted me as well, and everything simply seemed like too much bother to deal with.

So I was out with Hyōsuke, whom I'd allowed to pretty me up and bring me along to a get-together with his friends at a bar near his university, when my phone rang. Just as I suspected, it was Nagase-san.

"Have you been feeling poorly lately?" she asked, trepidation filling her voice, to which I replied, "The fact is, I just felt like quitting."

She sounded flabbergasted in response.

"You're *quitting*? Why?"

I got up and left the big table where I'd been sitting surrounded by Hyōsuke and his friends and walked down the corridor toward the restrooms, trying my hardest to sound as stupid as possible.

"Well, you know, it's a job where I have to stand all the time, and it gets hard after a while! The customers are all elderly, so that's not much fun. And the wage is pretty low, so . . ."

There was a beat, and then, perhaps because she was trying to suppress her anger, Nagase-san's voice was eerily gentle when she spoke.

"But to stop coming in without making even one phone call? Do you understand how much trouble you caused for everyone doing it this way? I was counting on you to run things when I wasn't there!"

Her calm, mature voice sounded in my left ear as the boisterous merrymaking of the students drinking around me filled my right. I knew she could probably hear them too.

"Well anyway, I'm quitting."

"I didn't think you were so irresponsible. This makes me think much less of you!"

Her voice was rising hysterically at the end of her words, as if she'd reached the end of her rope at last.

"You overestimated me from the beginning, Nagase-san! I told you!"

"And not one word of apology? I thought we were getting along so well!"

I didn't answer, and this seemed to prompt her to finally realize what might have happened. When she spoke again, her voice was low and quiet.

"Did I offend you by sending you all those books out of the blue like that? If so, I'm sorry. It was thoughtless of me."

"I mean, it's not that big a deal."

I stared at my pedicured toe sticking out of my sandal as I answered her. Hyōsuke had even gone to the trouble of painting the nail pink.

"It's just, I'd always avoided reading those kinds of books, you know. And the planarian stuff too, I'd never thought to do any further research on the subject."

Nagase-san was silent for a little bit, and then I heard her sigh, loudly.

"But, Haruka-chan, you told me it was your identity. Why wouldn't you want to learn more about your identity?"

An answer flashed through my head: *Because it's too hard to face directly*. I raised my eyes from contemplating my toenail and found myself staring at a couple making out in front of the restrooms, both surely still in their teens. The flimsy camisole dress the girl was wearing was something I knew I'd never be able to wear again for the rest of my life.

"No amount of research will make my nipple grow back or allow me to be reborn as a planarian, will it?"

"That's not really the issue—Haruka? Haruka-chan?"

But I'd already hung up without saying another word. My legs trembled as I turned to walk back toward my seat next to Hyōsuke, but I made it back to the table in time for there to be a lull in the conversation. Seizing the occasion of my return, someone asked, brightly, "Haruka, I heard you only work part-time. Why? Don't you want a proper job?"

"That's right. And I don't. Because I have breast cancer."

I was still settling into my chair as I said this, and Hyōsuke promptly fixed me with a fierce glare. This was his cohort we were drinking with, after all, and he'd warned me beforehand that if I brought up my cancer tonight, that would be it for us.

Despite having just sat down, I got up again from the suddenly silent table and walked away. The restaurant was huge and I was pretty drunk, so I soon lost my bearings. I grabbed the sleeve of one of the waitresses walking by and asked, "Where's the exit?" The waitress, a young woman who looked like a part-timer herself, recoiled at my touch, then raised her arm to point somewhere off into the distance.

Here, Which Is Nowhere

It was four days now that my daughter hadn't come home. She'd call in every evening, though, either out of fear I'd report her as a runaway or simply out of guilt, to casually tell me, "I'm staying at a friend's house tonight, okay?" But tonight I'd had enough.

"Don't give me that. Where have you really been staying all this time?"

"I *told* you! With a friend!"

I heard girls laughing in the background of her exasperated reply, along with train announcements. Was she calling from a platform somewhere?

"And I'm just supposed to accept that? Anyway, I want you to come home tonight!"

"You're so annoying! Oh, my train's here, gotta go. See you tomorrow. Maybe."

"What do you mean, 'maybe'? Are you even going to school, Hina?"

But she hung up without answering. The fact was, I'd called her school earlier that day to see if she'd been attending class. Her homeroom teacher had said, "She's late a lot, but I don't see any absences," seeming rather put out to have to go to the trouble. "I'll try to tell her to be on time," I apologized, and then, just as my daughter had done, I hung up without waiting for an answer. My daughter was in the second semester of her senior year. She'd already informed the school that she didn't intend to go on to university or directly into a career, so from the school's perspective, as long she didn't cause any trouble, there wasn't much left for them to do but wash their hands of her.

"You know, Mom, even when you get mad, no one's really scared of you."

My son, home uncharacteristically early, decided to lecture me from where he lay sprawled on the couch.

"No offense, but it's always been like that. You're not fooling anyone—we know you're not really angry. When I was little, I was like *Oh, Mom, she's so nice!* But now I see it's more like you don't care, not really. So Hina's just gonna keep walking all over you."

My son, twenty years old now, had pulled the bottom of his shirt up a little and was absently scratching his belly as he talked. He'd always been one to go on about things, even when he was young, and whether or not he'd been staying home from school to avoid playing sports on Field Day or for a more serious reason, like when he nearly succumbed to school-refusal syndrome from being bullied, I often found myself on the receiving end of his sophistry. Perhaps it was just a symptom of his cleverness, though, as he'd earned gratifyingly good grades all through school and tested well enough to get into a top university. But he, too, seemed to prefer hanging out somewhere else, as there were more and more nights he didn't come home either. The sound of a door sliding open came from the bathroom, announcing that my husband was done with his bath.

"You're planning on eating dinner with us, right, Shū-chan?" I asked.

"How many times do I have to tell you—stop calling me *chan*! And who wants to eat with their mom and dad, anyway? I'm going to the store to get something."

My son launched himself from the sofa and headed for the door. It had been like this more and more. He'd come home early and I'd make sure to cook enough for dinner to include him, but then he'd end up getting a cheap bento at the convenience store and eating it in his room. I could understand being tired of our faces, but didn't he miss having a home-cooked meal once in a while? Or was there a girl in a little apartment somewhere cooking for him now?

"Did Shūichi leave?" asked my husband, entering the living room as if changing places with his son. It wasn't even seven at night, but he was already in his pajamas. I knew he was just unwinding after his bath, but still, it got on my nerves.

"Where's Hina?" This new question came before I could answer the first one.

"I think they're both eating elsewhere tonight."

"I wonder if they're okay."

His tone, which seemed sincerely worried, stopped me short as I stood at the stove stir-frying vegetables. I looked over at my husband as he reached into the refrigerator for a beer, gripped by the urge to repeat his line right back to him, but I restrained myself.

Dinner itself turned out not to be particularly strained or lonely, though, the two of us eating peaceably together beneath the oddly modish tangerine light fixture that had come with our modest apartment. We were used to a childless dinner table by now. NHK on the TV. The seven o'clock weather forecast. The foam on the beer in the glass we got from the liquor store. The smell of ginger sprouts dipped in dark miso.

"Is it about time I took the winter pajamas out?" I asked, his cotton ones striking me as a bit chilly for the weather. My husband grunted his assent, nodding slightly as he continued watching TV. His face in profile was exactly like his son's.

I finished washing the dishes, went to take my bath, and then, suppressing the urge to slip into some pajamas myself, changed only my underwear, putting the shirt and sweater I'd been wearing all day back on. I looked at the clock on the wall and saw it was already past nine. I needed to hurry.

"All right, I'm off!"

I called out to my husband as I left him sitting in his habitual spot on the sofa with the TV on, spending yet another evening in a blank stupor. I took the elevator down to the bottom floor and walked into the parking area only to see my son's mountain bike sitting next to the one I used for shopping. He'd failed to return after saying he was going to the corner store, so I'd assumed he'd taken his bike to the train station, but apparently he'd gone off somewhere without it. He wasn't even wearing a jacket on this chilly evening—where had he gone?

I zipped the fleece my son had decided not to wear up to my chin, shouldered a camouflage backpack my daughter had at some point stopped using onto my back, then got on my bike and pedaled off into the October night.

I rode through the residential streets and then onto the paved path running beside the highway. I'd dreaded this ride when I'd gotten out of the bath, but now that I was out here breathing hard, it became increasingly bearable, even fun. I'd never been one to go out at night before, so perhaps that was why it seemed so refreshing. It all still felt new to me: the vending machines floating up out of the dark as I passed them; the children gathered in front of them on their way back home from cram school; the vivid neon of the pachinko parlors; the retirees going for walks in their weirdly sophisticated sportswear. But this sense of freshness, too, would surely pass before long, everything fading back into a routine landscape around me. Last week I was fine, but tonight the cold bit into my hands and ears as I rode. *I should look through my children's discarded things and find a hat and some gloves to borrow.* Preoccupied with these thoughts, I made the final turn on my route and saw the wholesale outlet store swing into view like a cheap movie set, the lone structure lit up in the dark. Glancing at the watch on my wrist, I saw I'd cut it close: only five minutes left till ten. I hurriedly parked my bike and ran through the employee entrance, taking my time card and plunging it into the punch clock as fast as I could. One minute after ten. When you're late, the time on your card is stamped in red; three red stamps and you're docked a day of pay.

"Hey, Katō-san! Nice sweater!"

One of my young coworkers called out to me as I opened the door to the employee changing room.

"Hello, everyone! I'm afraid I'm running late."

"Is that a cherry print? So cool!"

"It's an Atsuki Onishi original, it says so right there! Her backpack is camo-patterned too."

"Just hand-me-downs from my daughter..."

The girls who worked with me at my part-time gig, their hair all dyed either reddish blond or blondish red, blurred together in my mind; even after a month working here, I had trouble telling them apart. I put my bag in my locker and shut the door, then tied the fluorescent-yellow staff apron around my waist.

The girls lost interest in me, returning to their previous conversations as they huddled around the sole ashtray, a chimneylike tower that stood in the corner of the room. My arrival seemed to have coincided exactly with their break time.

Rushing to the front of the store, I saw, just as I feared, that only two of the six registers were open, with lines building up at both of them.

"You're late, Katō. Go to your register."

I bobbed my head in meek apology at the floor manager's scolding, installing myself at my register and turning it on. The moment I entered the number on my name tag into the system, a line of customers materialized in front of me. It was still a bit of a shock to me how many shoppers there were this late at night. The store sold just about any nonperishable item you could think of; the first customer in line pulled a wide array of goods from their basket: shampoo, disposable diapers, cat food, condoms . . . I did my best to run each item over the barcode reader without looking the customer in the eye. (I hardly had time to raise my eyes from my task anyway.) I'd really only had trouble when I first began working here, though—as jobs go, it wasn't a hard one.

I worked the late shift three days a week, from ten at night till two in the morning, working the registers for ¥1,000 an hour. A housewife like me needed to be able to do errands during the day, so the night shift made more sense for me. The hourly rate was much higher than during the day as well, adding up to about an extra ¥10,000 a month.

The bustling aisles started to calm down around midnight, and, besides helping the occasional customer who did show up, I was largely left to stare absently at the empty store. The employees in charge of stocking the shelves stood around talking and laughing with one another. I was watching with a certain sense of wonder as a girl about the age of my daughter talked like old friends with a man about the age of my father, apparently a part-timer like myself, when a young man who worked full-time appeared in front of me.

"Hey there, Katō-san! Nice sweater!"

This again. It was just something my daughter had gotten tired of that happened to fit—why was everyone making such a big deal about it? But years of habit took over, and I responded with a pleasant laugh.

"It was my daughter's. Does it really look so weird on me?"

"Didn't you hear me? I didn't say 'weird'—I said you looked nice!"

A broad smile spread across his babyish face; he wasn't young at all, really, but a full-grown man in his midthirties who, now that I think of it, had a wife and a kid who'd just entered kindergarten. My daughter would've surely put him squarely in the "middle-aged" category, but to me he was neither "middle-aged" nor even quite an adult.

"We're all going out after closing tonight, you should come!"

I stared at the characters spelling out *Hamazaki* on the name tag pinned to his apron as I manufactured another smile.

"Oh, that's just for young people. Go and have fun without me."

"What are you talking about? Matthew and Saorin will both be there!"

"Matthew" was *Mat*suda, the part-timer in his seventies, and "Saorin" was Saori Inoue, the floor manager. Hamazaki, by the way, was called the Hammer. Not long after I started working here, someone decided to share with me, unprompted, that Saori and I were the same age. Unmarried and living alone, she looked a full decade younger than me, without a hint of the hausfrau about her, though of course that only made sense. As for me, no matter how many of my daughter's discarded Atsuki Onishi sweaters I might wear, I'd always look exactly like what I was: a forty-three-year-old housewife with a son already in college. Why else would everyone be making such a fuss over a trendy top?

"C'mon, just for an hour."

The Hammer wasn't letting me off the hook.

"I have to wake up early tomorrow."

"That's right, you're a mom, aren't you? What time do you have to get up?"

"Five thirty."

"What? Only three hours of sleep?"

Hamazaki made a show of being shocked. But why was this kid dogging me like this in the first place? I lost the will to keep laughing him off and didn't respond, remaining expressionless as I avoided his gaze.

"I should tell my wife about you. Sometimes she sleeps in and doesn't even take our daughter to school!"

"Is she a full-time housewife?"

"No, she works. She's an *entertainer*, if you know what I mean. And she ends up making a lot more than me, so I'm hardly in a position to complain, you know?"

Saori walked by then and rescued me, saying, "Less talking, more working, Hamazaki."

An entertainer, if you know what I mean—what kind of thing was that to say, anyway? One more thing about Hamazaki that made me think less of him.

It was fifteen minutes till quitting time, so I started closing out my register. When I first started, I tended to be scolded for having too many discrepancies when I cashed out, but today I was relieved to see that everything lined up down to the last yen. I was a part-timer, so as long as I didn't have any problems with my register totals I was allowed to leave right at two, but full-timers were obliged to stay on to serve any lingering customers, clean up the store, and take part in an after-hours debriefing.

"Have a good night!" I called out to Saori, but she didn't respond. She just stared at me wordlessly, cocking her head to the side. It seemed like she had something to say, and as I hesitated, wondering if I should ignore her and head out anyway, she broke into a rare smile.

"Watch out for the Hammer, okay?"

"I will," I replied reflexively, and it wasn't until I was untying my apron in front of my locker that it occurred to me to wonder, *Watch out for what?*

Leaving the store, I ran into a group of young people who looked to be in their twenties hanging out in front despite it being closed. I stood there for a bit, watching them talk and laugh together, either crouched down drinking canned coffee or paired off into couples, their hands slipping below each other's waists as they held each other. Finally, after assuring myself that neither my daughter nor my son was among them, I unlocked my bike and began the twenty-minute ride along the late-night highway back home.

My husband woke up at 5:30 a.m. every day except Saturday and Sunday. It took about two hours to get from our apartment in the suburbs to work, but he hated the crowded trains at rush hour, so he left the house at six to avoid the worst of the crush.

Even if I managed to go to sleep right after getting home, three hours never felt like enough. I knew my husband had gone to bed soon after I'd left for work, so he should have been well rested, but he hardly looked cheery as he stood at the sink to shave.

I put the coffee on and the bread in the toaster, then fried some eggs and shredded some lettuce. Every weekday morning since we'd been married—twenty-one years of mornings—I woke up at five thirty to make breakfast for my husband. If I told people that, they'd surely react with the same admiring shock the Hammer had displayed last night, but the truth was, I'd always been an early riser, so it never felt like that much of a burden. Though after starting my part-time gig, it began to feel a bit more onerous, I admit.

"How's work?"

I knew that if I didn't make a point to ask, my taciturn husband would never tell me anything.

"Getting used to it. How's the store?"

"Getting used to it as well. I don't get yelled at nearly as much anymore."

"Neither do I."

We laughed together at that, and then I went into the kitchen to make up the lunches. I'd never thought I'd be spending my mornings packing lunch boxes at this age. I put leftovers from last night's dinner in each of the three boxes, along with some bite-size cutlets I'd fried up first thing that morning. One was for my husband, one for myself, and the last was for my mother.

By the time I was wrapping his lunch box in the checkered cloth I used to use for my son's lunches back when he was in high school, it was five minutes before six. My husband finished watching the

NHK weather forecast, then got up to go. Sixty percent chance of rain tonight. I handed my husband a foldable umbrella along with his lunch.

"Feels like we're newlyweds again," he said cheerfully.

I forced a smile in response.

"It does."

Five minutes after my husband left, I was on the sofa trying to catch up on my sleep when I heard someone unlock the front door. I rose to my feet and, rubbing my eyes, caught my daughter peeking through the door. It was cracked just wide enough to allow one eye to appear, surveying the scene. *You know, Mom, even when you get mad, no one's really scared of you.* My son's words came back to me as I tried to decide, in my sleep-fuzzy state, if I should respond to my daughter's reappearance with kindness or anger.

"I met Papa outside," she said first, sheepishly, leaving me no chance for anger. But the fact was, it was a relief not to yell at her. My son was right—I wasn't good at raising my voice at anyone, even my own children.

"Come on in, honey, it's fine. Did he yell at you?"

"A bit. He said I shouldn't make you worry so much."

Now that she was through the door, I could see that my daughter was wearing her school uniform, with an oversize Hello Kitty bag hanging from one shoulder. I had a million things I wanted to ask, but I couldn't decide where to start; I also knew that a volley of questions would only put her in a foul mood. I'd tried again and again to scold her when she first began staying out all night during summer vacation, but I was so bad at it that I eventually lost the energy to keep after her. All I could think was *Whatever, it's fine*, I'd *rather get some sleep than deal with this.* Which might well make me a failure as a mother.

"Are you going to school today?"

"Yeah. Can I heat the water for a bath?"

"Yes, sure."

"And can I grab something to eat?"

"Hina, this is your house. You can have anything you want, of course."

Her face darkened, and she stomped sullenly from the room. Kindness put her in a bad mood. As did lecturing her. In other words, there was nothing I could say that wouldn't irritate her. Exhausted by the absurdity of it all, I lay back down on the sofa.

My eyes closed, I idly wondered if my daughter was a delinquent. Her hair wasn't dyed, her makeup wasn't trendily outlandish, her school uniform's skirt wasn't rolled up to be scandalously short. On the other hand, it seemed unlikely she was still a virgin. The delicate curve of her neck, her habit of pulling absently on her bangs—these were the features of a young woman, not a child. Thinking this far, I found myself getting worried again. Where on earth was she spending her nights? The girls I worked with at the outlet store were dropouts, and I knew they tended to meet guys at bars or karaoke places and end up going to love hotels with them; I knew because they had no compunction talking to me about it. They were someone else's children, allowing me to respond with a simple *Sounds fun!* But thinking about my own child doing the same made me anxious. The world is filled with people worse than you could possibly imagine. Thinking about the dangers my daughter might face on the streets at night made me want to lock her in her room and throw away the key. She was too young to be out in the world like that. Too innocent.

Hina finished her bath and came into the living room dressed in a T-shirt. She opened the refrigerator and greedily drank milk straight from the carton.

"At least tell me where you've been staying at night."

I rose from the sofa and said this to my daughter's back.

"I *told* you! I'm staying with a friend!"

"Don't treat me like a fool. Your father and I are really worried about you."

"You don't have to worry about me."

Her response left me momentarily speechless.

"You're still in high school. Of course I have to worry about you!"

"Oh, shut up! This is why I hate coming home! If I quit school and got a job, would you finally leave me alone?"

"What kind of thing is that to say?"

My daughter walked over and opened the refrigerator again without answering, presumably looking for something to eat this time.

"I made a lunch, do you want that?"

"Isn't it for Grandma?"

Hina took out some slices of bread and put them in the toaster.

"How about some egg salad?"

"I'm fine. Leave me alone, okay?"

Rejected so squarely, I massaged my neck and sighed. I knew I was the one who'd given birth to this child, but it seemed so long ago now that it felt like a lie. My own daughter was as inscrutable to me as the girls I worked with at night. I lay back down on the sofa and closed my eyes, then popped them open again.

"Oh, Hina, I meant to ask you!"

"What is it now?"

"Do you have any gloves or hats you're not using?"

My daughter, having braced herself to be lectured, reacted with frank bewilderment. "What?"

"My hands and ears get cold when I ride my bike."

"Can't you buy your own?"

"You have so many, I thought you might spare me something."

A thoughtful look crossed my daughter's face, and she took a good look at me from across the dining room table.

"I knew I'd seen that sweatshirt before. It's one of mine, isn't it? From back in middle school?"

Hina giggled. It had been a while since I'd seen her smile. I looked down, my eyes meeting those of the Winnie-the-Pooh on my chest.

"Do I really look so funny?"

My daughter didn't answer, drinking the rest of the milk instead. I mentally added *milk* to the shopping list I kept in my head.

I spent the rest of the morning running the washing machine and hanging four people's worth of laundry out to dry on the balcony, then dusting everywhere that seemed dingy and vacuuming the floor. It was already eleven thirty by the time I finished, so I put the two remaining lunch boxes in the basket of my bike and pedaled off. The woolen hat and gloves my daughter had eventually lent me were pleasingly warm, but both sported Ralph Lauren tags that troubled me anew—how had she managed to get her hands on such expensive things? But I decided not to think about it further for now. Both of my children had part-time jobs (of course I'd asked them what they were, and of course neither deigned to tell me), and they'd been buying their own clothing for a while. I considered no longer giving my daughter an allowance, but then it occurred to me that all I'd be doing would be giving her one more reason to focus on working at the expense of her schooling. Though the allowance for my son was another matter—he was already twenty years old! Perhaps it was about time to stop that one.

It took about thirty minutes to bike to my mother's house. Going by bus and train would have taken almost an hour due to the number of transfers I'd have to make, as it was oddly hard to reach via public transportation. The fares involved were no laughing matter either, so taking the direct route by bike just made more sense, as well as taking half the time.

I made the trip about once every three days, so I felt comfortable enough to wind my way through a tangle of residential streets, take an illegal shortcut through the grounds of a huge textile mill, and then slide beneath a private rail overpass to make it to my mother's house in twenty-six minutes. A new personal record.

"What's up with you, panting like that?"

My mother looked up from cutting her toenails on the small porch running along the front of the house to fix me with her gaze.

"Could I get a drink of water, Mom?"

"I never asked you to kill yourself coming here by bike like that..."

Muttering to herself, my mother rose unsteadily to her feet and disappeared into the house. Inwardly anxious, I kept my eyes on her throughout the process, then locked up my bike and headed in through the front door. The interior was largely unchanged from how I remembered it growing up, save for two new features in the living room that bothered me every time I visited: a memorial shrine for my father, and a sofa set placed directly on the tatami. When my father was alive, the only furniture in the room had been a traditional kotatsu with some cushions around it.

"I brought lunch."

My mother was coming back from the kitchen with a cup of water as I presented the two lunch boxes, one for each of us, wrapped in cloth.

"Thank you very much. I appreciate the trouble you go to for me."

"You're very welcome. It's no trouble at all."

We bowed our heads to each other in exaggerated formality, like strangers, and then I drained the cup in one draft.

My father had passed away three years ago in a car accident during a trip. He and my mother had gone to a hot spring resort to celebrate my mother's seventieth birthday; he'd lost control on a sharp curve in the mountains and smashed into the guardrail. While he suffered an unlucky blow in the crash that killed him instantly, my mother escaped with just some scrapes and a broken leg.

My father had loved cars, and in his extensive driving history, he'd never had an accident or moving violation. He may have been seventy-five, but he was in good shape and never drank or had any problems sleeping. And of course he showed not the slightest sign of senility. There were no witnesses to the accident, and my mother had been no help either, spending the aftermath incoherently weeping, so its cause was never definitively found. The police said there were tire tracks on the road that indicated sudden braking, so perhaps a monkey or raccoon dog had jumped out of the woods, causing him to swerve.

At first, my mother lived in a state of weepy mourning for her husband of so many years, but eventually her wounds healed and the money from his life insurance policy came in, allowing her to enjoy a relatively calm, stable life again. I was an only child, and while my husband indicated his willingness to move her in with us so as not to leave her all alone, she refused, saying she preferred to stay in the house where she'd lived most of her life. It wasn't really an option to move our entire four-person household into her forty-year-old single-story house either, so I ended up paying her regular visits like this instead.

Sipping the miso soup my mother had prepared for us, we sat side by side on the sofa and opened up the lunch boxes I'd brought. My mother's right leg was less mobile than it was before the accident, and it was my husband who'd suggested buying her a sofa to make it easier to sit down and stand back up.

Her leg wasn't *that* bad, though—she had a small hitch in her step that slowed her down, but she made food for herself without trouble and made regular trips to the supermarket. So there was really no more reason for me to go to the trouble of making her lunches and bringing them over like this, but somewhere along the line, I'd missed the opportunity to stop. Now that I had my job, though, it was becoming harder for me to keep up the pace, so I was considering trying to extend the gaps between my visits to four or five days instead of one or two.

"So those two are getting a divorce? Huh."

She said this with her eyes fixed on the television, where a daytime tabloid show was playing. She was talking about a pair of celebrities, of course, not anyone she actually knew.

"Kids these days have no resilience. Oh, that reminds me—did Rumiko Koyanagi ever officially get her divorce?"

"I wonder . . ."

"Remember Madame Dewi? Do you know if she's still someone's 'Madame' these days?"

"I'm not sure . . ." I murmured, and then I was assaulted by sudden drowsiness, enough to make me drop my chopsticks. I hurriedly picked them back up. *What's going on with me? I'm like a little kid who tires himself out so much he falls asleep midmeal!*

"Are you okay? You look tired."

I hadn't told her about my new late-night job. It was less that I didn't want to worry her than that I didn't want to be subjected to incessant questions and remarks about it.

"I haven't been getting enough sleep lately is all."

"Well, you know you don't have to put yourself out just for me."

My mother had taken to saying things like this lately. *You don't have to visit me if it's so much trouble. It's no fun to see you run yourself ragged trying to be nice.* It reminded me of things my son would say as a child about his father, who clearly doted on his daughter more than him. *It's fine, I don't need Dad to play with me anyway!*

"So, how's Katō? Does he like his new job?"

Perhaps sensing that I'd been put off by her remark, my mother changed the subject with pointed cheerfulness. By Katō, she meant my husband, as if that wasn't my last name now too.

"He's fine. He says he's largely gotten used to the new company."

"Such a pity, though, a good worker getting *restructured* like that."

My mother sighed ostentatiously. My husband had recently been transferred from the pharmaceutical company he'd worked at for years to one of their subcontractors. I'd meant to keep this from my mother as well, but my husband had let it slip one day when we'd dropped by for a visit together, breezily remarking, "Looks like that restructuring everyone's talking about has reached me too!" My mother, seemingly not really understanding what *restructuring* might mean, made a big show of sympathy at the news, apparently under the impression that it meant *My daughter's husband has been fired!* At the same time, her constant questions and concerns were oddly heedless, as if my husband's employment troubles were just another scandal like the ones she followed on TV.

"What's the pay like? You'll get through the year all right?"

The fact was, his base pay was much less and there was no overtime, so his yearly income was essentially cut in half. There would probably be no bonus this year either, which meant that the extra mortgage payment we usually made at the end of the year might not be possible. Making our regular payments was hard enough, draining our savings and leaving us without a clear plan for how to pay for our son to go to university next year. That was why I'd taken on a part-time job—it would at least help pay for groceries and day-to-day expenses.

I was on the verge of voicing my worries aloud, but then I looked into my mother's eyes as she leaned toward me in unseemly anticipation and lost my will to speak. If I explained what was going on, she might be moved to dip into what she was getting from Dad's life insurance to lend us some money, but there was something unnatural about the prospect that made me unable to accept it.

"We'll be fine. We just need to tighten our belts."

"Indeed. Shū-chan and Hina-chan still need you to support them, after all, at least until you manage to marry them off. Oh, that reminds me! I just heard Furukawa-san's daughter is getting married!"

Who's Furukawa-san? I wondered as I gathered up the empty lunch boxes and stood up from the sofa. I brought them over to her small sink and began washing them, listening to my mother bad-mouth "Furukawa-san" all the while. *She's always smiling, but I know she makes fun of everyone behind their backs! She can't clean a house to save her life. And the lunches she brings are always so awful!* As I listened to her, it finally dawned on me that Furukawa-san must be the aide sent by the city to help out elderly residents—in other words, a volunteer worker who stopped by a few times a week to help her keep house.

"You shouldn't be so hard on her. She's doing her best."

I'd poured some tea for us at this point, bringing it with me as I sat back down next to my mother.

"You've only met her a couple of times, you don't know."

True enough, I thought. It was twenty-one years ago that I'd moved out of this house, and even though I ended up settling down not so very far away, for all that time, I'd only ever see her on major holidays like New Year's and the Bon Festival. So it had been a bit of a shock to find out that my mother was the kind of person she was. She was supposed to be one of the people I was closest to in the whole world, and I'd always thought I knew her, but it turned out I was sadly mistaken. The mother I remembered didn't talk so incessantly; she was more thoughtful, more patient. I chalked it up at first to the trauma of my father's death, but it seemed to me lately that the faults in my mother's character were more foundational than that. I appreciated my father's forbearance all the more for putting up with her for the many years they'd spent together. Was he a saint? Or just good at tuning her out?

"Oh, one more thing. Are you still having to go visit Katō-san's place?" asked my mother, her tone vaguely spiteful.

Katō-san referred to my husband's father, and his "place" was the hospital. I nodded, fighting off another bout of drowsiness.

"I guess you don't have it easy either," she replied, peeling a tangerine.

I'd had a day off from my job last night, so I'd finally been able to get a good night's sleep. My son and daughter both came home too, even if it was quite late, which meant they both went off to school (hopefully) at a normal time. I spent the morning replacing the summer clothes in the closets with winter ones. I ironed my husband's white shirts, hung the laundry inside to dry, and then got ready to go out. I was about to pedal off on my bike when the mailman arrived on his little scooter, so I took the mail from him and put it in my bag.

As I made the ten-minute trip to the station, I thought about what to have for lunch. In a rare turn of events, my daughter had actually eaten the rice I'd made for breakfast, so I couldn't make onigiri like I usually did. *Should I grab some soba at the stand-up noodle place on the station platform?* But I needed to hurry. I tended to think of our area as the suburbs, but it was closer to living in the sticks—if you missed a train during the day, it would be nearly half an hour before the next one came.

Today was my day to visit "Katō-san's place." My husband's father had been hospitalized for four years now. He was first admitted due to chest pains, but almost as soon as he entered the hospital, he became completely senile. No one thought at the time that he'd last all that long, seeing as how he was plagued by every old-age condition in the book, but he defied the doctors' predictions and lived on anyway. Unable to recognize his own son's face, he was cared for around the clock, which meant there was really no need to visit him regularly; on the other hand, it seemed wrong to simply send money to the hospital and leave it at that. His wife had passed away quite a while ago, so it fell to his children and their children to work out a rotation. As these plans were being made, I was seen as "a full-time housewife with grown children and time on her hands," so I ended up with more shifts in the schedule than the others. I was obligated even now to visit him once every five days. It took an hour on the train and ten more minutes by bus to reach the hospital.

It was almost time for the train to arrive when I reached the station on my bike, so I hurriedly grabbed a bun stuffed with yakisoba at the grab-and-go bakery nearby, bought a ticket for the minimum possible distance, and then ran onto the platform, barely catching the train before it pulled away. The car was completely empty, and I sat down on the side where the sun streamed in through the windows. It was actually quite warm. I munched on my yakisoba bun and watched the rows of houses slide by through the window. Sipping tea from a thermos I'd brought with me, I reached up and grabbed a newspaper that had been abandoned on the rack above my head and began to idly peruse it. Drowsiness assaulted me again, but, remembering when I'd fallen asleep once before and ended up in the next prefecture, I slapped myself on the cheek to keep myself awake.

Oh, that's right! I thought, remembering the mail I'd stuffed into my bag as I'd left the house. I took it out and began looking through it. Most of it was junk mail: an ad for a department store sale; a change-of-address notification from someone whose name I didn't recognize, addressed to my husband; an announcement of new arrivals from a video store for my son. There was also an envelope from NTT that contained the phone bill, and when I opened it to take a look, all remaining sleepiness left my body. The total was over ¥40,000.

"What? What is this?"

I muttered my surprise aloud in the empty train as I went over the bill again and again. There must've been some mistake! I didn't remember it ever being over ¥5,000! Then I recalled that my son had bought a computer last month. He'd connected it to the phone line, so maybe that was what was going on. I decided to confront him about it when I got home. There was no way I was paying that kind of money.

I stared out at the landscape again, watching the buildings gradually give way to fields and hillsides, and thought over our expenses. We'd used up almost our entire savings back when we bought our apartment, leaving us only the minimum breathing room if anything came up. But that was back when my husband had had his previous job; thinking back now, we'd been living in the lap of luxury. I'd avoided spending too much on myself at the time, but we were able to buy the sorts of clothes and video games our children saw other families provide for their classmates, and we could afford tutors and cram schools to help with their education.

But now, with my husband making half what he did before, we barely scraped by with help from my modest part-timer's income. Our mortgage payments were ¥150,000 a month. My husband's spending money added up to ¥20,000 a month. My son's monthly allowance was ¥10,000, while my daughter's was ¥5,000. Our electricity bill was around ¥30,000, and my husband's life insurance cost about ¥20,000 a month. We also paid our share of the cost of my father-in-law's hospitalization, and our day-to-day household expenses were nothing to sneeze at. We were scrimping and saving however we could, but our December mortgage payment, which included the end-of-the-year bonus payment, was coming up; costs for the whole month would end up totaling nearly ¥400,000. That would likely be it for our savings.

As I allowed my body to sway with the movement of the train, my thoughts turned to the nature of banality. When I got married, it had seemed like my husband's income would continue increasing forever; it never occurred to me that I'd find myself in my present situation. To think I'd have to run out at my age and find a part-time job because my husband was "restructured"! I no longer read books. I didn't understand the wars happening in distant countries. I'd always felt at least somewhat connected to the outside world through what I watched and read, but these days, I didn't even have time to watch TV. All I thought about was my children, my husband, my mother, my father-in-law; all I wanted was more money and more sleep. At this point, the banality of the humdrum married life I'd imagined would be a relief.

My head was filled with these thoughts as the train pulled into the station. I got out and then, instead of heading for the exit, sat down on a nearby bench. I was even farther out in the sticks now, so the platform emptied quickly around me. There weren't any employees around either, so I seized the moment and walked with feigned casualness to the platform's edge. A railing ran along it that was a little taller than I was, and I reached up, grabbed the top of it, and pulled myself over as quickly as I could, paying no mind to how my skirt hiked up in the process; soon I was standing on the ground outside the station. The only witness was an old man gawking at me, eyes round as saucers, from the opposite platform. I ignored him and walked quickly to the bus stop. The loop-line bus that would take me to the hospital pulled up almost immediately, and I stepped right on.

And that was how I saved myself most of a train fare.

When I arrived at the hospital, my father-in-law was sitting up in bed, staring into space like usual.

If you said "Good afternoon," he'd say "Good afternoon" back. If you asked "How are you?" he'd answer "How are you?"; if you said "It's gotten cold lately, hasn't it?" he'd respond "It's gotten cold lately, hasn't it?" My father-in-law made conversation like a parrot, simply repeating back whatever was said to him.

A young nurse passed by and called in through the open door.

"Your appetite has really improved lately!" Her voice was filled with good cheer.

I patted the blanket pulled over my father-in-law's knees and smiled.

I took the train back from the hospital, and then, leaving the station, decided to do some shopping at a nearby supermarket on the way home; coming back out, I felt a sprinkling of rain. Luck wasn't with me—I had a shift at the outlet store that night. It was already almost seven, so my husband might've been back from work. I decided to use a pay phone to call home, only to be surprised when it was my son who answered.

"Shūichi! I need to talk to you!"

I raised my voice without meaning to.

"What is it now, *Mother*?"

His tone was sarcastic.

"Do you realize that this month's phone bill's more than ¥40,000? It has to be your computer. I can't pay all this. You need to take care of it yourself."

"What? You think it's my fault? What about Hina hogging the phone all the time?"

"It's not her and you know it. Unlike you, Hina pays her own PHS bill. Is your father home?"

Even on this pay phone in the middle of a loud, crowded supermarket, I persisted. But he'd stopped answering me.

"Are you still there? I'm coming home. I don't care if it's you or your father, but someone needs to put the rice on for dinner!"

I yelled this last part, as angry as I'd ever been, and then slammed the receiver down. *I wonder if I sounded believable this time,* I thought as I loaded the milk and the discounted daikon and everything else into my bicycle's basket and rode away.

When I got home, I found my husband lying on the sofa reading the evening paper. He was in his pajamas. It seemed he'd already had his bath, and now he was drinking a nice cold beer in the cozy afterglow. Volcanic anger rose up in me again, but I managed to control myself. My husband greeted me like nothing was the matter. "Welcome home!"

"Where's Shūichi?"

"He said he was going out. I put the rice on."

So he had passed along the message. And then run away. I glanced at the clock on the wall and saw it was nearly eight. My husband sat with the TV blaring, his eyes back on the newspaper in his hands. Peeking into the kitchen, I saw that while the rice cooker was indeed steaming, nothing else had been prepared for dinner. Though getting one of them to switch the rice cooker on at all was reason enough to rejoice, I told myself.

My husband wasn't the domineering sort; rather, he was more kindly than not. Weak-willed, even. He was the kind of guy who did what he was told without question but never thought to do any more than that. *Is that why he ended up restructured?* But of course I'd never say such a thing aloud. After all, his weakness was also a strength, a thing I liked about him. Ever since his transfer was made official, though, he'd been more closedmouthed and withdrawn than usual—if I didn't ask him a direct question, he'd go for hours without saying anything at all. He wasn't sulky, exactly, but it was clear he was preoccupied. And every morning he'd rip himself out of bed at 5:30 a.m. like a ritual punishment.

One day my husband mentioned that his new workplace didn't

have a cafeteria like his old one did and that eating lunch out was costing him a pretty penny, so I took it upon myself to start making up a lunch box for him every morning again. His mood improved noticeably after that. But it did seem like he could maybe stop staring off somewhere that wasn't here every once in a while and notice when I was too busy and make something for himself.

I intentionally made as much noise as I could in the kitchen as I transferred various things from my shopping bag onto the counter and chopped up the pickled vegetables, but my husband didn't notice a thing. "Dinner's ready!" I said, and he came to the table and sat down. It irritated me to have to always be the one to have to start the conversation, so I didn't say anything further and simply started eating.

"Was this a day you visited my father?"

He remembered that much, at least. I decided to stop giving him the silent treatment and smiled.

"He seemed to be in a good mood. I think he's doing well."

"Good. I'm sorry to make you do that. I'll try to go myself next time I have a day off."

We smiled at each other, lightening the atmosphere. I'd wanted to get after him to take more interest in our kids and the household budget, but now that I was actually talking to him, my anger melted away like usual. "All right, then," I said, getting up from the table. It was nearly nine already. No time to take a bath before going to work.

"I'll wash up tonight."

I was already at the sink, holding a sponge in my rubber-gloved hands, when he said this. I was shocked—he never offered to help out like this.

"Thank you. I think I'll take you up on that!"

"It's raining. Why don't you treat yourself and take the bus tonight?"

My husband smiled kindly at me as he added this last bit. I smiled back, saying "Thank you" once again. It was so like him to forget that by the time I finished work, there were no more buses left to take me home.

I put a plastic poncho on over my clothes and held an umbrella in one hand the whole way, but by the time I arrived at work, I was completely drenched anyway. *These convenience store ponchos really are worthless*, I thought, and then, from the corner of my eye, I saw the proper raincoat the parking lot security guard was wearing. *I should have tried to get my hands on one of those.* The rain had made my commute longer than usual as well, and when I punched my time card, the stamp was red: thirty seconds late. All the strength left my body as I stared at it and imagined ¥10,000 disappearing from my hands into thin air.

"Oh my gosh, Catherine, you're soaked!" exclaimed one of the girls as soon as I entered the changing area. *Who's Catherine?*

". . . Hello, everyone."

"What do you mean, 'Hello, everyone'? Do you have anything to change into?"

A girl with silver-dyed hair asked me this. I looked over and saw that she was taking a sweatshirt out of her locker and offering it to me. A towel came flying at me from another direction, hitting me in the face and then falling to the ground. I went in the corner and peeled off my dripping top, switching it for the bright hibiscus-print sweatshirt I'd been given.

Going out onto the floor, Saori greeted me with "You're late," and then stopped to take a good hard look at me.

"Sorry I'm late."

"Don't you own an umbrella?"

"I do, but I came by bicycle, so . . ."

Still drying my hair with a towel, I went to my register and turned it on. A customer who'd been waiting impatiently came up and slammed his basket down in front of me. I felt Saori staring a hole in my back from the register behind mine. Worked up and embarrassed, I found myself shouting, "Thank you, come again!" in an abnormally loud voice. As soon as it got less busy, Hamazaki appeared like he always did to give me a hard time.

"I see you're wearing a *very fashionable* shirt again today, Catherine!"

"Catherine" was me, apparently. As in *Katō-rin*. I smiled ruefully at this name I'd been given at some point when I wasn't aware of it.

"Mari . . . *anne* lent it to me. My other one got soaked in the rain." I remembered just in time that the girl who'd given me her sweatshirt was named *Mariko Andō*.

"It suits you. You look cute. You have a baby face, Cathy—when you wear things like that, you look younger than my wife!"

I wasn't really listening, though, as I'd been preoccupied since I'd arrived by the discount bin full of men's pajamas placed near my register. They were flannel and had been originally priced at ¥3,000, but now that all the more popular colors were gone, they'd been marked down to ¥2,000 and dumped into the bin. It looked like there were only a few sets left. My husband's winter pajamas were getting pretty threadbare, so I couldn't help eyeing them hungrily.

"Hamazaki-san, does the employee discount apply to things in the discount bin too?"

"Hmmm? Oh, yes, we get half off everything, no matter what."

"I really want to get some pajamas for my husband. Can I ask you to get them for me?"

Part-timers didn't get the employee discount, but we all just asked full-timers to buy things for us and then paid them back.

"Of course! You really are family-minded, aren't you, Cathy? I'm happy to do this for you, but I admit I'm also a little jealous."

Hamazaki's words seemed to hold a hidden meaning. *I should have asked Saori*, I thought, regretting my request a little.

I'm going to have to bike through the rain to go home too. The thought weighed heavily on me, but I took consolation in the fact that a hot bath and a warm bed were waiting for me once I made it there. I put my still-wet poncho back on and headed out, jogging over to where I'd parked my bike only to find it wasn't there. I searched and searched for its brick-red frame among the other bikes—the ones parked there by customers and fellow workers, the ones abandoned forever by their absent owners—but to no avail. It was gone.

I was in such a hurry, I must have forgotten to lock it up! Remembering that I'd attached my umbrella to it, I sighed in despair. I'd ridden bikes my whole life and had had them stolen more than once or twice. But to have it happen during a tremendous downpour like this—that was a first.

I knew it was hopeless, but I walked around the store looking for it anyway. Unsatisfied after the first trip, I made a second one. The parking lot security guard's shift ended right at two, so he was already gone. I was making my third futile trip around the store when I saw someone exiting the delivery entrance in the back. It was Hamazaki.

"Cathy! What's wrong?" He rushed over immediately, grabbing me by the shoulders when he got close. "Why are you crying?"

"What?"

I hadn't realized I was crying until he said it.

"Well, it seems my bike and my umbrella were both stolen, so . . ."

"You're kidding! You've checked everywhere?"

Before I could answer, Hamazaki was already running over to the bike racks. I hurried after him.

"What kind of bike is it? A 'mama chariot'? Does it have your name on it?"

"My name and address are painted on it. It's dark red, with a basket in front—look, I've already looked all over for it. It's not here."

Hamazaki didn't even acknowledge me as he continued searching through the bikes, making a show of jostling each one as he worked his way down the line. Then, ignoring my attempts to stop him, he said, "Wait here," and ran off. Left beneath the warehouse eaves, I found myself increasingly annoyed at Hamazaki's soap opera–worthy "heroic young man" routine. If the bike was gone, it was gone; all there was left to do was give up and walk home. I wanted to get going, not stand here forever waiting for him to do whatever he was doing. My fingertips were starting to get numb from the cold.

"You're right, it's not here. I checked the convenience store and video store parking lots too."

I'd been waiting a good fifteen minutes by the time he returned. I was chilled to the bone—even my internal organs seemed to be shivering. I'd thought about going back into the store, but it felt rude to do so while Hamazaki was running around in the rain on my behalf.

"Thank you so much. I'll just walk home, it's fine."

"You don't even have an umbrella! If you can wait a few more minutes, I'll give you a ride in my car."

I didn't immediately know how to answer. If I were ten years younger, I would have refused right away. But I was a middle-aged woman with a college-aged son. He wasn't going to try anything with the likes of me, and besides, I was so tired at this point I was ready to lie down and sleep right there. I did put up some token resistance, though.

"Maybe I could borrow an umbrella instead?"

"Of course, but listen—I'll be done here in about ten minutes, and then I can take you home. Why don't you wait in the car till then? It'll be better than walking, trust me."

It seemed like too much trouble to resist any further, so I nodded my assent. Hamazaki selected a key from the huge ring that always jangled at his side, then used it to unlock the passenger-side door for me. I obediently climbed in. I didn't know much about cars, but his seemed expensive, a white domestic model. It didn't really suit Hamazaki's inveterate boyishness, but I was reassured by the stuffed animals and cassettes of kids' music scattered around the interior. Returning after exactly ten minutes, Hamazaki got in and started the engine. Hearing my address, he laughed. "Oh, that's not far at all!" He seemed so sweet and sincere that I started to feel bad about my previous unkind thoughts. Was he a good person after all?

We drove down the highway as rain sheeted down, the wipers moving rapidly back and forth across the windshield—*seka-seka-seka*. The rain-refracted lights of the pachinko parlors and vending machines I usually rode by on my bicycle emerged from the darkness only to disappear quickly behind us. The route I hurried along as fast as I could on my bicycle passed by in the blink of an eye. We pulled up to a red light. No cars crossed in front of us. Just a few more lights and we'd reach the family restaurant where we'd make the turn that would take me right to my house.

"Do you have to get up at five thirty tomorrow?" asked Hamazaki, taking a break from humming along with the radio.

"Yes. But for once I don't have anything else scheduled during the day, so I can go back to bed and catch up on my sleep."

He was doing me a favor, so I didn't want to seem sullen; I worked hard to sound bright and cheerful as I answered.

"Ahh, I see! In that case, how about we stop for a quick drink before going home?"

I'd thought he might try something like this, so the question didn't rattle me.

"I'm so grateful for the ride, but the truth is, I'm totally exhausted."

And that *was* the truth. As soon as the light in front of us turned green, though, Hamazaki stomped on the accelerator. The sudden g-force pinning me to my seat and the tight grin pasted on Hamazaki's face both sent chills down my spine. I hugged the bag containing the pajamas for my husband to my chest.

"Let's go for a little drive."

Hamazaki didn't look at me as he said this. It was a development so predictable that any fear I felt was accompanied by simple annoyance. It was ridiculous. Hamazaki was obviously a man who watched too many bad TV movies. I decided to keep silent. We blasted past the right-hand turn I'd told him would take me home. Signs showing how to get back on the highway started to appear, as did an increasing number of love hotels. Despite what was happening, all I could think of was my daughter; I imagined her facing a similar situation at that moment, and even as I knew it was hardly the time or place, I found myself gripped by concern for her.

"I'll get you home by five thirty, don't worry."

Hamazaki's tone was pleasant again, perhaps because I hadn't offered any outward resistance. I smiled at him. I couldn't really believe that something like this would still happen to me at my age. I thought of myself as a dowdy middle-aged lady, but in thinking about it objectively, it occurred to me that this very fact might make me seem like an easy target. Hamazaki drove into the parking lot of one of the many love hotels lining the road without the slightest hesitation.

"You come here often?" I asked as I released myself from the seat belt.

"Well, I wouldn't say *often*, but . . ."

But what? I thought, but kept quiet as I opened the car door and climbed out. I realized I was nervous. Hamazaki walked ahead of me toward the hotel's entrance. I gave silent thanks he hadn't tried to take my hand or force a kiss. To be honest, the Hammer didn't strike me as dangerous. Just sleazy.

I slipped my self-defense alarm from my pocket and pulled the string. Its loudness resounded in the dark parking lot. Hamazaki looked around wildly, seemingly unable to comprehend what the sound might be.

Soon enough, someone came out of the hotel to see what was going on. I pointed at Hamazaki and said, as loudly and clearly as I could, "This man is a pervert."

In the end, I was able to make breakfast and everyone's lunches the next morning as if nothing had happened, though I hadn't gotten a wink of sleep; after seeing my husband off to work, I crawled immediately back into bed, still in my clothes. I'd planned to sleep the entire morning, but the phone rang at ten, waking me up. It was my mother.

"Were you asleep? Must be nice," she said, hearing my sleep-groggy voice. "Are you coming over?"

"Oh, sorry, but I'm pretty tired. I'll come over tomorrow."

I almost hung up, but then I heard her start to cry on the other end of the phone.

"But I don't have anyone else to talk to! And now you're abandoning me too?"

Her sobbing intensified as I brought the receiver back to my ear. *This again?* I massaged my temple with one hand. At first when she'd accuse me of abandoning her, I'd drop everything and rush over, assuring her that nothing could be further from the truth. But how many times had she done this now? Maybe it made me a bad daughter, but the more she accused me of abandoning her, the more I was tempted to really do it.

Weeping all the while, my mother worked her way through her usual litany of complaints: *Your father always did whatever he wanted and now he went and died and left me all alone, he always took care of me so I never worked a day in my life and now I don't have any friends, I don't know what do with myself, what's going to become of me?*

"Well, do you want to come live with us?"

"How many times do I have to tell you, the thought of squeezing myself into that little apartment if yours makes claustrophobic! I couldn't bear it!"

I'd lost count of how many times we'd run through these lines with each other. I knew by now that telling her I'd be right over wouldn't solve a thing. Once I arrived, she'd greet me with some tea and a sour look on her face, muttering, *You didn't have to put yourself out just for me.*

Would this be me at some point? Assaulting my daughter with a warped version of love and dependence? The receiver pressed to my ear, I used my free hand to gather stray hairs off the floor and contemplated the future. There was no guarantee I wouldn't end up like her. I felt a mixture of anxiety, loathing, and pity as I listened to my mother go on, but there was something else too. A sense of distance, as if she were a stranger. I understood her situation. I understood how she felt. Yet it was like it had nothing to do with me—I felt a kind of peace. It wasn't unlike how I'd felt last night with Hamazaki. I understood he wanted to cheat on his wife. I understood he thought I was an unworldly part-timer and an easy target. I even understood that the kindness he'd shown me earlier had been sincere. But his pushiness had left me cold.

"Mom, I think there's a deliveryman at the door, I'll have to let you go."

I hung up without waiting for an answer. She was likely to call back, so I pulled the cord out of the wall, jack and all. Whatever else happened, I wanted more sleep.

I lay on the sofa and closed my eyes; drowsiness washed over me immediately. I looked over at the window and saw the laundry the neighbors had hung out to dry on their balcony glowing white in the unseasonably warm autumn sun. *I should hang some laundry out too*, I thought. *And vacuum the floor.* But my body refused to move.

Even so, I found myself suffused with contentment. I was experiencing the ecstasy of the housewife: a weekday morning spent dozing in a sunbeam. As my mother's weeping receded from my mind, Hamazaki's face last night rose up to replace it.

The Hammer gawking at me as the earsplitting alarm echoed off the concrete. The man from the hotel, who looked to be in his sixties, grabbing him by the wrist, and Hamazaki crying out just from that. The man was pretty compact, but perhaps he'd done aikido or some other martial art. It was only later that I learned he was the love hotel's owner.

"Don't call the police! I wasn't going to hurt you! You didn't say anything, so I thought it was fine!" Hamazaki prostrated himself before me, tears in his eyes as he scraped and bowed. "Please, I can't lose my job!"

"Guys who say things like that are always the worst," said the hotel owner. "You want me to call the police?" But I was too exhausted to deal with that, and besides, if it became a big deal at work I'd likely lose my job too, so I decided not to make an official complaint. The owner called a taxi to take me home then, so I didn't know what became of Hamazaki after that. It was still unclear whether he was just an immature sleazebag or someone worse than I could possibly imagine. But I wasn't scared of him, and I had no intention of quitting my job.

Now that I thought about it, though, my children had both failed to come home again last night too. My son could go off and never come back as far as I was concerned, but I couldn't help worrying about my daughter. If something like what had happened to me last night happened to her, would she be able to get out of it? I was surprised at how effective the little alarm had been—*Maybe I should buy one for her.*

I was getting sleepier and sleepier as I lay thinking, and was on the verge of drifting off completely. At that exact moment, though, right when I was about to sink blissfully into a deep slumber once and for all, someone started shaking me.

"Hey, Mom, wake up!"

"Leave me alone . . ."

I reflexively brushed her off, but then thought about it more and opened my eyes. Hina was standing there looking down at me, appalled. Looking over at the door, I saw a young woman standing there watching us. *Is that a teacher from her school?* I sat up, trying to force my sleep-deprived mind and body back into action. The stranger at the door bowed crisply toward me. She seemed like a conventionally fashionable, conventionally professional woman. I felt like I might have met her before, but I couldn't remember where. She spoke.

"I apologize for interrupting you at this busy time."

". . . Uh, it's okay. As you can see, I was taking a nap."

"We tried calling, Mom, but you never answered! Out to lunch as usual!"

My daughter had lost none of her habitual disrespect. I was still trying to figure out what on earth was going on when the unknown woman came up and touched my daughter's back, prompting her to turn and nod at her, then turn back to face me.

"Mom, I need to tell you something."

"That reminds me—you didn't come home last night! Again!"

"Mom, please. I need to tell you that I'm leaving home today. For good."

"What?"

"I only have a little bit of school left to go anyway, so I wanted to ask if you would allow me to graduate early. I'm trying to save up enough to get my own place, but until then, Itakura-san has kindly agreed to let me stay with her."

My daughter looked me straight in the eye, waiting for my response. I scrambled to my feet.

"What are you talking about?!"

"Please, ma'am. Calm down."

I shook my head in disbelief.

"Who do you think you are? Who are you to tell me to calm down?"

"She's not doing anything wrong. Please hear us out. We can explain everything."

"What's going on? It's about time you thought about someone besides yourself! Do you realize how much your father and I worry about you?"

As I got more and more emotional, I felt the presence of another self within me, a cool, calculating self that told me that now was the time to be believably upset. It wasn't the time to play the understanding mother.

"I told you before—I need you to stop worrying about me!"

Just as I'd predicted, my hotheaded response prompted a similar one from my daughter.

"This place is like a prison! You and Dad are nice, and I'm grateful to you for making sure I got an education. But coming home each night depresses me so much. I can't stand your face anymore—I get annoyed just looking at it!"

"Hina-chan . . ." said the other woman, warning her to stop. But she didn't stop.

"I don't ever want to become like you, Mom! I need to start working as soon as I can so I can be free of this place. I can't stand seeing the way you live!"

Her angry, tear-soaked face looked exactly the same as it had when she was a child. Little Hina-chan had been a mama's girl, dissolving into hysterics if I stepped out even for a moment to pick up something at the store.

My daughter, wiping her tears roughly from her face, said, "I'll be back," and then ran from the room; soon enough came the sound of the front door slamming. The strange woman and I found ourselves left alone together in the living room. The woman looked at me calmly, as if she'd anticipated this turn of events, and bowed her head at me once more, saying, "Sorry for that." *Itakura-san.* That was what Hina had called her.

And that was when I remembered where I'd seen her before.

Itakura-san had been a young nurse just starting out when she'd taken care of Hina back when she'd had her appendix removed in middle school. Now that I thought about it, they always did seem to have a good connection despite their age difference and kept in touch even after she left the hospital.

Natsumi Itakura. Twenty-five years old. She said she worked now at a university hospital downtown. In her time since the hospitalization, my daughter had apparently paid a few visits to the apartment where she lived alone, but they had never been particularly close. About a year ago, though, Hina had come to her asking for advice, saying, "I want to drop out of school and find a job." My daughter had already amassed around ¥300,000 in savings by then from her part-time jobs and her allowance. She wanted to leave home, and she had come to ask Itakura to be her guarantor so she could get an apartment of her own.

I bowed my head to Itakura-san, thanking her for refusing my daughter's request. She girlishly waved her hand in front of her face, blushing and saying, "Oh, it was nothing. I told her she needed to wait until she graduated and do a proper job search then. And also that she needed to talk to her parents about it. But

I didn't do it out of a sense of morality or kindness. I just didn't want to say the wrong thing and then be responsible if something bad happened."

My daughter had started staying out two or three nights at a time that summer. She'd stay with Itakura-san sometimes, but she also stayed at her classmates' houses or at twenty-four-hour manga cafés and other all-night businesses.

"I started to get worried at that point. Though I knew it wasn't my place to intervene."

Itakura-san seemed genuinely sorry as she went on to explain that she'd been afraid that Hina was getting desperate enough to quit school and move in with any guy she could find, even if she didn't even like him that much, just to get out of the house. She felt she couldn't watch the situation deteriorate any longer without doing something, so she offered her a place to stay on the condition that she finish school and stop staying out all night.

"But that's so much trouble for you to go to . . ."

This woman was a complete stranger. How could I ask her to indulge my daughter like this?

"It's fine, really. I work the late shift, so most nights my apartment is empty anyway. And besides, it's not like I'd let someone stay at my place if I didn't like having them around."

Despite there being a sofa in the room, we'd ended up kneeling directly on the carpet to talk.

"Even so, it doesn't feel right to just say okay like it's no big deal. I need to talk to my husband about it at the very least."

"Of course. But I wanted you to know that Hina would be staying at my place from now on, so you didn't need to worry about her. And also—well, I hope you don't find this rude, but Hina can't take seeing you like this anymore. It really weighs on her."

Itakura left me her address and the phone number for the hospital where she worked, as well as the numbers for the two places Hina worked: a bookstore and a bread factory. Apparently, my daughter worked in the evening every weekday at the bookstore and all day every Sunday at the bread factory. Itakura told me that once she graduated, Hina planned to quit the factory and work full-time at the bookstore.

Even after Itakura left, I stayed where I was, kneeling on the ground and staring vacantly into space as the room darkened around me. What I'd thought was a simple case of skipping out a few nights to spend time with her friends turned out to be a thoroughly worked-out plan for living on her own. *I wanted to ask if you would allow me to graduate early,* she'd said—in other words, she wanted us to help her leave home as quickly as possible. I knew it was wrong, but I couldn't help but wish she'd dropped out. Then I could have given her conditions. *Not until you do your final exams. Not until you find a job.* I could have kept my daughter close at least a little bit longer.

There was only half a year left in the school year—did my presence bother her so much that she couldn't stick it out till then? Was seeing *the way I live* really that intolerable? Perhaps it struck her as cheap of me to run out and take the first part-time job I could find as soon as my husband's salary decreased; perhaps she couldn't stand seeing me scramble around like that after living so long dependent on him. It was true that working at a shitty little neighborhood outlet store was exactly what it looked like—a desperate measure. I fully planned on quitting once my husband's salary went back up and my children became financially independent. Was that what she saw and couldn't stand? Along with how all the other things I spent my time doing, like visiting my mother and my father-in-law, were grinding me down too?

Having reached this point, the thread of my thoughts snapped. All strength left my body, and I laid myself down on the carpet. For the first time, I understood how my husband must have felt when he'd been restructured. I'd tried my best, but in the end, I'd been restructured too. By my own daughter.

All of a sudden, the light switched on. My son was looking down at me, a shocked look on his face.

"What are you doing down there? Taking a nap? You startled me!"

Still sprawled on the ground, I looked up at the clock on the wall. It was almost time for my husband to get home.

"Shūichi."

I called out to my son, stopping him as he turned to head off to his room.

"What now? Look, if this is about the phone bill, I'll take care of it once I get my next paycheck. But I have the ski trip with my school club coming up, and I told my friend I'd buy his snowboard off him. So I need my New Year's money early, okay?"

He thinks he's getting New Year's money this year? It was my turn to be shocked as I slowly rose to my feet.

"Shūichi, I had my bike stolen at work last night."

"Uh-huh," he replied, plainly uninterested.

"Do you think I could borrow your mountain bike tonight?"

"I guess . . ."

"And you know, I was the one who actually bought that bike in the first place. I'm sorry, but I'm going to have to use it from now on, I think. So don't take it out without telling me."

"What? That was a graduation present! What the fuck is wrong with you!"

My son walked right up to me and started shouting in my face. Before I quite realized what was happening, my hand curled into a fist, and then I punched him as hard as I could right in the head. His mouth dropped open in disbelief—this was surely the first time he'd ever been hit, not just by me or his father, but by anyone. He leaned against the wall, blinking.

"We're not paying for your school anymore. We don't have the money. If you want to go to university, you're going to have to find a way to pay for it yourself."

I turned and walked into the kitchen. As I started washing the rice, I heard my son call after me, his voice pitiful with shock. "Mo-om?"

Strength boiled up within me, flooding my whole body. I'd never known how good it could feel to hit someone.

I got up the next day at five thirty, making up three lunch boxes and seeing my husband off to work like always. I spent the rest of the morning doing the laundry and my other usual housekeeping chores, and then I left to visit my mother just before noon. The way my son's mountain bike pitched me forward scared me at first, but I got used to it soon enough, and I pedaled along with increasing pleasure. I couldn't believe how light and fast it was—how had I put up with my heavy "mama chariot" for so many years? The mountain bike didn't have a basket, but I could put things in my backpack instead. I made it to my mother's house in twenty-three minutes.

My mother was her usual self when I arrived, as if yesterday's phone call had never happened. I listened to her as she went on and on, making appropriate noises as I fought off sleep. My father had surely done the same, slowly growing accustomed to her over the years.

That evening, I stopped at the supermarket on the way home, made dinner for my husband, took a bath, and then left for work. My son had spent the morning sleeping in as if he didn't have a care in the world, but at some point during the day he'd disappeared. The mountain bike was still in the parking area, though. So maybe some self-reflection had taken place after all.

I breezed through the night, riding along the edge of the highway instead of taking the path. I could go so fast now that I was afraid I wouldn't have time to dodge the pedestrians who would inevitably block my way on the path. Enjoying the feeling of speeding along like this, I suddenly felt something hit me in the face, and, panicking a bit, I squeezed the handbrake. I looked up and saw a fox-god statue looking back down at me, and next to it, a tall oak tree, its golden leaves fluttering in the breeze; it was one of these leaves that had struck me as I'd sped along. As I was standing there staring up at it with my mouth open, another leaf drifted down to land on my face. I contemplated the scene a bit longer, then got back on my bike. The wind hit my face once more. But thanks to the hat and gloves I'd borrowed from my daughter—which I learned had been presents from Itakura-san—my hands and ears were perfectly warm.

I got to work and headed into the changing area, returning the hibiscus-print sweatshirt, now freshly laundered, back to Marianne, along with a self-defense alarm as a thank-you gift, which for some reason elicited a big laugh when I presented it to her. Going out onto the floor, Hamazaki ran over like a lost little kid reuniting with his mother, holding his folded hands in front of his face and saying, "Sorry, sorry, sorry!" I almost laughed, but then, thinking it wouldn't do to let him off easy, I made my face as expressionless as possible as I acknowledged him with a curt nod.

"You're early today."

Saori greeted me from the register behind mine.

"I took my son's mountain bike, it's a lot faster."

I keyed my code into my register as I answered her.

"You have a son? Huh. How old is he?"

"Twenty."

"What—really? I don't have any children at all, even though we're the same age, Maho-chan."

Hearing Saori call me by my first name, I turned to look at her. I thought she was making fun of me, but her expression was neutral.

"Don't you remember? We were in the same homeroom our second year of middle school. I recognized you right away. *She hasn't changed a bit, that Maho-chan*, I thought. *Always going at her own pace.*"

I opened and closed my mouth wordlessly as I leafed furiously through my memory.

"Is that so? I'm so sorry, I didn't realize. I'll look in my middle school yearbook when I get home."

Saori was looking down, seemingly stifling a laugh. *Is she remembering something funny?* A customer approached right then, and I hurriedly turned back to my register.

How had I spent my days in middle school, anyway? I was so absorbed in all the various tasks I had to do that I couldn't seem to remember anything. Including where I might have put that yearbook. Including if I even still had it.

The Dilemmas of Working Women

We were celebrating my twenty-fifth birthday when my longtime boyfriend looked at me and said, "Well, I guess it's about time. We can get married."

Not "Marry me" or "Let's get married"—he said it as if granting permission. He was smiling from ear to ear, his face flushed from a single glass of wine. It was the flush of confidence, not bashfulness; he wasn't the least bit nervous that I might refuse.

"What do you mean, 'it's about time'?"

I didn't want to puncture the mood, so I worked hard to conjure a convincing smile.

"Weren't you the one who told me you wanted to get married by twenty-five, Mito?"

"Did I?"

"You're so forgetful..."

I tried as hard as I could to remember if I'd ever said anything like that, but I couldn't. More importantly, though, no matter if I ever said such a thing or not, the fact remained that we were hardly in the position to get married at the moment.

December had just begun, and the "casual dining" Italian restaurant next to his apartment was noisy with end-of-the-year celebrations. We were at a small table near the back, staring at each other, thinking our respective thoughts. He had a confused look on his face, likely due to my distinctly underwhelmed reaction, while I found myself unable to decide what to say next; my mind whirred frantically, trying to think of a way to get out of this as quickly as possible.

As it was my birthday, our table was covered with plates and glasses from the full-course meal and a bottle of wine we usually would never order. In the seven years we'd been together, we'd had our share of arguments, but this was the first time the atmosphere between us had become so charged and heavy. The waiter came by and asked if he could clear away my less-than-half-eaten plate of pasta. I apologized to him for leaving so much behind.

"Lost your appetite?" asked Asaoka-kun, his tone querulous.

"Not at all. I just want to leave room for the other courses and dessert."

"Last year you ate everything."

So what? I almost replied, but bit back the words. The topic had finally changed, so now wasn't the time to pick a fight.

"I've gained five kilos since I started working, you know."

"Don't people usually lose weight when they work? It must be stress. All the more reason why it's time you settle down and get married."

Back to this! I laughed ruefully and extended my hand toward the bottle. He reached over to stop me, then picked up the bottle and filled my empty glass himself. Getting desperate, I drained the whole glass at once. Asaoka-kun hardly ever drank, so we usually never ordered wine, but today was my birthday. It was time to get drunk. And then change the subject for good.

The main course arrived, and we both cut into the meat placed before us at the same time.

"Getting married doesn't interest you?" he asked with feigned naturalness.

"It's not a question of being interested or uninterested. After all, we're young . . ."

"Is it because I'm still a student?"

I couldn't very well say yes, so I put a piece of veal in my mouth and remained silent.

"What would be the problem with making it official? It's not like I don't have money. It makes a lot more economic sense to move in together than live separately, anyway."

That was when I understood why the subject of marriage had come up so suddenly—I'd recently said, "It's about time I moved out of my parents' place." When he said he had money, he was talking about the allowance he still got from his parents. I was vaguely appalled. *Don't go around proposing to people when you don't even earn your own money!* But I knew from experience that trying to argue with him would be more trouble than it was worth. He might have looked meek and reserved, but he was adept at arguing his point—I had no hope of winning a debate. I'd gone to work early and worked through lunch to make up for skipping out on my usual overtime to come to dinner, so I had no energy to match wits with him anyway.

I just nodded, and then made a show of looking at the menu to pick out dessert.

We left the restaurant and walked toward his apartment. Over the many years we'd been together, I'd usually go straight to his place rather than meet somewhere, and when we did meet somewhere, we almost never parted ways afterward without stopping by his place; there was no reason for me to expect this time would be any different.

His apartment was immaculate as always. It was an old-fashioned apartment near the university, a typical student's layout comprising a small three-mat room, a larger six-mat room, and a tiny kitchen, but he kept it up nicely, his vintage computer and piles of used books lending the space an intriguing atmosphere. He hated fluorescent lights, so there were warm-toned incandescent lamps set all around instead; the glass paperweight on his desk glowed softly in their light. It was less a student's apartment than a scholar's. The cups he used to serve us tea were Mashiko ware we'd bought on a trip together. Now that I was here, I had to admit I found the place soothing.

Sitting on his white cotton bedcover, sipping my tea, I suddenly remembered when I'd said I wanted to get married at twenty-five—it had been on that trip when we'd bought these teacups. I'd been just nineteen at the time, taking my first trip with my first real boyfriend, and had been so happy. Back then, turning twenty-five had seemed like something that would happen in the far-distant future.

He had no television (not because he couldn't afford one; rather, he said he didn't watch it anyway and it would be a distraction), but he did have a radio, a new model designed to look like an antique that was playing softly in the corner. When he wasn't pressing a point to win an argument, he was a man of few words. Once at his place, he tended not to say much of anything unless I asked him a direct question. I reclined against a pillow on his bed as I drank my tea, watching him look over the morning and evening editions of the newspaper. Gazing at the familiar contours of his profile, I felt my eyelids grow heavy. If I acceded to his wishes and we indeed got married, this would likely be how every day would end. So why was I resisting?

He was a grad student, currently in a PhD program after earning his master's degree. We'd been classmates as undergrads in the psychology department at the same university, but Asaoka-kun had seemed somehow different from the other students. He'd known he wanted to go on to grad school even as a first-year, and took the time to attend even classes he wasn't registered for, developing ideas for research topics and taking it upon himself to pursue professors who could help him with them. But as his girlfriend, I was the only one who knew he was so zealous in his studies—he kept this aspect of himself under wraps and got along well with his classmates. There were other bookworms in our class, of course, but they tended to just regurgitate the contents of the books they read in lieu of conversation or offered unasked-for armchair psychological analyses of everyone around them. He displayed none of these tendencies, at least not on the surface. At the age of twenty, he'd already cultivated an air of quiet reserve, listening more than speaking, coolly taking in the conversations happening around him as he made the appropriate sounds to keep people talking.

When we'd first started seeing each other, he'd seemed more mature than my other classmates, an impression I chalked up to him being a year older than me, as well as the fact that he'd been accepted into a law program at another school before changing his mind and entering this program; however, as I got to know him better, I realized his habit of regarding everyone from a distance, like an objective third party, extended to even me, his girlfriend. I wasn't exactly a complicated person, but he understood my psychology completely. And when I realized this, I found myself becoming docile, content to follow his lead. Surprisingly, it didn't feel uncomfortable to do so. I knew he could see right through me, so it relieved me of the burden of hiding things from him or trying to be calculating or strategic.

So we passed the years together peaceably, but lately, the balance of power in our relationship had begun to shift subtly. Was it because, unlike before, I'd started to try to hide things from him, to be more calculating and strategic? Perhaps the reason why I'd responded the way I did to how he proposed to me was clearer to him than it was to me.

The familiar comfort of spending time in the tranquil apartment of a longtime lover seeped into my work-weary body and mind. It was true that we'd spent our days together for years under the unspoken assumption we'd one day marry. But there was more to my resistance than that he was still a student. He'd taken it upon himself to give a name to the uneasiness I felt, and it would be easy just to go along with it. But he may well also have had an inkling of the true shape of my disquiet.

Dilemma. I repeated the word inwardly, deep in my chest.

"You look like a baby," he said, smiling, as he looked up from the newspaper in his hands at me on the bed.

"I'm getting sleepy."

"Go ahead and sleep. I have a paper to write anyway."

I still lived with my parents in the suburbs and was technically still forbidden to stay out all night, but my father was frequently away on business, and while he was away, my mother didn't mind if I stayed over at Asaoka-kun's place. I still hadn't introduced him to my father, but I'd invited him over to meet my mother a few times back when I was still a student. She took to his well-bred reserve immediately, and these days she surely assumed we were well on our way to getting married.

I had a drawer of my own in his dresser, where I kept my overnight things. I pulled myself to my feet, took out my face wash and makeup remover, and then dragged my heavy body to the bathroom. I removed my makeup and took a quick shower, then put on a pair of his pajamas. When I returned, he'd already installed himself in the little three-mat room he used as a study. Soft lamp glow and the faint sounds of typing leaked through the narrow crease along the edge of the sliding door dividing the rooms. His schedule had been inverted for a while, his nights becoming his days and vice versa. I reached for the alarm clock next to the pillow. It seemed to be still set for when he'd woken up the previous day: two o'clock in the afternoon. I'd seen him set it for ten in the morning sometimes, as well as five in the evening. I set it now for seven in the morning, an hour later than when I was at my parents' house, and then climbed into his bed and turned off the light. *What am I going to do when he brings up marriage again?* I thought, but not even five minutes later, sleep overtook me completely.

"Ahh, the same outfit as yesterday, I see!"

I got into the elevator at work the next morning and was greeted by the design consultant, who was already inside.

"Good morning to you too. It was my birthday yesterday."

"And you came to work straight from the party? Young people today!"

He was one to talk, coming to work in that ridiculous snowman sweater. Sure, he was an outside consultant, but he was also over forty—was it really appropriate to attend a business meeting wearing such a thing?

"Cute sweater."

"Isn't it? I knit it myself. Should I make you one too?"

I laughed, appalled at the suggestion.

"Have a lot of time on your hands, do you?"

"I'm too talented—my work's all done before I know it. Anyway, what are you doing tonight? Want to have dinner?"

It was just the two of us in the elevator, so he seemed to feel free to be bold.

"Isn't this sexual harassment?"

"Sure is. Email me before tonight, okay? I'll be waiting."

Just before the elevator doors opened, Snowman reached over and gave me a pat on the ass. Staring at his back as I walked out behind him, I found I couldn't even get mad. There was a tiny knit reindeer on his shoulder. He was surely joking about making me one, but the truth was, looking at it as I followed him down the hall, I kind of wanted him to. I felt myself gradually shift into work mode as I exchanged *good mornings* with various passing coworkers on my way to my desk. Mental preparations for the first meeting of the morning began to fill my head, blotting out everything else: Asaoka-kun's face this morning as I gave him a peck on the cheek when he took my place in the bed; a commute spent worrying about moving out of my parents' place and maybe having to get married to do so; the feeling of Snowman's hand on my ass in the elevator.

I worked in the User Interface Department at a major communications company that had recruited me right after graduation. Until I was onboarded and officially started working, I didn't have the faintest idea what such a department might actually do. But I learned quickly that, simply put, the department researched and developed ways to make the modes through which customers interacted with products—the buttons, the display screens—easier to understand and use.

They'd started recruiting people from psychology programs for this department only a few years before my arrival. My immediate superior was a man who'd earned a PhD in cognitive psychology at a major university, but everyone else had come out of engineering programs. At year three on the job, I was still the greenest in the department; while I'd gotten used to things now, at first I'd sit through meetings without understanding the first thing about what anyone was talking about. Everyone was Japanese, everyone was *speaking* Japanese, but no matter how much I listened to them while squinting at the meeting outline in my hands, nothing sank in. I considered running away with my tail between my legs after my first year, but my boss, strict as he was, wouldn't allow it. *If there's anything—anything at all—you don't understand, ask me*, he said, and I did, learning the basics of the business from him during my lunch breaks or after work, sometimes staying until it was time to catch the last train home. He would see through me when I tried to move things along, pretending to understand when I didn't, and he'd interrogate me until he was sure I comprehended each and every little thing. He didn't do this out of the kindness of his heart. He did it because, as I was his subordinate, his own research would suffer if my work was faulty.

My boss's patience and perseverance paid off, and I managed

to learn the ropes of the job well enough to largely escape his ire. I'd thought of leaving this demanding department for another place to work, but these days, the thought of relocating and having to learn a new job from scratch again made the prospect of staying here for the next ten or even twenty years seem infinitely preferable.

Today my boss, now in his late thirties, seemed to be in good spirits. He was dressed as always in a perfectly fitted suit, sipping a cup of coffee he'd made himself. I'd found a café au lait in the same kind of paper cup waiting for me on my desk. When he brought coffee for me before a meeting, it meant the papers I'd prepared met his approval.

We had a quick check-in, then headed together into the conference room. The engineers and industrial designers had been going back and forth about the interface for a telephone equipped with a terminal adapter that was to go on the market next year. Until recently, the simple act of opening the door to a conference room and having all the men inside turn to look at me had been enough to make me want to run to the ladies' room, but today I managed a smile and general greeting. Amid the sea of suits, Snowman's sweater stood out all the more. But this morning's insouciant smile was nowhere to be found. Every man in the room had a face that said he'd never give an inch to anyone. I chewed my lip, thinking how useful it would be to be able to make such a face myself.

That night, Snowman and I were in bed together. He'd told me once that the hotel we were in had been suffering as foreign chains crowded into the neighborhood, which left it conveniently underpopulated and primed for use in both business and pleasure.

Whenever he asked me to "dinner," we ended up here. This was about the fourth or fifth time it had happened.

This was an affair. No two ways about it. An absolute and total affair. Snowman had a family, I had Asaoka-kun. Neither of us had any wish to leave our partners either; Snowman, at least, also didn't appear to feel the slightest bit guilty about what we were doing.

"Are you sleeping with Kawai-san too, Mito-chan? Both of you shot down my ideas today."

Snowman, whose real name was Ōishi, asked me this after we were done, idly stroking my ass with one hand.

"He wouldn't make me work so hard if we were sleeping together. He's not someone you could win over like that anyway."

"Unlike me, you mean."

Okay, no more work talk, no more work, no more no more . . . Even out of his sweater, his body was as pale and bulky as a snowman's, and now he used it to cover mine. I giggled and buried my face in his ample chest.

It was a scene I had a hard time believing was real. I'd always thought of myself as a serious, even fastidious, person, but here I was, doing what I was doing. He was the man I had the most trouble dealing with at work, after my boss. My position put me between the designer in charge of a product's exterior and the engineer designing its interior; I was obligated to massage their stubborn egos while minimizing the time and costs involved. Ōishi had always been the biggest headache for me, pushing for designs that looked good but were impossibly hard to use no matter what I said—and then he invited me to dinner. And then to bed. I hated to admit it, but part of me had said yes hoping to use the situation to my advantage. But I also knew that if it had been the high-strung, unsmiling engineer who'd propositioned me, I'd have definitely said no. So I clearly didn't hate hanging out with the guy. And it wasn't like Ōishi had started changing his designs to conform to my wishes—though it was true that now that I had more direct access to his thoughts, work in general was getting easier. He was a man who had no compunction calling himself a genius, and the fact was, his designs really were consistently bolder and more eye-catching than those of his competition. So he had no trouble attracting clients and money. But what always saved it for me was his guileless good nature.

"You stayed over at your boyfriend's place last night. Does that mean your father's out of town?" he asked once we'd stopped messing around.

"Yeah, he's in Taiwan until next week."

"Can't you stay here tonight, then?"

"I can't, I have to go home. What would people say if I showed up at work in the same suit for a third day in a row?"

Besides, I'd never spent the night with Ōishi. Or with anyone else except Asaoka-kun, for that matter, outside the occasional business trip. I was never one to travel with my friends, not even in my student days, and I made sure not to stay out drinking past the last train. And no matter how late I got home, I never failed to exchange a short call or email with Asaoka-kun. An unbreakable habit from when we first got together.

"Did your boyfriend get you a nice present?"

Snowman asked me this in a distinctly uninterested tone as I, having caught sight of the clock next to the bed, got up and busied myself with preparations to go.

"We decided it would just create an endless cycle of obligations for both of us, so we don't give each other presents like that. Besides, he's still a student."

"I see. What does he study?"

"The Prisoner's Dilemma."

"The what?" he asked, his head popping out of his undershirt as he pulled it on. "Never heard of it."

"Not something you'd learn in art school, I guess."

"Hey, be nice! Anyway, is there money in it?"

The sincerity in his voice made me laugh. Asaoka-kun had once told me, "Mito-chan, you tend to laugh when you don't know what to say." I didn't really need him to point that out, but now that he had, I figured I should work on it. But there were so many instances when a laugh was the only possible response.

Ōishi graciously gave me a ride home. Despite the bumpiness of the ride in the rattletrap made-in-America car that was his pride and joy, I passed out in the passenger's seat as if my batteries had died. Sensing him navigating the familiar streets around my parents' house, I woke up, and then I heard a notification on my phone. I didn't have to look to know it was an email from Asaoka-kun.

The first time I heard the term *Prisoner's Dilemma*, it wasn't a professor talking, but rather Asaoka-kun. It was before we'd started going out, when we'd ended up going out drinking with a group of mutual friends. There were a lot of people under twenty in our group, but they seemed to go out and drink without a second thought. I could certainly have held my own with them, but my father had strictly forbidden me to drink in public until I was officially of age, so there I sat, obediently drinking my orange juice. The only other person in the group nursing a glass of vivid, artificially colored orange liquid was Asaoka-kun. Uncomfortable,

I sat down next to him and struck up a conversation. Everyone was talking so loudly, though, that we had a hard time hearing each other. "It's so noisy—you want to go somewhere else?" I asked, and he gave me a look as if I'd just saved him from drowning. It was right before Golden Week, the weather warm enough that we could sit outside comfortably in our short-sleeves, so we sat on the steps in front of a lecture hall on campus and talked about nothing and everything. I didn't remember how we'd gotten on the topic, exactly, but what I did remember was his face as he poured his heart into explaining it to me.

So, the Prisoner's Dilemma.

Imagine two people arrested as suspected accomplices in a crime. The police interrogate them in separate rooms. They say to each one, "If you confess first, we'll let you off easy. But if your friend confesses before you do, you'll get an even worse punishment." If neither confesses, there isn't enough evidence to convict either of them, so they'll get off scot-free. But if they both talk, the punishment will be quite severe for both. The best choice would of course be for neither of them to talk, but placed in separate rooms, they have no way to confer on strategy. Both end up thinking, *My friend might confess before me! That would make my punishment even worse. I better confess first and get off easy.* But the result is that both confess at the same time, and both end up punished. A case in which two parties focus on predicting each other's moves only to end up both losing out is thus referred to as a Prisoner's Dilemma.

Asaoka-kun brought up real-life examples like the Cold War showdown between the US and the Soviet Union and a time when photographic printing prices once dropped to zero.

He told me that he'd become so interested in the Dilemma that he'd dropped out of his law program to study psychology instead. The Dilemma itself came from mathematics and game theory, but he said he wanted to explore it from the points of view of psychology and sociology.

Listening to him, I couldn't help but be impressed. None of my other classmates were so committed to psychology that they'd quit a law program to pursue it, and the idea of the Prisoner's Dilemma was compelling—now that I thought about it, the world was filled with such conundrums. But there was still something about it that bothered me, young as I was, and I brought it up.

"If I were one of those prisoners, I wouldn't confess. After all, if I were conspiring with someone to commit a crime, I'd make sure it was someone I could trust. And besides, I wouldn't feel good about it if I confessed and got off easy while my friend was punished!"

Asaoka-kun didn't laugh off my concern, but rather answered earnestly.

"This is a thought experiment for when the parties involved are making short-term, hasty decisions. In other words, when you think in the short term, you end up in a Prisoner's Dilemma."

I think I laughed when he said this. *Oh, I see!* And then, his voice low, he said something I've never forgotten even after all these years.

"We're so often the ones who sow the seeds of our own downfall."

I looked hard at him then. He wasn't particularly handsome, nor did he have the air of a scholar, at least not outwardly. He was on the skinny side, but neither particularly tall nor short. You wouldn't call him manly, but neither was he feminine or androgynous. And maybe it was precisely because he was so unremarkable that he could see the world so objectively, as if from on high. I felt myself gripped by a sudden interest in him. It was only three days later that we became lovers.

I was sitting now in a campus coffee shop that overlooked that very lecture hall, staring absently at my surroundings after finishing my hot chocolate. It was Saturday, but the campus was still pretty crowded. Perhaps because it was almost time for winter vacation, the students' faces seemed brighter and cheerier than usual. I sat there, alone, surrounded on one side by a noisy group discussing a snowboarding trip they wanted to take at the end of the year, and on the other by a different group passing around bundles of photocopies to one another, presumably in preparation for a big test coming up in the new year.

I visited my alma mater from time to time like this; after all, Asaoka-kun still went there. I would borrow books for work from the library and end up waiting for him to get done with his errands. During these visits, I found myself thinking, *It's nice, being at a university*. No one batted an eye if you sat all alone; if you wanted to play around, you could play around, and if you wanted to study, you could study; you could dress however you wanted and not stand out.

Looking at the line of ginkgo trees, their branches now bare of leaves, I could see the clock on the lecture hall. *Seven whole years since we got together*, I thought. *And by spring, it'll be eight.*

It wasn't that I didn't like him anymore. It was more like we'd been together too long. There wasn't any particular reason to break up, not in our past or even now; it was more like the feeling you get waiting for a bus that won't come, wondering if you should give up and take a taxi or start walking instead but ultimately doing nothing.

"Sorry to keep you waiting!"

Asaoka-kun showed up twenty minutes late. I smiled and shook my head.

"I got sucked into a discussion with a student again."

Asaoka-kun had started teaching part-time this year. It was a lecture class for the general public covering the basics of psychology. The money wasn't any better than if he'd picked up a few shifts at an izakaya, but he'd never shown any interest in working at all before; progress was progress. He saw it as a form of advancement, saying, *Teaching is a good way to expand my skill set.*

"Oh, and before I forget . . ." he muttered now, pulling a small wrapped package from his bag. "I meant to give this to you before."

"What is it?"

I took it from him and unwrapped it, revealing a shiny silver ring. I was shocked. Not only a ring, but a "love ring" made by a trendy brand. It was quite like him to take it out of the box and present it raw like this, but at the same time, he'd never given me anything fancier than a souvenir key ring from a school trip before. I was speechless.

"Really, at this point . . ."

Right when we're about to break up? I almost finished, but swallowed the words just in time.

"I didn't know what kind of ring to get, so I asked a younger woman I know for advice. She said this would be perfect."

Say thank you! But words wouldn't come. With trembling hands, I slipped the ring onto my left middle finger. It got stuck at the second joint. Conscious of Asaoka-kun's gaze on me, I tried it on the ring finger of my right hand. It fit perfectly.

"Thank you. But it's so expensive!"

"Yeah. Glad it fits, I couldn't afford to get you a second one!"

He laughed bashfully. Last year—or, really, the year before that—I would have happily accepted it. As I looked at it now, though, the pattern of screwlike indentations in the silver reminded me of nothing more than a picture I once saw in an encyclopedia of an iron chastity belt. I couldn't accept it. I couldn't have it on my ring finger, it didn't matter if it was on my right hand. I knew he was lying when he had said he'd forgotten before. He just hadn't been able to bear it after how I'd reacted to his proposal. *I have to get this off me!* I thought, raising my eyes to look at him again, and then a man's voice rang out. "Asaoka-kun!"

I looked over and saw a professor standing there smiling at us. Asaoka-kun stood up to greet him. It was his advisor, the man who'd mentored him in undergrad and who was the head of the research group he belonged to now as a grad student.

I rose to greet the professor as well. "It's been a long time!" I'd never taken a class from him, but I knew he knew me as "Asaoka-kun's girlfriend." He nodded to me cordially, then excused himself to start a conversation with Asaoka-kun about gathering some research materials for the group. I quietly sank back into my seat and tried my best not to eavesdrop. I used to listen intently when Asaoka-kun discussed things with his professors or fellow grad students, but when I'd bring the things I heard up later with him, it would often become a debate that turned into a fight, teaching me that it was best to pretend I didn't hear anything.

So I sat there, staring at nothing in particular, as I waited for them to finish. Asaoka-kun's advisor, who looked to be in his fifties, was wearing a suit, but it struck me as being of a completely different sort from the ones I was used to seeing at work. But different how? I concentrated my gaze. Maybe it was that it seemed like a suit he wore again and again, making it less crisp than it should be. The wool waistcoat under his jacket seemed a bit worn as well. But these very qualities gave him a somehow scholarly air. He wrote both academic publications and books for a general audience, though he wasn't one of those "experts" who appeared on television. Still, he was rather famous in his field, and his lectures were always standing-room-only.

Am I looking at Asaoka-kun's future? I knew it was no simple thing to become a university professor. You needed to be good at not only research but politics as well, and you were likely to undergo various humiliations along the way. Asaoka-kun once even said, "I don't ever want to become a professor," but it was hard to know if he still meant it. Whatever the case, though, it was something to think about further down the road, not now.

Asaoka-kun's advisor finally left, and then so did we, exiting the building together without talking about where we were going. Whenever he started off like this without saying anything, it meant we were headed to his apartment. I kept my silence and walked along with him. The darkness of evening had begun to fall around us, and cold emanated from the stone-paved sidewalk all the way to our knees. I wanted to get to his apartment and have a nice hot cup of tea as soon as possible, but at the same time, I knew if I did that, avoiding a conversation about the ring and the marriage would become impossible. My father was still away and I didn't have work tomorrow, so Asaoka-kun surely assumed I'd be staying over.

"So, what are we doing for Christmas?"

His voice was gentle as he asked the question. And it was me who usually insisted every year that we needed to spend Christmas Eve together. But this year it seemed all too much to deal with. *How selfish can I be?* Intense self-loathing rose up inside me.

"It's a weekday, so I might have to work late. But I'll try to come by."

I recoiled inwardly; even to myself, I sounded like a man mollifying his mistress.

"Don't put yourself out. It's going to be New Year's soon, anyway."

"Aren't you going back home, then?"

He gave me a quick look. It was the same sharp look he'd get when he made fun of someone. I panicked a little, but tried not to show it.

"That's true. I just might, if I feel like it."

His tone was kind, unlike his look. I knew he'd sensed what I'd really wanted to say: *I want you to go.* His family lived in Yamanashi, close enough that he didn't need to make sure to buy a ticket beforehand, but far enough that you wouldn't just wake up and decide to go on a whim. He didn't get along all that well with his family, but he nonetheless made sure to show his face once or twice a year. I had, of course, never met them myself. Thinking this far, I realized I could use this to my advantage.

"Before, you said it wouldn't be a big deal to get married, but the fact is, I've never even met your parents!"

"All right. You want to meet them, then?"

That's not what I meant! I regretted my lack of foresight.

"I think you've got the cart before the horse, Mito-chan. First you need to be firm in your decision to marry me, and once you are, *then* you should meet my parents. I'm not expecting that getting your father's approval will be so simple either, you know. But we're old enough at this point that our parents' approval isn't the most important thing. Our marriage is something we should decide for ourselves."

"That might be true. But still, to jump into a marriage with someone without having ever met his parents even once..."

"Well then, do you want to meet them?"

Around and around we went. If I went home with him and met his family, that would be it. No way out. I didn't answer him, so he decided to humor me by changing the subject.

"We don't have to talk about this today. Take your time to think it over."

Asaoka-kun was usually one to pinpoint every inconsistency or contradiction in what I said, so it was unsettling for him to be so accommodating. I was both relieved and a bit frightened. Being with him for so many years had taught me that he wasn't as warm and peaceable as he seemed. It hadn't happened often, but I knew from experience that when he felt threatened, he was more than capable of launching a merciless verbal attack.

That night, we stopped by a neighborhood eatery and had dinner, and then we proceeded to his place as if nothing were amiss. We gave each other a light peck, and then I went straight to bed, leaving him to type away at his computer till dawn. I couldn't recall the last time we'd had sex. A small mercy of its own. I found myself thinking that maybe Asaoka-kun was my only real choice for marriage after all.

"You can't accept a 'love ring' from a man you're not crazy about, much less marry him!"

I'd asked for advice from a woman at work who'd entered the company around the same time I did, and this was her immediate response. She'd been a midcareer recruit, so she was four years my senior. She was the kind of woman who overflowed with vitality and always gave clear, direct answers to anything you asked her, making her one of my favorite work friends; indeed, she was the only one I went to for advice about not just work, but love as well.

We were standing in front of the huge mirror in the bathroom of a Western-style gastropub. I was at one of her singles mixers; it wasn't something I'd normally attend, but I'd needed to clear my head. So I'd thought, *Why not?*

"You're still young, Mito-chan—cut that case of arrested development out of your life already! There are so many other men for you to meet."

So many other men? Did she mean those six guys out there waiting for us? Or all the men in the world? If she meant the six, well, I hated to break it to her, but there wasn't one of them I'd want to break up with Asaoka-kun to pursue.

"Yeah, but still—"

"I'm throwing another party on Christmas Eve, do you want to come?"

"I promised to go to his place that night."

"I don't get you, Mito-chan! You're so decisive at work, but so wishy-washy when it comes to love!"

She stared into the mirror, blotting her nose with oil-absorbing paper.

"Am I?"

"You don't realize? Well, anyway, what's the plan now?"

She was someone who seemed to know everyone; people at work called her the Mixer Queen. But I'd never heard of her meeting a special someone herself at any of the events she organized. Were her standards too high? Or did she just enjoy hanging out with strange men for the sake of it?

"I think I'm going to go home."

"I don't blame you. Not the best batch tonight. Be careful of Kenya, though, he's the kind who doesn't like to take no for an answer."

About two hours had passed since we'd arrived. We'd looked at each other and silently agreed to go to the bathroom together to discuss whether to continue the festivities at a second location. Kenya was a guy who'd made sure to sit right next to me from the very beginning. Kenya wasn't his real name, it was just that everyone called him that because he looked like Rumiko Koyanagi's famously younger ex-husband.

"You two were having a strategy session?"

Kenya asked me this as soon as I sat back down. He wasn't bad looking, I admit it. The Queen had picked him, after all, so naturally he also had a good job at a top company, was well-groomed, made pleasant-enough small talk, and, unlike Snowman, was single. But still, he left me cold. For the simple reason that the kind of guy who'd come to a mixer like this was exactly the kind of guy I hated. So why had I come at all? It was a mystery to me, even as I spouted pleasantries in all directions. As usual, the thing I failed to understand the most was myself. It was just as the Queen had said.

"These mixers are such a waste of time, don't you think?"

An unpleasant question from an unpleasant woman—I thought as much even as I asked it. Kenya peered back at me, seemingly amused.

"They sure are. A total waste."

"Why do you think so?"

I turned the question back on him despite being the one who'd brought it up in the first place. A technique I'd picked up from Asaoka-kun.

"I wonder . . . Maybe because they use up a lot of energy and money with very little return?"

His answer was so unexpectedly honest I couldn't help but laugh. I hadn't gone to so many myself, but it struck me that attending a mixer like this used more brain power than burying your head in a book. You had to smuggle your real intentions into superficial small talk with a group of men and women you'd never met before, subtly communicating interest in those you liked and avoiding the unwanted attention of those you didn't; it was hard to think of a more severe test of a person's ability to read the unspoken thoughts and intentions of others. *Asaoka-kun should give it a go as part of his research—he'd be sure to learn a thing or two.*

It was around then that the guy in charge of organizing the bill started gathering money from us (the men, naturally, were expected to chip in more than the women), signaling that it was time to leave. I said my goodbyes to the women there from my company and then hurried out, heading toward the subway.

"Mito-san!"

I heard a voice behind me. Kenya's. I didn't turn to look, instead quickening my pace down the sidewalk, but he caught up with me at the subway entrance anyway. I should have made a literal run for it—who cared what people might think?

"I'll walk you home."

Kenya was all smiles. He had his coat in his hand instead of wearing it. Had he run out after me so quickly?

"Oh no, it's too far."

"Far is fine."

"I can make it there alone."

"Does that mean you could join me for another drink somewhere before you go?"

Kenya laughed, blithely ignoring everything I said.

"It's my father, he's so overprotective. If I stay out too late, he'll call me on my cell and insist on coming to get me wherever I am. So I could go with you, but only if you're cool with getting punched in the face at the end of the night."

I was being deliberately irritating, running my words together as I offered my ridiculous excuse. But my elaborate attempts to be off-putting seemed only to egg him on. He was quiet for a moment, as if thinking something over, then said, "Well, if you're father's going to give you a ride home anyway, what's there to worry about?"

He really did ignore what people said to him. Undaunted by my words and demeanor, he threw an arm around me, pulling me close. Fatigue overtook me as I gazed at the twinkling Christmas lights over this strange man's shoulder.

Even though I had work the next morning, it was past one in the morning when I finally got home. I'd not only gone for another drink but ended up at a love hotel too, and now here I was, nearly flattened with exhaustion as I clumsily opened the front door.

"You're late."

My father's face appeared at the end of the dark hallway before me. I froze in the entryway, my breath caught in my throat. I'd been sure he'd be asleep at this hour.

"Take off your shoes and get in here. A young lady like you, stinking of alcohol . . ."

"You're still awake?"

"I was waiting for you! And I have to get up earlier tomorrow than you do. C'mon, hurry up."

Muttering to himself, my father turned and headed into the living room. Accepting my fate, I followed after my father as he walked ahead of me in his robe. I hadn't gotten in trouble for coming home late since I'd gotten a job, so I was caught off guard. My mother hadn't emerged from the bedroom with him, which meant he was truly angry. Even though she pretended to take my side in these matters, she never defended me when the chips were down.

"An end-of-the-year party?"

My father noisily lowered himself onto the sofa, then looked up at me. I noticed the white streaks standing out more than usual in his bed-mussed hair.

"Yes. I'm sorry for being so late."

"That's not a big deal. You have a job, so a late night or two is only to be expected. There's something else I want to talk about—I hear you want to move out and live on your own?"

He lit a cigarette as he talked. *Mom spilled the beans*, I thought.

"Did you really think I'd permit such a thing?"

"... No."

"You got that right. Do you know why, Mito? Think about it!"

His voice was getting steadily louder. Thank goodness it was winter. During the warmer months, open windows would allow the neighbors even three doors down to hear him yell at me back when I was a kid; my friends would tease me about it, saying, "Somebody got in trouble last night!" The idea that these same neighbors might hear a man his age still yelling at his daughter, now an adult, was too embarrassing to contemplate.

"You're my only daughter—the only way you're leaving this house is as a married woman! If you have a man in your life, introduce him to me already. Stop sneaking around!"

I'm not your property! I wanted to say, but I knew if I did, I'd be yelled at till dawn. Even as I tried to stop myself, though, a tiny word of protest escaped my lips.

"But..."

"But? But what? You sound like a child!"

My father jumped up, his feet banging against the floor. He was a big man, over 180 centimeters tall and a former rugby player; even as an adult, it made my legs tremble to have him yell at me from his full height. When I was younger, he'd sometimes even roll up his fist and give me a punch, but these days he kept his hands to himself. His restraint only made it more palpable how much anger he had roiling within him, though, now that it couldn't find an outlet.

"Please forgive me."

I apologized as meekly as I could. He was an emotional man, but like many athletes, he also had a guileless side. When he was scary, he was scary, but he was also easy to handle.

My father stubbed out his cigarette and let out a great sigh. As I stood there, my head still bowed, he reached over and patted my shoulder. "Let's try to get some sleep," he said, and then he headed up the stairs to his bedroom. All strength left me then, and I collapsed onto the sofa.

My father was the main reason I wanted to leave home, a fact that seemed to have never occurred to him. I wouldn't call him a domestic abuser, but it was true that when he got upset, he'd scream and yell and break things; my mother and I lived in fear of his moods. I knew he loved us, but as I got older, I began to question why things had to be like this. My father's way of being was a big reason why I decided to major in psychology. But being able to analyze his volatility using theories of the mind did little to solve the situation in real life.

I'd talked to my mother about living alone knowing full well she'd be unable to resist telling my father. I was too much of a coward to confront him directly, so I used her. I knew she must have told him about Asaoka-kun too. The fact that my father had pretended to be unaware of him all these years must've meant he had a greater capacity for patience than I'd thought. I hauled myself up from the sofa. It seemed all the clearer, though, that the only way to get out of this house was to get married.

In any case, I was too tired to deal with anything else today. I headed for the bathroom to take a shower and go straight to bed. I took off my jacket and my sweater, and then, as I prepared to remove my makeup, I looked in the mirror and saw a vivid hickey on my collarbone.

I'm the worst. Why am I like this? I couldn't look at the mirror any longer. I turned and went to bed without even washing my face.

It was nearly nine when I finally made it to Asaoka-kun's apartment on Christmas Eve. I'd ordered the traditional Christmas cake at the department store near my work, but by the time I arrived, the dry ice had disappeared completely and the now-tepid cake was starting to fall apart.

Even so, Asaoka-kun was happy. When we were still students, knowing he had a sweet tooth, I'd make the cakes for his birthday and Christmas Eve myself. I no longer had time for that now that I had a job, but it still fell to me to order the cake and bring it over. Figuring I'd be hungry after work, Asaoka-kun made curry. He usually never cooked, but on days when he knew I'd be bringing a cake over, he'd always make curry as a form of thank-you or recompense. We ate his sweet, unspicy curry filled with grated apples and drank our oolong tea, then cut the cake and ate that. Christmas songs played one after the other on the radio, and I found myself becoming talkative, laughing more and more. Asaoka-kun was laughing too. I kept thinking, *Why is he laughing so much?* even as I deliberately said things I knew would amuse him, a contradiction that kept building in the corner of my mind.

"What's wrong? Did something happen?"

I'd been laughing a little hysterically when I suddenly burst into tears, but he seemed determined not to let even this bother him. Not just Asaoka-kun, but anyone looking at me tonight would know my mental state was off.

"I don't want to go home."

I was sobbing uncontrollably, and he rubbed my head as if comforting a child. I'd told Asaoka-kun before about times in the past when my father would hit me when I'd stay out too late.

"Then just stay here. I'll make the call if you'd like."

I shook my head vehemently.

"It's okay. I'll take care of it myself."

"Really?"

I nodded emphatically, wiping the tears from my face. If he called my father now, I'd end up being ordered to bring Asaoka-kun to meet him for New Year's. A situation I desperately wanted to avoid.

Taking my limp body in his arms, Asaoka-kun lifted me and laid me on the bed. As I lay there weeping, wanting to stop but unable to, Asaoka-kun started rubbing my back.

"Are you in the mood?"

He whispered the invitation in my ear, and I shook my head. Not only was I completely not in the mood, but I also remembered the hickey on my collarbone from my night with Kenya. Was Asaoka-kun disappointed or relieved? I didn't want to know. I shut my eyes tight, keeping his expression a mystery.

The fact was, Asaoka-kun and I never really had sex. We had when we first got together, of course, but soon enough we both realized that it did very little for either of us. At nineteen, I couldn't really abide the idea of getting naked with some guy and doing weird things with our bodies; as it turned out, Asaoka-kun at twenty felt like it was easier not to have to do it with me either. Confessing our mutual distaste to each other, my first thought was *I really have found my soulmate!*

It wasn't that he had no sexual desire at all, or that he was impotent or gay; it was more like he preferred to gratify himself on his own, or leave it to professionals. He didn't clarify things explicitly, but reading between the lines I got the message: Don't worry about it. Surprisingly, this didn't make me dislike him—if anything, I was grateful he was willing to go off and take care of things himself so I didn't have to think about it.

I'd told him he was my first, but in truth, I hadn't actually been a virgin. I'd had a boyfriend in high school, but when we did the deed it just hurt and made me feel embarrassed, and I grew tired of being pestered for it at the end of every date. I concluded then that sex simply didn't suit me. But once I started working, I was shocked to find myself wanting to go bed with Ōishi, the designer. I realized I *could* enjoy sex—but only when it was carefree, with someone for whom I had no romantic feelings at all. It was a surprise to discover that I possessed sexual desire after all, even if it was a bit off-kilter. I had to imagine Asaoka-kun had made a similar discovery about himself at some point.

I began to doze off in his arms. I wondered what my father would say if I asked his permission to marry Asaoka-kun. His initial reaction would probably be to bellow "You expect me to give my only daughter to some *student*?" But I also knew that if Asaoka-kun bowed his head and let the initial storm blow over, my father would likely relent and give his blessing. The fact was, even if he had to buy Asaoka-kun and me a place to live, my father would almost certainly prefer to do that—and thus keep us under his thumb—than allow me to be financially independent and live on my own. I wondered, though, if I'd feel differently about Asaoka-kun if he had a normal job. I didn't know. Was it really right to marry a man who'd given me a love ring I didn't want, and for whom I had no sexual desire to speak of? I couldn't decide, and my eyes welled up once more.

"I can't go on like this."

It seemed that he'd finally lost his patience with my incessant tears. He slowly rose to his feet, went to his desk, withdrew something from one of its drawers, and returned. I sat up and took it from him. I could tell what it was immediately, despite it being meticulously folded. A marriage application.

"I've already filled it out. So keep it."

I felt myself stiffening, my tears finally forgotten.

"You're not being straight with me at all. I'm not joking around—I want you to actually think about it! I know you're busy with work, but you don't return my emails, you don't wear the ring . . . Do you think you can do anything you want to me and I'll never get hurt?"

"Stop! Stop it!"

I shouted without thinking, my outburst sounding childish even to myself.

"I'm taking you home. Rant and rave and cry all you want then, alone!"

"I didn't come here to fight!"

"You're the one who started this!"

I grabbed a pillow and, before I quite knew what I was doing, threw it at him.

"Why do you think we can get married, anyway? You don't even make your own money!"

I'd finally said it. It was a relief. I saw his lip curl into a sneer, and then my eyes dropped to take in the remains of the Christmas cake the pillow had knocked onto the tatami.

"Wasn't your concentration in gender studies, Mito?"

He spoke slowly and quietly; I didn't quite know how to answer.

"And yet look at you—you're no better than any other dumb girl out there. What if our genders were reversed? Does a man only have the right to get married if he has a full-time job to support his wife and family? Is a man really only worth the size of his salary? Would you respect me more if I wrote a bunch of stupid self-help books for money like my advisor does?"

He went on and on until I clapped my hands to my ears to block him out. It was Christmas Eve! Not a time when I wanted to hear all this—it was a night I wanted to think about anything but.

I pulled on my coat and fled his apartment without another word. I ran as fast as I could down the iron steps, escaping before he had the chance to yell after me to stay. My head ringing as if an alarm were going off in it, I kept running until I reached a major street and finally stopped.

I'd missed the last train. The occasional taxi passed, but as I thought about raising my hand to hail one, I realized I didn't know where to go. A taxi all the way back to my parents' house would cost almost ¥20,000. But it was less the money than that I simply didn't want to go. I sat down on the bench in a nearby bus stop and scrolled through the contacts in my phone, from the beginning all the way to the end. There wasn't one person who seemed like they'd want to hear from me this late on Christmas Eve. I was near the university, and groups of drunken students would sometimes pass by on the sidewalk behind me, but a woman crying alone on a night like this was a disturbing sight and they gave me a wide berth. I decided to give Ōishi a try. But of course it went straight to voicemail. Grasping at straws, I left him a message, telling him to give me a call if he heard this.

"Mito-san? Is that you?"

As I sat there on that cold bench in the pitch-black night, completely at a loss as to what to do next, I heard a voice. I looked up to see a young couple looking down at me, quizzical expressions on their faces. I realized I recognized the couple's male half as he stood there peering at me in his wool hat.

"Did you have a fight with Asaoka?"

I managed a small laugh. The woman, whom I didn't recognize and who seemed a bit young, crouched down to look me in the eyes, offering me a handkerchief and asking, "Are you okay?" Flooded with equal parts embarrassment and relief, I burst into tears once more.

Asaoka-kun and I made up shortly after New Year's. He sent me an email apologizing for the Christmas Eve fight on the evening of New Year's Day, so, telling my parents I was putting the New Year's card thank-you notes in the mail, I slipped out and called him from a pay phone. His voice was kind, as if our fight had never happened, and it hurt my heart when he told me he'd spent New Year's Eve in his apartment alone. I knew my father would pull a face about it, but I promised Asaoka-kun I'd go with him for the first shrine visit of the year the next day.

A light snow was falling, so despite it being only the second day of the new year, the shrine downtown was less crowded than last year. Asaoka-kun was wearing a sweater I'd knit him back in our student days. We huddled together against the cold like little animals as we made our snowy pilgrimage. At the shrine, I threw my coin and pressed my hands together, but I couldn't think of a wish. Finally, I settled on a simple request: *God, please just make things easier between us.*

On Christmas Eve, I'd ended up staying over at the young man's place; I'd recognized him because he was part of Asaoka-kun's research group. His girlfriend seemed more concerned about me than he did, insisting that she'd stay with me until the trains started running again if I kept resisting their invitation. I felt bad ruining their Christmas Eve, but the girl, who turned out to be three years younger than me, was so inexplicably kind. The man, for his part, laughed ruefully and said, "I'm sure dating Asaoka's no picnic."

Back at his place, he made me a hot lemon tea with ginger in it. "He suffers from low self-esteem," he said, sounding like a typical psychology student. I remained silent, thinking, *Really? He's always struck me as thinking pretty highly of himself.*

"Maybe it's because he didn't graduate properly from high school. But he's no dummy—he passed the exam to get in here on his first try, after all."

He dropped this tidbit casually, as if it were something everyone already knew. Shock ran through me, but I strove to remain calm on the surface as I mulled over this new information. Did this mean the story about withdrawing from the law program at the other school to come here was just a lie? Why did he hide the real story, which everyone else seemed to know, from me? I wasn't close with his grad school friends, but it was still a shock that they knew and I didn't. Did they keep it from me on purpose, or did they just assume I already knew? I was having a hard time organizing my thoughts, so I decided to change the subject.

"He doesn't get along with his advisor very well, does he?"

"He doesn't. They went around and around when he was writing his master's. In the end, Asaoka pretended to go along with him, but I think he's secretly still upset about it."

The girl stopped her boyfriend then, saying, "Shun-chan, that's enough." We ended up sitting beneath the kotatsu watching late-night TV and laughing together. It was so much more therapeutic to spend the night that way than if they'd asked me to talk about the fight. I went home on the first train the next morning, and before my father, who was getting ready to go to work at that point, could start yelling at me, I apologized. Maybe because I looked pretty exhausted already, he let me off easy, grumbling, "Pull yourself together" and leaving it at that.

Once our visit to the shrine was done, I suggested we go for a little walk to enjoy the pretty snow a bit more. He pretended to resist at first, but I could tell he was pleased. We began to walk together, each of us taking off a glove to hold hands skin-to-skin. I was wearing the ring now, but still on my right hand rather than my left. Asaoka-kun held it tight the whole time.

As we watched the snow gradually build up around us, covering the world with its whiteness, my worries began to seem less and less important. *I don't know what to do.* I'd been saying this over and over, but the fact was, I was starting to realize that maybe I did know. But what if even this could be buried beneath the snow? Wouldn't that make things easier? I felt my emotions grow calm and quiet within me as my head grew numb and my thoughts grew vague. *If only I could walk along like this with him forever, hand in hand, thinking about nothing.*##

During the first week back at work, I started noticing subtle changes in how people treated me. The men avoided looking me in the eye, while the women avoided me altogether. I was trying to think of what I might have done to cause this when my boss summoned me.

The purchase orders I'd rushed to complete before the end of the year were a mess. There were mistakes in the rows of figures and some of the dates were off by as much as a month. They were elementary mistakes, and he yelled at me in the middle of the office in front of everyone. He could be sarcastic sometimes, but he very rarely raised his voice at anyone in public. My body trembled like it used to back when I was a newbie, and even though I told myself I wasn't going to cry no matter what, tears began leaking from eyes. My boss sighed, then said it was his fault, too, for failing to check my work more closely, and after telling me to apologize to our clients and redo the orders as soon as possible, he returned to his office.

As I sat at my desk redoing the paperwork and calling around to make my apologies, I wondered if these mistakes were really the kind of thing that would make my coworkers treat me so differently. They were basic errors, of course, and therefore unforgivable, but they were also the kind of thing that everyone ends up doing once in a while. Yet right now, even coworkers who'd usually have a kind word for me were pretending they didn't see me when we passed in the hall. I had a bad feeling that another shoe was about to drop.

We had a meeting scheduled that afternoon about the telephone with the terminal adapter, which meant Ōishi would be coming to the office. He was usually very jokey and familiar when he came around, but today he passed by with barely a glance in my direction. And that was when it hit me. Ōishi and I must have been found out somehow. That would explain why everyone was acting so oddly. It was a trivial matter, really, but it made me want to quit right there and then. Asaoka-kun's words rose unbidden in my mind: *We're so often the ones who sow the seeds of our own downfall.*

That evening, I brought my redone paperwork to my boss for him to check only to have him ask, "What are you doing tonight?" This was only the third time Kawai had ever invited me to dinner. The first time had been back when I was first hired, and the second had been a different time I'd made a major mistake; both times, I'd had no appetite at all but forced myself to eat anyway, ending up sick all night afterward. Even so, it was an offer I couldn't refuse.

"I heard you're getting married soon. Is that true?"

We were in the kind of oddly pretentious shabu-shabu place that people only go to on the company dime when Kawai suddenly asked me this. I'd been about to put some vegetables in the vat of boiling water between us, and I put my chopsticks down before answering.

"Is that what people are saying?"

"It's useless to try to hide it from you, so I'll just say it: The rumor going around is about you sleeping with both Ōishi and some guy named Kenya."

Despair washed over me; I picked up the small glass of beer in front of me and gulped it down. It was the Queen. I'd trusted her and she'd betrayed me, but as shocked as I was, I had to admit I was hardly as pure as the driven snow myself. It must have irritated her to see a woman dithering about being proposed to throw herself at any man who came her way. It probably hurt Ōishi's feelings to hear about it too. Not only did it make the prospect of working together less appetizing, but also, now that I thought about it, I'd called him and left a message late on Christmas Eve. It was only natural he'd give me the cold shoulder.

I waited for Kawai to refill my beer glass, but he either didn't notice it was empty or didn't feel like being kind to me, and he ignored it. Figuring we were well past the point of observing niceties, I reached over and poured some beer into my glass myself. Watching me, a tiny smile came to his lips.

"I'm still undecided about getting married. But the rumors about me and Ōishi are true. I'm very sorry."

"I don't need you to apologize to me. I don't care what you do in your private life, but if this whole thing is going to interfere with your work, I'd rather that you got married and quit."

I bowed my head at his directness. I knew he was an uncompromising soul, but it still hurt.

"Are you married, Kawai-san?"

"I am. I have two children. My oldest is in third grade."

His voice was emotionless as he answered me, his hands busy swishing sliced beef in the boiling water. Watching him bring the beef to his mouth, I wondered if even someone like him became kind and sweet when he went home to his family.

"That's a pretty big kid."

"Yeah, well. We were still students when we got married."

Hearing that made my eyes widen. Now that I thought about it, he was the product of a psychology PhD program too.

"I don't mean to be rude, but it seems like things have really worked out for you. Does your wife work as well?"

"She does. She's a teacher. Why do you ask?"

"The man I'm considering marrying is still in grad school."

I was tipsy and had already half resigned from my job at that point, so I decided to throw caution to the wind and tell him about the whole Asaoka-kun situation. I didn't mention our sexlessness, of course, but I talked about everything else, from how we met to how things were going now, including the issues I was having with my father. It was a long story, but Kawai didn't seem bothered as he sat listening to me. Greeted with silence when I finished, I began to regret opening up so much. I'd surely repulsed him completely.

"This is less about your boyfriend or your father and more about your fear of success, isn't it? Your background is in psychology too, after all."

His brisk diagnosis made my shoulders slump.

"You really think so?"

"I think you think so too. Anyway, the solution is clear. If you're half-hearted in your work, it'll just cause problems for everyone. So apply yourself at work with the idea that you need to take care of this man of yours as well."

"I don't want to do that."

"What have you been studying all this time? Your poor parents must be crying, seeing how you're wasting all that tuition money they paid!"

We both laughed at that point. It was a small thing, but it seemed like the first genuine laugh I'd had in a long time.

"This reminds me of something—the Prisoner's Dilemma. I don't know if this might shed some light on your situation, but every Christmas, my family faces the same problem."

Laughing seemed to have restored my appetite, and I reached for some beef with my chopsticks.

"My wife pushes herself once a year to make a cake for Christmas. We're a family of four, so naturally we split it four ways. But I don't really like sweets, so I just a take one bite from my piece and give the rest to the kids. The idea is that they should split it evenly between them, but every year they fight about it, each convinced that the other got a bigger piece."

"Sounds like you have a lovely family," I said, smiling, and Kawai coughed self-consciously.

"That's not why I'm telling this story. Anyway, last year the squabbling was particularly bad, so my wife thought up a solution. What do you think it was?"

I cocked my head. *Hmmm.*

"She made the children cut the cake. Specifically, she had the older child cut the cake and the younger one choose which piece to take first."

I nodded. *Of course.* Since both children wanted as big a piece as they could get, the child cutting the cake would try to cut the cake as evenly as possible. If one was clearly bigger than the other, the other child would end up taking it.

"Your wife is so clever!"

"I told you, that's not the point of this story!"

As we ate a final course of udon noodles, Kawai gave me one more lecture about applying myself at work. I rode the train home thinking about what he'd said about my fear of success. I was scared of Asaoka-kun hating me. If I went along with this marriage and became the breadwinner of the two of us, I knew that at some point his prodigious pride would end up wounded. I had zero confidence I'd be able to deal with it if that happened. The fact was, I wanted to remain the weaker one in the relationship. It had always been that way, after all: Asaoka-kun was the smart one, the adult in the room whose wisdom I could trust unthinkingly. I wanted to remain content to follow his lead.

The white in my father's hair had, at some point, spread all over his head. The day would come when even he would be the less powerful one in our relationship. The prospect frightened me.

Looking at the salarymen dozing in the train car around me, I thought about how powerful men were, and how pitiful. Just by being born men, they were expected to take the lead both at work and at home. They could never say they'd be fine getting the smaller piece of the cake.

Asaoka-kun and I were basically just a couple of warped children, each trying to get the other to take the bigger piece of cake. I had the thought again: *We're so alike.*

On my next day off, Asaoka-kun asked me to come over. I didn't really want to, but, mustering my courage to ask him about his fabricated education history, I went anyway. When I arrived, though, I was surprised to find an older woman there with him. His mother. I bowed my head respectfully to her. I'd thought I'd gotten used to Asaoka-kun's various modes of attack, but this one caught me flat-footed.

"Thank you for everything you've done for my son. I'm sorry for any trouble he's caused you."

Perhaps because my own mother resisted dressing her age, Asaoka-kun's mother looked old enough to me that I wouldn't have batted an eye if he'd said she was his grandmother. I bowed again, saying, "Pleased to meet you," and snuck a questioning glance at Asaoka-kun.

"She just showed up! You could have called first, Mom."

Despite his words, Asaoka-kun seemed fine with it, even pleased. Had she really "just shown up"? She'd never done anything like that before, so, even if he wasn't technically lying right now, it seemed impossible that he hadn't said something to prompt this visit.

"It's 'Mito'-san, right? Wonderful to meet you. I'm so sorry for intruding, I was about to go anyway."

"Not at all! I'm the one who should go, I didn't mean to interrupt."

"I won't hear of it. I'm the one who came over out of the blue. Please sit down. I'm so sorry for all this."

His mother's incessant apologizing was starting to get on my nerves. *What is it you really think I need to forgive?*

"Oh, Mom, I only have coffee! Shoot. I'll run out and get something you can drink," said Asaoka-kun. He sounded like an actor on a stage. I almost offered to go to the store instead, but then, realizing this must have been his plan all along, I stopped myself. My curiosity about what I'd learn about his true intentions once I was alone with his mother outweighed my discomfort at being set up.

Once Asaoka-kun threw on a jacket and left, the apartment became deathly quiet. I thought about going over to turn on the radio, but I restrained myself, not wanting to seem overly familiar with the apartment in front of his mother.

"Please excuse my son."

There she went, apologizing again. Her carefully done silver hair and her cashmere cardigan both smacked of money; the gap between her manicured appearance and her humble words was disorienting.

"Excuse me for asking, but did something happen that led you to come here today?"

Not wanting her to think me rude, I tried as indirectly as possible to ask her what she was doing here.

"Oh no, nothing happened. My son simply let me know he was getting married, so I came right over."

Of course. I stifled a sigh.

"I know my son can be selfish and must cause so much trouble for you, so I just wanted to thank you for accepting him into your life."

She bowed to me then. Startled, I spoke quickly to dissuade her.

"Wait a minute—we haven't officially decided to get married!"

"You haven't?"

Right then, the kerosene heater in the corner of the room sputtered noisily, then clicked off. Asaoka-kun's mother and I both turned to look at it.

"Oh, it must have run out of fuel. I wonder if there's any more around?"

Sounding dazed, Asaoka-kun's mother started to rise to her feet, but I stopped her.

"Please listen to me. Your son and I are in no position to get married."

"What do you mean? I heard you have a great job at a good company, Mito-san, and we'll be sure to give our son more than he needs to live on while he's still at school," she assured me, her tone even. "Now where's that kerosene?"

She got up and started poking around the apartment.

"We may be country folk, but we own several apartment buildings, which gives us more than enough to get by. We plan to leave them to our son, so there's really no reason for you to worry about money."

Asaoka-kun's mother said this with her back turned to me. I knew it already, but now I felt it in my bones—this was where it all came from, the money he used to treat me to my birthday dinner, to buy me a love ring, to go visit a *professional* whenever he had the urge. But was I really so different? I lived in my father's house, I'd gone to school on his dime—even the money I used on my little dates with Asaoaka-kun, if you traced it back to its ultimate source, came from him.

"Excuse me," I said. She'd finally found the kerosene, and now she stood up, the red plastic container in her hand. It was my turn to apologize.

"I'm very sorry, but can I ask you to leave now?"

She turned to face me then, her eyes wide. Sputtering indignantly, she began speaking in dialect. I didn't understand much, but I managed to catch it when she said she was the one paying for the apartment we were standing in. "I'll go, then," I said, and then pulled on my coat. Closing the door on the apartment's kerosene stink, I headed for the bus stop.

I was just about to step onto the bus when I saw Asaoka-kun running toward me. I considered ignoring him and getting on anyway, but that seemed like a little much, even for me.

"What are you doing, leaving like this? You're being so rude!"

Huffing and puffing, Asaoka-kun finally got close enough to grab my arm. I shook him off.

"I'm rude? How about you? Making your mother do the dirty work, like a child!"

My voice sounded cold even to my ears. Asaoka-kun, who usually had a snappy comeback ready no matter what I said, seemed taken aback.

"C'mon, you must have known how I really felt! Didn't you notice I've been having an affair this whole time?"

All the color drained from his face. I felt myself suddenly on the verge of tears.

"Were you going to break up with me if I said I didn't want to get married?"

"Why would we need to break up?"

"So, you wouldn't have? Asaoka-kun, you have to realize that no matter what you do, I will never marry you."

I could see on his face that he was furiously calculating what he wanted against what he thought he could get. Just like a child given a knife and told to cut a cake in two. I realized it was the same face I must have been making for years now.

The next bus came, and I got on. Asaoka-kun, left standing there on the stone-paved sidewalk, simply watched as it carried me away.

A Tomorrow Full of Love

It wasn't my dream to open an izakaya. It had never crossed my mind, even as an idle fantasy, before I quit my office job.

Whenever I finished the prep work and washed my hands before opening, smoking a cigarette after exchanging my dirty happi coat and apron for clean ones, a strange feeling would come over me. The ancient counter, the cheaply constructed walls and ceiling. The even rows of condiments, the aluminum ashtrays next to them. In less than an hour, the place would fill with the smell of kushiyaki sizzling on the oak charcoal grill, mingling with the cigarette smoke and conversation wafting up from the customers occupying the scant number of seats—only twelve in total, all at the counter—available in this tiny hole-in-the-wall bar.

The feeling that would wash over me in these moments before opening, imagining all the things that might happen that night, was a mix of comfort and unease. There lingered in the back of my mind a bitter sense that this wasn't how my life was supposed to turn out, but it was covered over by a soft, pillowy layer of satisfaction, along with something like resignation. It was a feeling not unlike the dessert I liked to eat from time to time, sweet custard with a thin layer of bitter caramel at the bottom—a nonsensical association that came to me every time.

Seeing that the old-fashioned clock mounted on the wall read five o'clock, I stubbed out my cigarette and rose to my feet. The door opened, and a young man walked in: Takurō, my sole employee. His usually blond hair was now bright pink.

"Is that the fashion now? Pink?"

"Good evening!"

"You look like those dyed baby chicks they used to sell at the night market."

"I'm so hungry. What's family meal tonight?"

"Are you even listening to me? Anyway, I made some mapo tofu, and there's also some stew left over from last night, you're welcome to either."

We were conversing like two ships passing in the night, but I let it go and brought the noren out to hang over the entrance. Setting the guitar case he'd brought with him down on a seat, Takurō hurried over to take the lid off the rice cooker. I stepped outside and looked up at the sky. The low, heavy clouds looked ready to drop a load of cold rain at any moment. Counterintuitively enough, a little rain tended to drive more customers into the place, but the noon weather report had said it might turn to snow as the night wore on. The vermilion lantern hanging in the entrance had seen better days; I switched it on and went back inside, only to be greeted by Takurō at the counter wolfing down a bowl of tofu-topped rice. For such a skinny kid, he sure could put it away. I didn't know whether to chalk it up to his youth or his poverty.

At exactly five past five, the first customer of the night walked in. He was a taciturn old man who presumably lived in the neighborhood and showed up at the same time almost every night. He seemed to stop by on the way back from the public bath, as he was always carrying a plastic washbasin with a towel and his wallet in it. He never ordered beer, even in summer, preferring instead to get two orders of heated sake accompanied by snacks; he'd spend two hours quietly imbibing and then leave. An ideal customer, as far as I was concerned.

"Welcome! Cold out, isn't it?"

"Yep. Supposed to snow tonight."

The old man took his seat at the counter opposite from where Takurō still sat silently shoveling rice into his mouth, and after this remark, he stopped talking completely. As more familiar faces started filtering in, Takurō finished up, went into the storage area in the back to stow his guitar case, came back out, washed his rice bowl, and pulled his happi coat on. The first wave consisted mostly of retirees or the owners of businesses in the neighborhood, as the after-work salaryman crowd didn't start showing up until after seven.

The door opened again, the sound of it accompanied by a woman's voice.

"It's *free-eezing!*"

Another voice, a regular's, answered.

"Oh-ho! Sumi-chan!"

I kept my head down, concentrating on chopping shallots. It would be strange to say nothing at all, though, so I raised my voice in the standard greeting while studiously avoiding meeting her gaze. "Welcome!"

"Brrrr—there's a few flakes coming down already. Majima-san! Hot shōchū, please!"

"I told you not to call me by name!" I clucked my tongue inwardly. Of course, it would put my teeth on edge to hear her call me Master, but something like Chief or Mister would be fine, or even Old Man (okay, maybe not that). I wordlessly cut the shōchū with boiling water and placed it in front of her.

"Aren't you cold in that flimsy thing, Sumi-chan?"

The man who owned a nearby produce market was on her like white on rice.

"It's all right. I'm still young!"

"Would you like Daddy to buy you a nice new sweater?"

"Are you being serious? The department store in front of the station is open till ten these days, you know. Maybe we could go together later!"

Sumie looked up at me, her expression wordlessly communicating triumph: *Yes!* I returned her gaze with a reproachful one of my own, but she didn't seem to notice as she used her chopsticks to poke at the pickled plum she'd put in her shōchū to flavor it.

She was a customer who wasn't really a customer. The reason being that we were currently living together. The other customers might've had their suspicions about us, but I didn't think any of them realized where she slept at night. Takurō and I knew how to keep our mouths shut, but I was less sure of Sumie. The fact that the regulars weren't saying anything about it, though, told me she must not have said anything either. I couldn't help but think that this was due less to her discretion than to the fact that it would be harder to charm things out of them if they were wise to the situation.

It was now the time when customers besides the regular crew started coming in. Right as the rush started to hit, a couple of young women wandered in, seemingly lost. They looked timidly around the place, clearly coming in for something besides a drink. I made a point of ignoring them, but they timorously approached Takurō as he flipped skewers on the grill, mustering up the courage to ask, "Excuse me, but we heard we could get our fortunes told here . . ."

Takurō answered wordlessly, thrusting out his jaw to indicate the far end of the U-shaped counter. Sumie was sitting there, chatting up the produce shop owner. Against my own instincts, I murmured, "You have a customer," to her in a low voice. She looked up and saw the two girls, who looked like typical office ladies, standing near the entrance and waved. "Over here, over here!" she said as if greeting a couple of old friends, and then she picked up her drink and moved all the way to the back to sit at the only table in the place. Piled high with condiment caddies and chopsticks and a bunch of other stuff, it wasn't somewhere I usually had customers sit.

Sumie and the two girls squeezed into the space, facing one another across the corner of the table that seemed least cluttered; Sumie passed along their drink orders to me, and then one of the girls, clearly nervous, extended her hands hesitantly toward her, palms up. She didn't remove her coat or take a sip from the beer Takurō brought her—she just stared raptly as Sumie, taking her palms in her hands, began to talk to her in a low voice. The other girl, who seemed to be simply along for the ride, occupied herself by looking uncomfortably around the place as she took tiny sips from her beer.

"What's going on over there, Master?"

The question came from a salaryman who'd started coming in recently.

"Palm reading. Get a fortune and a snack."

"Really? Did you hire her?"

"No, she just started doing it all on her own."

"But you get your cut, right?"

"Not at all. She doesn't do it for money, that one."

I was used to it by now, but it must have been a strange sight for the less regular customers.

"Fortune-telling, huh? Like astrology? 'You put up a strong front, but inside, you're a sensitive soul'—stuff like that?"

Distaste was written all over the salaryman's face.

"You could say that. In the old days, vagrants would go from bar to bar playing their guitars for money. This is no different. It's just entertainment."

Whenever the subject of palm reading or fortune-telling came up, people had one of two responses: piqued interest or outright disgust. I'd always been more on the "disgust" side myself, and when she first started doing it, I'd said, "Don't do that shit in my bar." Little by little, though, she'd worn me down, and now it was part of the routine.

Thirty minutes later, the girl having her palm read began to sob. This, too, happened all the time; one more thing that probably discomfited customers who weren't used to it yet. It wasn't that Sumie said anything purposely cruel to the people who came to her. It was more that the kind of woman who would come to a place like this for a palm reading usually had something fairly serious on her mind, and as she unburdened herself of her troubles, even if it was to a sketchy palm reader in a tiny izakaya, it would be like a great weight being lifted from her shoulders. On top of that, Sumie was unusually good at pinpointing her clients' problems and reputedly gave eerily accurate advice. An elementary school teacher who came in regularly once told me, "That woman has a real knack for listening." Though I had my doubts. She always struck me as someone unusually immune to listening to others—or maybe just to me.

The two office ladies paid the bill for their drinks, including Sumie's, and left. That was what she charged in lieu of a fee: a drink. She brought the bowl of snacks the girls had left untouched back with her to the counter and started munching on them like nothing had happened.

"What was worrying tonight's client?"

The produce man, red-faced with drink, sidled up to Sumie.

"Girls like that are all worried about the same thing—love. More importantly, though, that store's about to close, Mister! We should get going."

"Heyyy—I thought you'd forgotten!"

Sumie quickly ate the rest of what there was to eat and drank the rest of what there was to drink, and then cheerfully left with the produce man. "Master—you're so accommodating!" said one of the regulars, mocking me. I smiled in response, but it didn't reach my eyes, which fixed him with a deathly stare; he looked away quickly, striking up a conversation with the man beside him about something else entirely.

It was eleven o'clock. Closing time. Takurō waltzed out the door, leaving all the cleanup to me. I only paid him to be here from five to eleven, so I could hardly blame him, but I admit it still sometimes irked me when he left like that. I was washing dishes alone when I heard Sumie's drunken voice sing out, "I'm ba-ack!" She took off the baseball jacket she was wearing to reveal an ugly, cheap-looking pink sweater.

"He really got it for me!"

"Along with a bunch of drinks, it seems."

"I'm a big girl, I can handle it."

"Nothing costs more than something free, you know."

"What the heck does that mean? Ja-pan-ese is so ha-a-ard!"

Smiling at her own joke, Sumie removed her new pink sweater. Dressed in just a T-shirt, she walked behind the counter, took the sponge from my hand, and began washing dishes. I never told her to do it, but sometimes she took it upon herself to help out like this. She'd done prep work in the past, and when Takurō and I found ourselves overwhelmed with a rush, she'd been known to bring out orders and clear away dishes for us. But it was entirely a matter of when the mood struck her—there were plenty of times when things got busy or when Takurō had the night off and she would flit off with a customer to another bar without a second thought; she wasn't someone to rely on.

I lit a cigarette and sat down in a nearby seat. I watched as she washed dishes, humming a drunken little song to herself. Sure she was inside, but it was still February—how could she be comfortable in just a T-shirt? Takurō was a skinny guy, but Sumie was as spindly as a preteen. She was flat as a board in both front and back, and her arms and legs were as thin and pale as a doll's. Her hair, clearly growing out from being dyed, was lusterless and covered in split ends. Even so, though, her roughness wasn't entirely unpleasant. *Her life might have turned out differently if she were a real beauty*—I'd had the thought before, but of course I'd never say such a thing aloud. And it wasn't as if she wasn't cute: Her pale face bloomed with freckles, her eyes were narrow and widely spaced, and her mouth, which could seem either innocent or vulgar, was in any case quite large. It was the kind of face men loved. Real beauty was impenetrable; Sumie's was filled with gaps and cracks. She was cheerful by nature, and good at handling drunks—if she ever got it together to open up a place of her own, she'd make a great hostess bar mama.

"Are you hungry? We have leftovers."

"Nah—Mr. Produce fed me some yakiniku."

"Oh he did, did he? Not to be a broken record, but—"

"Nothing costs more than something free? I know. But Mr. Produce is hardly the sort to rape or traffic me, don't worry."

That's not what I meant, I almost said, but I swallowed the words before they came out. I had my doubts about her womanly virtue, but I was hardly in a position to criticize her for it.

Keeping my opinions to myself, I cleaned the floors and the restroom, and by the time I was done, Sumie had finished cleaning everything behind the counter, so we closed up and walked out together. A thin layer of snow covered the asphalt, but what was falling from the sky was no longer snow but cold rain mixed with sleet. "Brrr!" I said, opening my umbrella, and Sumie huddled beneath it, wrapping both her arms around mine. However tightly we kept our mouths shut, sooner or later the regulars were going to catch on that we lived together. Maybe it shouldn't matter, but at the same time, it made things awkward to have your girlfriend among your customers. If she'd agree to become a proper employee, that would be one thing, but she'd flatly refused when I'd brought it up. *Work for you? No thank you! And if you try to make me, I'll be gone.* Her voice had been gentle, even filled with a certain sympathy, as she threatened me.

We reached my apartment in about ten minutes, and once inside, she switched on the kerosene heater, put the kettle on the stove and lit the burner, and then went into the bathroom to turn on the gas to heat the water for a bath. Every heat source in the place was now on, but the place hardly had a chance to warm up before she stripped off both her jacket and the sweater Mr. Produce had bought her, just as she had back at the bar, followed by her socks and her jeans. *Does this woman ever get cold?*

Dressed in only her T-shirt, she walked over to the stove to make tea; I reflexively reached for her as she passed. Pulling her to me, I smelled the dry scent of her body. She laughed, turning within my arms to face me, and our lips touched. I felt my lower half respond immediately. I should have been completely fed up with women by now—what was I doing? I slipped my hands beneath her T-shirt through the sleeves and unhooked her bra, which I'd bought for her. My hands cupped her breasts, covering them entirely, and she sighed, smiling. Who was this woman? What was I doing with her? I pulled her to me, my pleasure accompanied once more by the taste of bitter caramel.

Sumie had appeared in my bar about half a year ago. I was coming up on two years of running the place at that point; when I'd first begun, things were so tight I'd worry about being able to afford Takurō's meager part-timer's pay, but now the place was on the road to stability, taking in a little over ¥2 million a month, and I could finally breathe a bit easier.

She arrived on the arm of a man. They both had reddish dyed hair and were dressed in tank tops, shorts, and beach sandals, flirting and making out without a care for what anyone else might think. In short, your run-of-the-mill couple of punks. They came in a few times for a drink, and then, just when I thought I'd seen the last of them, Sumie showed up one night alone. The left side of her face was swollen, and while it had already started to heal, she clearly had a black eye. One of the regulars asked about it, to which she replied in a cheerful tone, "He said he was moving out of town, and when I refused to follow him, he socked me!"

Truth was, my first thought at that point was *Oh man, what a pain*. I already found it hard to deal with female customers who came in alone; a customer like her, with trouble following her around, wasn't the kind I wanted. Contrary to my expectations, though, the regulars went over the top in their sympathy for her, and from that point on someone always made sure to pick up the bill whenever she came around. It was as a form of thanks that she first started reading palms. It wasn't clear if she'd ever been properly taught how, but she managed to impress the men with her accuracy anyway, making them cry out in disbelief as she correctly divined the age they got married or how many kids they had or at what age they'd put their relationship in jeopardy by having an affair. *Your love line is so pronounced, I don't think you'll be able to stop cheating. But look at your marriage line—it's strong too. So I don't think you're going to get divorced either. Remember to treat your wife right, though. Doing bad things adds up, and eventually it can even change your fate.*

So Sumie became beloved by the other customers. I could hardly tell her to stop coming around, as everything she ate and drank ended up paid for. She started coming every night, reading the palm of a customer who ended up paying her bill and then, more often than not, going off somewhere with him afterward. The impression of her I'd had back then was of a strange, rather easy woman. She was far from being my type, so I kept my distance while also keeping an eye out for the first sign of trouble, at which point I planned to tell her to leave and not come back.

This all changed one day in late August when Takurō came in

and said, "I think that woman's been sleeping outside in the park." Takurō, who was gay (I once asked, "What, you're a homo?" only to be promptly corrected: "I'm *gay*.") and had no real interest in women, nonetheless felt for her on a human level; he looked upset as he said, "Staying out there all night like that will only lead to trouble." The truth was, Takurō always seemed a bit out of sorts, but it was rare for his worries to be about a customer.

The natural thing to do would've been to send Takurō off after closing to go check on her, but he had band practice after work and disappeared before I could ask him to. *It doesn't have anything to do with me,* I reminded myself. She was a customer, so if she went off with a fellow customer to have a drink somewhere else, it shouldn't matter to me if she ended up sleeping at his place or in a park or anywhere else. But Takurō's words got to me anyway, and after cleaning up, I decided to stop by where he said he'd seen her. It was a sizable green space between a library and a children's center, featuring a thick stand of trees, and as I approached, I saw it was pretty lively even this late at night. The benches were covered with sleeping drunks and homeless people, and from the shadows beneath the trees came the occasional moans of unseen couples.

Aren't there any policemen? Or at least a security guard? I began my search, muttering to myself. I looked everywhere, mosquitoes biting me all the while, and then finally stumbled upon her. She was near the playground sandbox, sleeping soundly inside a slide shaped like an elephant. I couldn't believe it—I never dreamed she'd be in such an exposed, easy-to-find place. The elephant's trunk formed the slide, while its hollow body was a tunnel for children to climb through; this was where Sumie was curled up, using the small bag she always carried with her as a pillow. I tried to wake her by shouting *Oi!*, but to no avail, so, left with no other option,

I reached out and gave her shoulder a shake. She jerked awake, her eyes flying open. Seeing that the man shaking her was just the proprietor of her regular drinking spot, she relaxed and smiled. "What's going on?"

"If you have nowhere else to go, come sleep at my place." I hadn't actually planned to invite her over, but seeing the fear that had flashed in her eyes when I shook her awake made me unable to leave her there. Sure, it might not have anything to do with me, but I still didn't want to wake up to the news that one of my regulars had been raped during the night.

She didn't reply to my invitation with "Are you sure?" or "If it's not too much trouble," but with "Ooh! My lucky day!" Her blithe good cheer was at odds with her earlier fear, but by then it was too late to regret being a damn fool.

We reached my apartment, and when she saw the nameplate with my name carelessly brushed onto it by my landlord, she burst out laughing.

"Makoto Majima! Really?"

"What's so funny?"

"A serious name for a serious man! Can I call you Majio?"

"Oh, be quiet!" I grumbled, but she merrily ignored me, walking into my rundown apartment—no more than a kitchen and a single six-mat room—and saying, incongruously, "It's so big!"

Looking at her more closely, I saw that her hair was pretty unkempt and her feet were grimy. *This is how someone wakes up one day a street person*, I thought, heating up the water for the bath and telling her to have a soak. She happily took her time, and then emerged dressed in one of my T-shirts and smelling of my special tonic shampoo. I'd been bursting with questions—What was her full name? Where was she from? How did she end up unable to find anywhere but a city park to sleep in?—but she immediately walked up and threw her arms around me. "Thank you for being so nice to me."

"Stop it!" I said, pushing her off me. She persisted, coming close to press her lips to mine. I put up more of a fight, but mostly for show; within ten minutes, she was on top of me. *I'm going to get a disease from this,* I thought, as well as, *Who's being raped in the night now?* But once the flame was lit, there was no going back, not for her and not for me either. It had been so long since I'd been with a woman who wasn't a professional. With her face cleansed of makeup, she looked unaffected as a child as her slender body moved in sync with mine. Seeing her brows knit as she moaned sweetly beneath me, I got more and more excited. I didn't even have time to put a condom on before I came.

This didn't put the horse back in the barn, however, and I mounted her again and again until there was no strength left in my body. Satisfied at last around dawn, I looked over at her as she slept beside me, seemingly without a care in the world, and thought, *I bet this is how she's gotten what she needs for a while now.*

But maybe that was exactly why she was the right woman for me. For the first time in a long time, a feeling of real peace washed over me as I drifted off to sleep.

Was it Valentine's Day? I couldn't remember. In any case, the clock read ten minutes after five, but the old man who always came by after his bath still hadn't shown up. Well, there was the occasional evening he didn't show, I reminded myself, but I was still worried. What if he'd caught a cold or something? As I worried, I realized I didn't know where the man lived or even what his name was.

I had quite a few regulars at my place, but I wasn't the type to take it upon myself to start up conversations with them or inquire too deeply into their lives. I hated those places where the regulars acted like "family." I wanted to run a place where a customer coming in all alone would feel welcome, so I made sure to treat both regulars and first-timers the same way. I made my menu as unpretentious as possible, offering the same things off the grill every day along with whatever sashimi I had on hand; I refrained from stocking the fancy sakes that were so trendy these days, offering instead a single house brand each of sake, shōchū, and beer. A place like mine, in all its humbleness, felt necessary. Or at least necessary to me. People on their way home from work on a cold night would look up and see the vermilion light of the lantern out front floating in the dark and feel a warmth inside that they'd never get from the neon sign of a convenience store. My place was somewhere you could go to be among people you had no connections or obligations to, where you could have a nice conversation or keep to yourself, a place to have a drink and disappear for a while. My ideal watering hole.

Tonight, though, it was already six o'clock and my ideal watering hole had yet to attract even one customer. Sumie, who'd made the rare decision to come in to help out with prep, was in the corner with Takurō, absorbed in conversation across the counter. I wasn't trying to, but it was impossible not to overhear them; they were talking about some British band that had been all the rage back in their school days. It seemed that both of them had coincidentally attended the same concert when the band had come to

Japan, and they were excitedly sharing their experiences. I'd never had the slightest interest in music myself, and I felt a bit left out as I occupied myself dusting sake bottles. I didn't know how old Sumie was, but from the way they were talking, it seemed she must be around the same age as Takurō.

Indeed, Sumie and Takurō got along surprisingly well. When Sumie first started to stay at my place and help out at the bar, I sensed a bit of resentment from Takurō. He must have cottoned on that she was living with me, but he kept whatever he might have thought about it to himself. We never, as a rule, stuck our noses in each other's business outside work, but Takurō was well within his rights to speak up about anything affecting the bar. He ignored Sumie for a while (though in truth, outside of taking orders and calculating bills, he tended to ignore everyone), but she would attempt to strike up conversations with him from time to time just as she did with everyone else. After a while, he began to make perfunctory signs that he was listening, and then, after another while, they began making small talk during downtimes. They were amusing to watch, two alley cats working out how to share the same territory.

Yet, even though I knew he had no sexual interest in her, it still wasn't my favorite thing to watch them converse so happily with each other. After all, at least from the outside, Sumie looked much more suited to be with Takurō than with me.

I first met Takurō well before I opened my own place, when I was working at a yakitori franchise to support myself and earn a cook's license. Takurō was working part-time at the same place, and despite his close-cropped blond hair and the piercings in his ear, eyebrow, and lip, he was a serious worker, applying himself to the job without a lot of needless conversation. I'd always thought

I'd try to hire him myself one day, but I didn't want to arouse suspicion before I was ready to do it, so I refrained from getting too friendly with him on the job. Still, when it did come time for me to strike out on my own, he didn't seem all that surprised when I asked him to join me. He'd likely seen through me all along, sensing the real reason why I was using this franchise job to acquire as much know-how as I could about the business; I might have been careful not to talk about it, but it had surely been obvious anyway.

Takurō explained, in his affectless way, that he couldn't come on full-time, as he needed to devote as much time as possible to his real career: his band. He was willing to work in the evenings from opening to closing, but no more. And he had one more condition—he needed the night off whenever he had a show. I'd wanted to take him on full-time, but I also knew he'd do the job well without me having to train him, and besides, it would be easier to balance the budget if he were a part-timer. As I was presenting the contract to him, I joked, "With a handsome guy like you around, all our customers are gonna be girls!" To which he replied, smiling, "Don't worry, I'm gay." And that was when I said, unthinkingly, "What, you're a homo?" and was corrected: "I'm *gay*." *What's the difference?* I thought, and then Takurō added, as if reading my mind, "You like women, right Majima-san? But that doesn't mean you'll go out with any woman you meet. The same way, I like men, but not every man who crosses my path."

Something made Sumie and Takurō both burst out laughing, and at that moment, the door opened. An older gentleman poked his head in and looked around, then broke into a smile when he caught sight of me. "Oh-ho!"

"Yodobashi-san! It's been a while."

I jumped to my feet behind the counter.

"Sure has. How've y'all been doing?"

"How have *you* been? When did you get out of the hospital?"

"Last week. They told me no alcohol, but come on. One warm sake—but not too warm, y'hear?"

I wondered for a moment if I should really serve a customer whose doctor had told him to stop drinking. But wasn't it really his problem, not mine, if he'd rather shorten his life and be happy than live a longer one bereft of pleasure?

Sumie was still technically a customer, so she had a big stein of beer and some snacks in front of her. Yodobashi sat down beside her, leaving a seat between them.

"Hey there, beautiful! Are you Takurō's special lady?"

He raised a pinkie to underline his question.

"Oh, no. He's gay, don't you know?"

"Oh yeah? Well, are you Majima's, then?"

"Why do you want to know who I'm doing what with so bad, kind sir?"

"Because you're a beaut! Ever considered becoming a second wife?"

"Your first wife passed away?"

"Three years ago now. Time for another lady in the house, don't you think? She'd understand."

"Do I look like her?"

"I wouldn't say so. She was the kinda woman who looked more animal than human, like a cow or a hippo."

And with that, they were off, the two of them trading zingers as they got more and more chummy. It was exactly the kind of trick I was used to seeing Sumie pull off by now, but this time it was with Yodobashi. I couldn't help but feel nervous.

Yodobashi used to own the place, and he had a habit of showing up like this every once in a while as if suddenly remembering our existence. He'd first appeared as my savior three years ago, when I'd been having trouble finding a location for my bar. Everyone who wants to open a drinking establishment wants the same things: a cheap rent and a prime location. I was looking for somewhere fifty square meters or less in an area that was neither overcrowded nor deserted, located near a station linked to the downtown core, facing the street, and costing less than ¥250,000 a month—conditions that, as my search dragged on, seemed increasingly impossible to meet. I was just at the point of deciding which to compromise on first, the location or the price, when my real estate agent called me up all excited, saying that the perfect place had just come on the market. The owner of a well-established izakaya located about an hour's trip from downtown had lost his wife and was interested in selling.

The location was in your average residential area, but the new department store in front of the train station had made the surrounding businesses prosperous as well. It faced an alley one street back from the main row, making it a bit hard to find, but it was an area undergoing aggressive redevelopment, and the new office buildings and condos going up meant that chances were good it would attract new customers before long. Yodobashi, as owner, had lost the will to run the place after the sudden death of his wife, but he was still involved in the sale. While he had no official say about what the eventual buyer would do with the place, he nonetheless made it very clear that he wanted the spirit of the place he'd created to live on after him.

Seeing it in person, I realized it was my ideal location—I couldn't think of anything more I'd want. The narrow entrance, the timeworn lantern out front. The indelible traces on the counter left by decades of customers. Anyone can construct a clean, brand-new place if they have sufficient funds, but the feeling conferred by years of loving patronage is something money can't buy. I decided to buy it on the spot, and besides modernizing the food-prep area, I kept everything exactly as it was, down to the name. Yodobashi had tearfully shaken my hand when the deal was done, saying, "I'm glad I could hand the place over to such a good guy."

I thought Yodobashi was a good guy too, then, but that was the last time. The day the contract was signed, we went out for a customary drink together. The first stop was a cozy, unpretentious sushi place in Shitamachi, but things spun out of control after that. It was partly my own fault for the idealized image I'd had in my head of him as a salt-of-the-earth, hard-headed barman, but when we went on to a second place, it turned out to be a rundown little hostess bar in a deserted part of town where he was apparently a regular. The drinks poured like rain, and then, getting in trouble for being overly handsy, he took me to a third place, a cabaret bar where touching was allowed. "I think it's about time for me to go home," I said, to which he whacked me on the head and insisted we go on to a fourth place: a Filipina hostess bar where, it seemed, he had an "official" girlfriend. Once there, he forced me to buy bottle after bottle, and then skipped out somewhere in a car with his girl. From the initial sushi place on, all the bills had come to me. I'd have felt taken for a ride even if the places he'd taken me had been the "nice places" he'd promised to show me. *What a dirty old man,* I thought, planning how to get my payback, but his years of carousing must have caught up to him, as last year he'd ended up in the hospital with liver problems.

I heard the door open and looked up to see a pair of young women peeking through the noren. *Why do girls always come in pairs?* I thought, irritated despite the fact that I didn't particularly like female customers who came in solo either. The short-haired, cheerful-looking one spoke up first, looking me in the eye and asking, "We heard there's a palm reader?" Sumie called out, "Over here!" and then, since the place was basically empty, guided the two women to the back part of the counter. The other woman, who had long hair in a permanent wave, hesitantly extended her hands toward Sumie. There had been so many customers like this coming in that I'd put a new item on the menu: The Palm Reading Special—a draft beer and some snacks that automatically came out when Sumie got to work.

I thought Yodobashi would have something to say about this, but he seemed completely unbothered as he took in the scene, and then he turned back to me and struck up a conversation about a series of completely unrelated subjects—how his Filipina girlfriend had dumped him, how he'd been too handsy at the hospital and the head nurse had yelled at him, and so on.

After a while, the long-haired woman burst into tears, collapsing onto the counter. That in itself wasn't so unusual, but then she suddenly leaped to her feet and, screaming, "Who do you think you are, saying that to me!" threw her still-full beer right in Sumie's face. Before I could even yell *Stop!* she'd fled the place, still in tears. It all happened in a matter of seconds, and the whole place fell silent in the aftermath. Every eye in the place was fixed on the short-haired woman still sitting at the counter.

"Don't worry, it happens all the time," said Sumie with forced casualness, and then Takurō silently handed her a towel and his sweatshirt.

As soon as she disappeared into the restroom to change, Short-hair looked at me and apologized. "Sorry about that."

"I'm not . . ." I started to say, and as I trailed off, Takurō finished the thought without turning to face the woman, his voice cold.

"He's not the one you need to apologize to."

A bit flummoxed, Shorthair nodded and asked for the bill. I charged her for two Palm Reading Specials and Sumie's beer.

"I'm so sorry, but could I get a receipt?"

Despite her words, her tone wasn't apologetic in the least, and then she dropped the name of a publisher so big that even I'd heard of it. Seemingly unaware that the atmosphere in the place had become even tenser than when her friend had thrown the beer, Shorthair took the receipt I handed her and left, her sunny smile never leaving her face. Despite what Takurō had said to her, she never apologized to Sumie.

"What a shit customer," murmured Takurō, flipping skewers on the grill after Shorthair was gone.

"Majima, you need to be careful of her."

Yodobashi had remained silent throughout the whole incident, but now he spoke up, nodding toward the restroom where Sumie was still changing. He wasn't wrong. I couldn't allow this kind of thing to happen in my establishment.

"That's the kinda woman who'll pick a man like you clean."

I'd assumed he was referring to Sumie's amateur palm reading, but now it seemed he was talking about something else. Yodobashi took a plate of freshly grilled wings from Takurō and peered at me, his eyes twinkling with amusement.

"She's too much for you. You want me to take her off your hands?"

"Take her or don't, she's not mine to give."

"You got that right."

Yodobashi laughed, his gap-riddled teeth tearing into the greasy meat he'd ordered. Sumie finally emerged from the restroom.

"Wow, what a mess! She really got me."

Her wet hair was smartly gathered into a ponytail, but her smile looked pained; the incident had clearly gotten to her.

"Hey gorgeous, how're you feeling?"

"It's fine, it's fine. I told you, this kind of thing happens all the time."

"Your reading was spot-on and she didn't like it, I bet. Don't worry your pretty head about it."

"Thanks. Yeah. All I told her was that if she doesn't break it off with the married guy she's seeing, she'll never find the right man."

"Oh-ho! Well of course she didn't like it! That's why she came to see you, 'cause she can't bring herself to do it. Anyway, whattaya say, you wanna take a look at an old man's palm?"

Yodobashi extended his hands toward her; they were surprisingly fleshy for a man of his age.

"Wow, what an unusual palm! It hasn't been easy for you, has it?"

"I've never been happier to be called *unusual!*"

The two of them put their heads together, peering at his palm and laughing together. Soon enough, Yodobashi's hands began wandering, touching Sumie's arms and then her back. After a bit, he said, "Your hair still smells like beer," and then he brought up a nearby "health spa" he knew. And then they left together.

Yodobashi's visits were always on the house. It wasn't any kind of official agreement, nor a sign of gratitude for selling me such a nice place. It was simply that the first time Yodobashi dropped by for a visit, he'd said, "Put it on my tab," and I felt I couldn't refuse. I didn't know the details, but apparently Yodobashi couldn't return home to his native Kansai, as there were some people he owed money there who were no joke; he'd used the money from selling his bar to pay them back but couldn't manage the whole amount. He was barely getting by on a meager fixed income, and when I went to visit him in the hospital, he'd been overjoyed, as it seemed I was his only visitor, and he had me buy all sorts of things for him in the concession stand—sweets and snacks, dirty magazines, even a new toothbrush. Looking at him still drinking like he did, the fact was, though it might seem heartless, I had a hard time seeing him surviving another ten years. So I couldn't bring myself to take money from the old man.

Watching now as the two of them walked out arm in arm, I cursed my own softheartedness. The place was empty again. Takurō opened his mouth wide in a yawn.

I was staring at the palms of my own hands. I'd woken up strangely early and was still lying in my perpetually rolled-out futon in a hungover daze, staring at my hands in the light that streamed in through the gaps in my dusty curtains.

Could you really see the future in the folds of a palm? It seemed to me that if that were true, I wouldn't be scrounging around in a place like this, and Sumie herself would be able to enjoy a more stable lifestyle than she seemed to. Or was this my inevitable destiny? To lie here at thirty-six years old on a rice-cracker-thin futon in a cheap apartment, irritably waiting for a woman who wasn't coming home?

But no—destiny isn't real! If the path of a life were really set from the start, what point would there be in human effort? If I'd never saved up what I could, would I be the manager of some franchise now instead of owning my own place? Would Takurō never do more than put out a CD or two on an indie label before giving up and selling his guitar? But Sumie always said that the fate spelled out on a palm could change over time. And in any case, I'd never had her read my palm in the first place.

I'd grown to dread the customers who came in to see her. It wasn't just young women anymore—these days, there were men, too, who were old enough to know better. Why in the world would these people want to go to the trouble of having a total stranger predict their future? Not just a stranger, but a sketchy palm reader in a bar? *What will happen in six months? In a year? In five years? Should I break up with my boyfriend? Should I change careers?* Decide for yourselves! People came in on their own but ended up getting intolerably smug looks on their faces when Sumie got something wrong; others, like the woman yesterday, heard something they didn't like and got hysterical. There was the palm reader but there was also the palm read, after all. Why couldn't people laugh it off like they would a magazine astrology column?

It wasn't like I didn't understand feeling uneasy about not knowing what might happen in the future and of wanting someone to tell you if you're making a big mistake. I'd had times in my own life when everything around me seemed shrouded in fog and I wanted someone, anyone, to tell me what I should do next. I knew well from my salaryman days that it's infinitely easier when someone tells you do this or do that than if they tell you to live freely and make your own decisions. Even my ideal watering hole, which should have been continuing to make money now, had seen its profits sag since the beginning of autumn.

"Work, work, work," I muttered, staring at my palms, until I felt foolish enough to finally get up. Last night I'd gone out with some regulars who showed up around closing time, something I never usually did. I may have worked as a barkeep, but my alcohol consumption was generally confined to the occasional beer a customer bought me, and it had been a while since I'd last drunk a real drink. I remember someone saying at some point during night, *Oh, Master, you're really tying one on!*

Pulling myself out of bed, I went to the bathroom to wash my face and brush my teeth, and then went to the stove to heat up some water in the kettle; right at that moment, I heard the key turn in the lock. The entrance to my apartment was right next to the kitchen, so my eyes met Sumie's at close range when she came in. The smell of alcohol came off her in waves.

"I'm home! Yodobashi got sick last night while we were out, I had to take him back to his house. Though maybe I should have taken him to the hospital instead . . ."

"I don't need your excuses, Sumie."

"My excuses? What do you mean?"

Sumie looked at me, surprised. Was she pretending not to know what I meant? Or did she really not get it?

"If you're making coffee, I could sure use some!"

"I'd like you to apologize first."

"Apologize? For what?"

Sumie took off what she'd been wearing and then pulled on a pair of my sweats, both a top and bottom, that had been hanging out to dry after being washed. It made me ill to make coffee for a woman who came back in the morning after staying out all night without a hint of regret, but I made it nonetheless, even making sure to put in the milk and sugar I knew she liked. "Thank you," she said cheerily as she took the mug from me. What I wanted to ask was if she'd had sex with Yodobashi or not, but my self-respect wouldn't allow me to actually say the words.

"So Yodobashi paid your way last night?"

"He sure did! I know, I know—*nothing costs more than something free!*"

"I've told you before, you need to get a real job."

"What? Don't be a drag."

"I want you to think about it."

"Man, I'm starving! Mind if I make something?"

Completely ignoring me, she went to the refrigerator and took out some vegetables and eggs. She was surprisingly skilled in the kitchen. I'd even caught her sharpening my knives at home, though she didn't do it at the bar. Did she have experience working in a kitchen?

"Why don't you take a few shifts at my place? I don't care how many. I can't pay you any more than I pay Takurō, but still."

She stood with her skinny back to me as I made my proposal, and all I got in return was a dismissive giggle.

"Well, if you don't want to work for *me*, why don't you set up shop somewhere as a proper palm reader? Everyone says your readings are accurate. Even department stores have fortune-telling corners these days. You should be earning your own drinking money, don't you think?"

"I already am, reading palms in your place, aren't I?"

Sumie glanced at me as she scooped leftover rice into the pan to fry it.

"That's not what I mean! Don't you think you should have some money of your own?"

She didn't answer, busying herself instead with using the cooking chopsticks to deftly mix the eggs into the vegetables and rice already in the pan. Sumie got people to buy her drinks and charmed my regulars into buying things for her, but she never seemed to have actual money. Yet she somehow managed to buy her own cosmetics and feminine hygiene products. Which may have meant she had some kind of savings, but not nearly enough to fund her forever. How did she think she was going to get by?

"I'm just saying, Japan has laws about this. You have to work. If you're able-bodied but don't, that's technically a crime."

Sumie put the egg-fried rice, now done, on the kotatsu, placing the hot pan on a folded towel along with two bowls. She scooped some of it into one of the bowls with a paddle and held it out to me.

". . . That looks really good."

"Doesn't it? Can't beat fried rice when you're hungover."

"Have you been listening to me at all?"

"I have. Tell me, if I'm just living my life, not working or earning money, do I still owe taxes?"

The unexpected response stopped my spoon halfway to my mouth.

"You pay for your National Pension and health insurance, don't you?"

"Hmmm."

"Don't you?"

"How would I?"

This rendered me momentarily speechless, and then I thought, *Well, I guess that does make sense.*

"You mean you don't have a National Insurance card?"

"No."

"What would you do if you got in an accident or got sick? Do you realize how much medical care costs without insurance?"

A small smile came to Sumie's lips, and she picked up the remote and turned on the TV. A morning news show was on, talking about yet another kid who'd up and killed someone. Saying nothing, I reached over and hit the switch on the TV itself. Sumie's smile disappeared, replaced by an annoyed glare in my direction.

"If I'm getting on your nerves, I can always leave."

"Fine. Do what you want."

We ate the rest of the fried rice in silence. Once we were done, Sumie took the pan and the bowls and put them in the sink. As I gazed at her cascade of split ends while she worked, a hard-to-describe mix of confusion and anxiety came over me. Was I scared of losing her? Did I need her? Or was it that I wanted her to need me?

"Hey. You wanna read my palm?"

Sumie turned and looked at me, surprised.

"What's going on? I thought you hated that stuff!"

She was right. One day when she first started coming around, there weren't any customers around to cajole, so she turned to me and asked if she could read my palm for a drink since she didn't have any money. "I don't want any part of that crap," I replied, my voice rising. "Go wash some dishes instead!"

"Things change. I want to give it a try."

"Really? Well, all right, but just promise you won't get mad."

"Get mad? Over something like that?"

We sat back down to face each other over the kotatsu, and then Sumie took both my hands in hers and began peering at them. My life had been a rather wild ride so far, all told. I admit I was a bit nervous what she might say to me.

"Kinda normal."

"Normal? You mean boring?"

"I told you—you're mad!"

That shut me up. I wasn't any different from the customers I despised, the ones who came in wanting a reading from her and then, when they got what they'd asked for, got angry. At the same time, though, I was beginning to understand how those customers might feel.

Sumie picked up a toothpick from the table and traced the shallow path of the most vertical of the three branches fanning out across my palm.

"This is your fate line. The rest of these branches are deep, which means you have a strong sense of identity, but your fate line is shallow and split-up, which means you've gotten to your thirties still wondering what to do with your life. Did you get married or live with someone when you were about twenty-four? And then break up four years later?"

She'd hit the mark so precisely I couldn't think of an answer. I didn't want to admit how right she was.

"How about business?"

I changed the subject with deliberate roughness.

"Right. Look here—this part of the fate line is nice and long, which makes me think your business will do just fine. Your palm is pretty positive overall."

"All right, that's enough."

There was actually a mountain of things I still wanted to ask her about, but it was precisely because I wanted to ask about them so much that I couldn't bring myself to. I lay down, my legs still beneath the kotatsu, and Sumie got up and began washing the dishes.

"We're closed tomorrow, remember."

I didn't want to bring it up, but I had to. So I did it with my back to her.

"I know it's short notice, but can I ask you to be out of the house tomorrow afternoon?"

I heard the faucet turn off. "What?" I heard her say, and then, "You have a woman coming over?"

I closed my eyes and replied in a small voice.

"Something like that."

I'd asked her to make sure to be out tomorrow afternoon, but as soon as she was done washing the pan she'd made the fried rice in, Sumie took a little nap, put on some makeup, and then disappeared—I saw neither hide nor hair of her in the bar that night, nor the next morning at home either. Yet her bag was still here, and her underwear still hung from the drying rack, so it didn't seem like she'd decided to leave for good. Or at least that was what I tried to tell myself, though I couldn't help but worry. Even though I knew worrying wouldn't accomplish anything. And besides, I didn't have time for all that, as today was the day when—for the first time in six months—my "woman" was coming over.

I spent the morning washing everything in the place, including my curtains, vacuuming the floors, and hiding all of Sumie's things—her face wash, her toothbrush, her bras, her panties. I cleared the nail clippers and ear picks off the kotatsu, shutting them in a drawer in the bathroom, and gathered up the various manga weeklies and sports magazines scattered around the place, tying them up with string and stacking them in the closet. I ran the bath and scrubbed myself from the top of my head to the tips of my toes, and then cleaned the bathroom as meticulously as I could. I changed into the relatively fashionable sweater and corduroy pants I'd bought on sale for the occasion, and even made sure to have on a fresh, clean pair of socks. Last, I swept the kitchen floor, laying out a plastic picnic blanket when I was done and placing a chair on

Yamamoto Fumio

it. Glancing at the clock on the wall, I decided to try and arrive at the station a little earlier than when we'd agreed. I took a peek at myself one more time in the bathroom mirror, checking for any stubble or stray nose hairs I'd missed, and then left the apartment.

It was sunny out, but the north wind was still bracing as it hit my face. Despite the cold, my hands in my jacket pockets were slick with sweat. Her visits were supposed to be every three months, but last time, something had come up on her end and the visit was canceled; now, another three months later, I found myself that much more nervous.

I arrived at the station ten minutes earlier than we'd agreed, but my daughter was already there, waving at me from where she stood in front of the turnstiles. She was smiling. She wore a charcoal-gray coat I didn't recognize, and held, as always, a box in one hand that I knew contained our customary dessert. I restrained myself from running to her and sweeping her up in my arms, and instead walked toward her as slowly as I could make myself.

"Aren't you early?"

"You're the one who's always early, Dad! So I decided not to make you wait."

She was only eleven, but she was already able to look me straight in the eye.

"You've grown."

"Yeah, it happened all of a sudden. I'm tallest girl in my class now."

She sounded a bit unhappy as she said this. Now that I thought about it, my ex-wife was pretty tall too. Maybe I was biased, but it seemed clear to me that within the next five years, my daughter was going to grow up to be as stunning as a model.

My daughter made inconsequential small talk during the

fifteen-minute walk to my place: about school, about cram school, about video games. Was this for the benefit of her inarticulate father? Since a young age, she'd always been the kind of child careful not to hurt the feelings of the adults around her. It wasn't that I wanted her to be a delinquent, but it might have made me feel better if she'd been willing to be a bit more selfish and moody with me. There was something sad about a girl so considerate while still in grade school.

"Excuse me, I'm coming in," she said, sounding uncannily adult, as she slipped her feet into the brand-new slippers I'd set out for her. She stepped up from the entryway and then sniffed the air. *Does it still smell of a woman?* I broke into a cold sweat. I handed my daughter a hanger to put her coat on, and then walked over to put the kettle on. She started laughing when she saw I'd put out the sheet and chair like usual.

"We can have tea later—why don't we do my hair first?"

She slipped out of her cardigan and then, just in her blouse, plunked herself down onto the chair. I wrapped a towel around her shoulders, then a smaller cloth around her neck to catch any stray hairs. Brandishing my scissors, I became a young barber again. I sprayed her hair down to get it wet, and then, watching as it fell between her shoulder blades, noticed there were layers cut into it. Had she gone to a hairdresser?

"I'm sorry, Dad, I ended up getting a haircut! But just once, I promise!"

"Why are you apologizing? It's your hair, honey. Do with it what you like."

My daughter nodded. I'd be lying if I said it didn't make me feel sad, but on the other hand, I'd always known this day would come.

My mother had been a small-town hairdresser, while my father had spent all his time playing pachinko, every inch the feckless stereotype of a hairdresser's husband. I'd helped my mother out growing up, trying my hand at braiding and even cutting my little sister's hair. After a while, I graduated to cutting my mother's hair as well, as she was often too busy to take care of it herself. I found hair fascinating, and I continued pursuing the craft, paying no mind however much my friends made fun of me. "You have talent," my mother told me, and I sincerely planned to open up a barbershop of my own when I grew up. This didn't end up being the course my life took, but I still knew how to do a basic haircut as an adult, so when I got married and had a child, cutting her hair became my special task. Or rather, since I was so busy with work that I hardly did anything at home, cutting her hair was literally the least I could do. And before our marriage fell apart, I remember that I would often wash and care for my wife's hair too, enjoying the feeling of braiding it or putting it up for her. In the end, though, she became unable to stand even having me touch her shoulder, much less her hair.

We separated when my daughter was four, and officially divorced when she was six. The immediate reason was my wife's affair (though she contended to the end that it was never an affair, but in fact true love), while the indirect reason was that I was always working and almost never home. I'd wanted more than anything to avoid being like my own father, so I'd gotten a job at a major company and worked as hard as I could to provide for my family, but that became its own kind of problem. One day, my wife simply went off with our daughter to stay with her parents. She left behind a note that was over twelve pages long, but the long and the short of it was that she'd met someone else and wanted to separate.

Even while we were separated, I made sure to visit my daughter every three months to cut her hair. I'd also thought I might repair things with my wife, but every time we met, she'd simply sit there, silent as a stone. Finally, my wife's father came to visit me, bowing his head tearfully as he apologized for his daughter's selfishness and even offered me a monetary settlement for my trouble. This, at long last, made me realize it was well and truly over.

If our child had been a boy, I might have gone to court to try to keep him, but as painful as it was to accept, I couldn't help but think a young girl needed to be with her mother. My wife came from a prosperous family, and both her mother and father were good people. Even if I managed to wrest my daughter from my wife's custody, I had comparatively little to offer her. So I let my wife take her.

Once the divorce was official, though, my six-year-old daughter had said, "I want Dad to keep cutting my hair!" My wife wasn't exactly pleased about it, but she couldn't bring herself to refuse her daughter's wishes.

When she was little, I would cut her hair at her mother's house. But starting last year, she began coming here for her haircuts. *It's a drag when Mom's around, and besides, I can ride the train all by myself these days,* she'd said, so that was what we did.

I looked now at my daughter's hair, the weight of its eleven-year growth lightened by carefully placed layers. There was no question it looked more sophisticated—more adult—this way. Thinking that an amateur like me no longer had the ability to make his daughter beautiful, I couldn't help but be sad.

It was so healthy, so lustrous and full from having never been dyed or permed. *Is this going to be last time I cut it?* The thought made her hair all the more dear to me, and all the more painful to contemplate. I remembered that when she was a baby, her hair had been as wispy and thin as a baby chick's; my wife and I had worried it would always be like that. How many months old had she been when I finally had the courage to use some thinning shears to trim her bangs? And now it wouldn't be long before her thick, perfectly straight hair would be cut into a trendy style and touched by the hands of some man she hasn't met yet. I combed her bangs to trim them, and my daughter closed her eyes. The afternoon sun made her cheeks glow like a pair of peaches. Her lips were shiny; she'd touched them up with lip gloss. These things, too, would one day be an unknown man's to have and to hold.

As a warm rush of feeling rose up in me, there came a sound at the door—someone was turning the key in the lock. Startled, I dropped the scissors onto the floor. I bent down to pick them up, and then, as I straightened back up and looked toward the entrance, there was Sumie. Of course. Her eyes met my daughter's, and then, surprised, they both looked at me.

"You're busy?" asked Sumie, inanely.

"Busy cutting hair, as you can see!"

My voice was irritable, even as I knew it was childish. But what was her plan if she really had interrupted me "busy" with another woman? Or had she meant to do that all along?

"Good afternoon. Thank you for taking good care of my father."

My daughter rose from her chair. Strands of cut hair fell all over the floor.

"You're his daughter?"

"Yes. He and Mom got divorced a long time ago, but I still come by every once in a while to get my hair cut."

An ironic smile came to Sumie's lips as she looked back at me.

"So you're a licensed cook *and* hairdresser? Impressive!"

"I don't have a license or anything like that. I just picked up some skills growing up because my mother was a hairdresser."

Perhaps sensing the tension in the air, my daughter glanced over at me, a concerned look on her face. I quickly tried to explain, making my voice as gentle as possible.

"She's my employee. She works at the bar as a palm reader."

"A palm reader?"

My daughter sounded suspicious. I was nervous what Sumie might say, but she put a mature look on her face and improvised an answer.

"Since you're his daughter, I can give you a reading for free! Come by anytime. So anyway, uh, *Master*, Takurō-san lost the key to the bar. Can we borrow yours?"

I played along, surprised at Sumie's quick thinking.

"I have a spare in the top drawer over there, give him that."

"All right!" she replied, our little cover story coming together nicely, and then she went over to the small dresser sitting in the middle of this apartment she knew so well, retrieved the key, and then went back to the entryway to slip her sneakers back on to leave.

"Master, now that I know about this skill of yours, maybe I'll ask you to cut my hair sometime. Okay, I'm off! Sorry to have bothered you."

And with that, Sumie was gone. My daughter sat back down in the chair. "So you *are* seeing someone," she muttered.

"No, she really is an employee!"

"I'm glad. I've been worried about you. Can I tell Mom about her?"

My daughter obviously didn't believe a word I said. But even an eleven-year-old could see that a woman who barged into my apartment using her own key wasn't just an employee. I decided to stop trying to convince her otherwise.

I finished cutting her hair, made us some tea, and then ate the sweet custard my daughter had brought with her. Perhaps due to my gruff exterior, people were surprised to learn I had a sweet tooth; my daughter knew, though, and always brought a custard with her when she visited. Today's was decorated with a spring-appropriate array of strawberries and whipped cream. I could always get sweets whenever I wanted from the convenience store, of course, but if I made myself hold off until my daughter visited, they tasted like heaven itself.

"Your mother's remarrying, I hear."

I decided to broach the subject myself, as I knew it might be hard for her to bring it up. My daughter was looking down as she brought her spoon to her mouth, and she nodded.

"How are you feeling about it? Do you get along with your new papa?"

"He seems like a nice person."

My ex-wife had called me last week and told me about her upcoming remarriage. It had been five years already since we divorced. The news seemed neither good nor bad. But what bothered me was that her new husband was a medical researcher of some sort, and he planned to move them to the US at some point next year and stay there for at least a few years.

"You're going to America?"

"Yeah. I'll start middle school there."

Don't go. Stay with me here in Japan. But thinking about her future, I realized she was going to be happier this way, just like when I decided not to fight her mother for custody during the divorce.

She'd grow up bilingual, for one thing, which would open so many doors. And a youth spent in an elite school in the US would surely be better for her than the dreary education she'd get in today's Japan. I didn't want her to end up like me. Or like Sumie.

After we finished our custard, we left the apartment together. We rode the train downtown. I'd asked her what she wanted for dinner and she'd responded with a typical child's choices: sushi or yakiniku. But was she just playing the baby again, for my benefit?

All during dinner, and then later as I delivered her to her mother's house, she chattered nonstop but never brought up my ex's remarriage or her impending move to America or even Sumie. "Till next time!" she said, waving at me in front of the fancy condo where her mother lived. "Till next time," I replied, laughing.

I rode the train back home, picking up some beer and snacks along the way, only to find the lights still off in the apartment when I arrived. Sumie's things were all gone as well. The key I'd given her to the apartment was sitting on the kotatsu, right next to the spare key to the bar I'd handed her earlier under false pretenses.

I didn't see Sumie again during the next three days, nor the next week either. Even Takurō ended up asking about her. *What happened to Sumi-chan?* When I responded with a dismissive *How should I know?* he just shrugged and didn't bring it up again. Several customers came in looking to get their palms read, and when they learned Sumie wasn't there, they turned right around and left. Some persisted before leaving, though, pressing me to give them her number.

I was working behind the counter, having just hung the noren up out front after finishing the prep work, when I heard the door open. Startled, I turned and saw it was the old man coming back from his bath; I hadn't seen him for quite a while.

"Welcome! It's been too long!"

I'd actually been afraid he'd dropped dead or something, and indeed, his face seemed a bit drawn.

"Yeah. Caught a bad cold. Finally feeling better now."

"I admit I was a little worried about you."

"Sorry 'bout that. The cough just wouldn't go away, so I stayed home and made do with my own tub for a while. Didn't want to go to the public bath and cough all over the place, you know?"

"You have your own tub?"

"Of course. I just like the public bath better."

Usually so taciturn, the old man was quite chatty today, even smiling a bit as he talked. It made me inordinately happy to see him. Right then, the bar's phone rang. Takurō walked over and answered it as curtly as usual, saying nothing but the name of the establishment. *Is it Sumie?* I thought, sneaking a sideways glance at him as I started heating the old man's sake. I watched his expression grow as dark as I'd ever seen it, and then he held the phone out to me.

"Who is it?"

"That bitch," he replied as if spitting the words out. *What if she heard you?* I thought as I took the receiver. The voice on the other end began speaking, dropping the name of a major publisher right away. I didn't write out a lot of receipts, so I recalled who it must be immediately. Shorthair.

"An interview?"

I repeated the last thing she said back to her.

"Yes. I visited your establishment once before, and now I'm doing a special issue on fortune-telling. I'm planning on making up a guide to unusual places around town where you can get your fortune told. I'd love to include your place as a 'psychic izakaya.' Is there a good time to come in this week to talk and take a few pictures?"

Shorthair's voice was cheerful, clearly never imagining I'd ever refuse. *Are you kidding?* I almost said, but then I remembered my sagging profits lately, and I was suddenly gripped by the impulse to do anything I could to get ahead no matter what for the first time since my salaryman days.

I'd worked for a construction company back then, and when my divorce was finally official, I quit without a second thought. Taking clients out until all hours as a form of bribery or corporate spying, all in the name of helping the company "thrive"—I could stand it when I was doing it to provide for my wife and child, but once they were gone, I couldn't see why I should continue sacrificing my sleep and nerves that way. That was when I'd first thought of opening an izakaya. I'd always found that my work-fried nerves were best soothed not by some sleek, elegant bar, but by taking my time drinking alone in a timeworn izakaya somewhere that looked like it had never been renovated, a place where no one seemed to ever think about making any more money than it took to simply keep the lights on.

I slammed my hand down on the counter as if to ward off the killer instinct rising in me.

"I don't want to do an interview or a photoshoot! We're not a 'psychic izakaya' or anything like that. The palm reader you saw was just a customer who does that on her own. Please don't call here again."

Shorthair seemed faintly appalled at the severity of my reaction.

"Well, in that case, could I interview just the palm reader?"

"She's a customer, I don't know anything about her."

"But she comes to your establishment every night, doesn't she? I'd like to talk to her about this myself."

"She hasn't been around in a while. I don't want to see you around here either."

I slammed the phone down. Surprised, the old man looked over at me.

"What's this about an interview?"

"Oh, it's for Sumie. But she's stopped coming for a while now, so . . ."

I shrugged, laughing ruefully, to which the old man replied, as if it were nothing, "I just saw her, though. She was handing out tissues in front of the train station."

I heard Takurō start to say something behind me, but I'd already run out into the street. *What are you doing, abandoning the bar like this?* I thought, but even as I did, I found I'd already reached the bus terminal in front of the station. The sun was starting to go down, and the area in front of the station was crowded. Among the mass of commuters were three or four women dressed in white windbreakers and matching white miniskirts that looked like tennis shorts. As I got closer, I saw that one of them was indeed Sumie.

"Oh, Majio-san! Here, take one."

I reflexively took the tissue packet she handed me, and then turned it over to see what it was advertising. A newly opened "sauna," apparently.

"You—you—"

"Do you need something? I need to hand all these out by six, I can talk to you after that."

"Why are you doing this? If you need a job, come work for me!"

My voice rose, surprising even me. Sumie ignored me, continuing to hand out tissues to passersby with a cheery smile. I grabbed her by both arms.

"Hey, that hurts! Let me go! What do you want?"

Even I didn't really know why I'd grabbed her like that, and I scrambled for an answer.

"Uh, well, the thing is, we just got a call from a big publisher, and they want to interview you for a magazine . . ."

"I don't wanna."

"Right, of course. I thought so too."

"Now let go."

Scared she was about to shake me off, I pressed my fingers harder into her arm.

"Marry me!"

Sumie's jaw dropped, her narrow eyes widening as much as they could.

"Majio! What are you saying?"

"I don't think I said that quite right. How about this: Sumie, will you marry me? Please."

"I never thought about it before, but I don't wanna sounds a lot like marijuana, doesn't it?" She burst out laughing at her own dad joke. My blood boiled, both from my dearest wish leaping unbidden from my mouth like that and from her apparently mocking me for it.

"You're my woman!"

"What?"

"We've had sex every night for six months! You're mine! And I'm yours!"

An older woman passing by turned her head to look at us, shocked. But I plunged on.

"Don't leave. Come home with me!"

Seeing I was serious, Sumie was no longer smiling.

"The fact is, I don't understand you at all. Which makes me even more unable to let you go."

"I'm the one who doesn't understand *you*, Majio-san. Though I'm seeing now that you're a pretty pushy guy."

I'd experienced plenty of jealousy and unhappiness since meeting Sumie, but this was the first time she'd said anything so cold. All the strength left me, and I let go of her arms.

"Are you with Yodobashi these days?"

The smile returned to Sumie's face, and she nodded.

"I see. Sorry to be so *pushy*. I'll go now."

Dispirited, I turned my back to her and began walking away, only to hear her call out "Majio-san!" I stopped and looked back at her.

"Hey, do you think you could cut my hair? I don't have the money to go to a salon."

Who does this woman think she is? I suppressed the urge to walk back and punch her in the face. It was getting to be the time of night when people started coming into the bar. I'd run out of the place in just my happi coat, and the frigid air was suddenly pressing in on me. *Isn't Sumie cold in that little skirt?* I wondered, but then I realized I no longer cared.

The next Sunday, I packed up my comb and scissors and left the house, cursing my sense of integrity and obligation all the while. I'd never gone to Yodobashi's place, but I wrote down the address from the contract in my desk drawer from when I'd bought the bar from him.

I got on the train heading away from downtown and got off ten minutes later; it seemed like there must be a bus that could take me the rest of the way, but since I'd never made the trip before, I took a taxi instead so I wouldn't get lost. I showed the address to the driver and he dropped me off before the meter had begun charging mileage, saying, "I think it's somewhere around here." I showed the address to a passing mother and child, who kindly told me that it was the same building they lived in. It was a big old Showa-era apartment building with laundry and futons hanging out to dry on every balcony. I plodded up the stairs to reach unit 203, and then let out a great sigh when I got there.

YODOBASHI HAS MOVED. PLEASE FIND HIM AT:

These words were scrawled on a piece of paper stuck to the door, followed by the new address. It was right near my own apartment. He was free to move wherever he wished, and it wasn't like I expected a change of address notice from him, but thinking of the transportation fees I'd just wasted, I couldn't help but feel a little angry. I forwent the taxi and walked back to the station, then rode the train back to my own neighborhood. Yodobashi's new place was just on the other side of the station from mine, and I figured I could find it simply by wandering around, but this part of the neighborhood hadn't modernized its numbering system, so I ended up completely lost in the tangle of streets and alleys, asking passersby where the address might be but getting no help. Tired and hungry, I was on the verge of going home when I looked up at a telephone pole and saw that the sign tacked to it showed the same set of numbers as the piece of paper in my hand. There was an old-fashioned one-story house standing there, but the nameplate read Kagawa. Still, the number matched. Wanting to get to the bottom of this once and for all, I let myself in through the wooden gate and walked up to the entrance only to be confronted with yet another notice stuck to the door. *To whom it may concern: We're in the back garden*. It was enough to make me think someone was screwing with me on purpose.

A stone walkway lined with potted plants led behind the house. Following them, I began to hear voices. It sounded like a group of people talking and laughing. Rounding the back corner of the house, I saw a narrow porch running along the backside of the house facing out onto a small garden.

"Excuse me," I said, peeking my head around the corner.

"Oh-ho! Majio!"

Yodobashi hailed me as soon as he caught sight of my face.

"Hey, there he is! Welcome, welcome!"

Sumie smiled at me, no trace of ill will in her demeanor.

"I thought you might be coming by, so I waited up. Are you going to cut our hair?"

The biggest surprise of the day was who said this—the old man who always came by the bar after his bath. All three were sitting on the porch with the door to the house wide open, huddled around a Japanese chessboard. A huge pile of chess pieces were piled on top of it, seemingly on verge of falling over.

"What's all this? What are the three of you doing here?"

"We're playing dominoes with chess pieces!"

Sumie's cheerful response left me deflated.

"Not that. I mean, why are you here, Yodobashi?"

"Well, Sumie and I can't really afford to get by on our own, so Kagawa here offered to put us up in a spare room at his place!"

The old man, whose name was apparently Kagawa, handed me some tea and sweet bean-filled cookies. I was so hungry I ate three immediately, one after the other.

"Kagawa's an old regular from back when I ran the place."

I washed the cookies down with the tea as I listened to Yodobashi's explanation. It made sense, now that I thought about it. But to offer his house not only to Yodobashi but to Sumie too? These two parasites, who seemed like the last people on earth who'd do anything for you in return?

"So are you gonna cut our hair or what, Majio?"

"Okay, first of all, don't call me Majio! And second of all, I don't cut men's hair."

"Why not? You only cut people's hair to seduce them?"

"No, it's just that men's haircuts are more difficult than women's."

Sumie and Kagawa had brought a chair out of the house and set it beneath the plum tree in the yard, happily readying a towel and some sort of cloth that looked like a scarf. I stood up, thinking, *Might as well get this over with and go home.*

"The plum blossoms smell so good. Did you know it's Keichitsu today—the day the insects awaken?"

It was a bit of a shock to hear a highfalutin word like Keichitsu come out of Sumie's mouth. I wrapped the towel around her neck as she sat obediently in the chair, then lay the big scarf over it like a cape. Looking at it closer, I saw it was Hermès.

"Hey, what's this?"

"It was Kagawa's wife's, before she passed away."

"It's much too nice to use, isn't it?"

"It's much too nice *not* to use."

Persuaded by this even if I didn't really understand the logic, I began combing out Sumie's hair. Unlike my daughter's, her hair was damaged and stiff, a mass of split ends. The truth was, I'd wanted to do her hair since the first night she stayed over. But I knew if I did, I'd become attached. My mother, my sister; my wife, my daughter.

My hands remembered the feel of their hair even now. My palms were stained with love as indelibly as with the fate foretold in their creases. So I'd always been scared to cut Sumie's hair.

"How short do you want it?"

"About shoulder-length. It's annoying if it's too short to tie up."

That would mean cutting about ten centimeters off. Enough to get rid of almost all the damaged bits. I sprayed her hair down and began cutting, then noticed that the two old men watching from the porch were whispering to each other about something. Were they talking about us?

"Ahh, it feels so good to have your hair cut by a man you love! I can understand why your daughter can't give it up."

My hands stopped.

"You . . . love me?"

"Of course I do! Why else would I have sex with you every night for six months?"

Look here, I started to say, but realized I didn't know how to end the sentence. So I changed the subject.

"You're so young, why are you here? Aren't you ashamed to live off a couple of old men like this?"

"You're always talking about how young I am! I'm thirty-six years old!"

"What? You mean we're the same age? Are you some kind of vampire?!"

My voice rose again, prompting the old men to call out, "Hey, no fighting!"

Sumie giggled.

"Look at you, Majio-san! Getting so *angry* every time things don't go exactly the way you expect!"

I had no response for that. I stood silently, staring at the nape of Sumie's neck.

"Can you do me a favor? I'd like you to stop treating me like someone who needs to be rescued. If you're gonna get angry if I don't get a job or get married, you might as well be my father." I looked up at the plum branches, thinking. And then the sheer blueness of the sky made me blink.

"Is that why you ran away from home?"

"That's part of it, but you know, I don't have the kind of tragic past you and some other people seem to think I have. More a brain problem, you know?"

"You think I have a brain problem?"

"No, no, I'm talking about myself! My brain's weird. All these people coming to me for palm readings, they're upset, they're lonely, they're desperate and needy. But the thing is, I don't really understand those feelings. I don't have them. I used to think there was something wrong with me, but these days, I feel like it's a good thing, something to be thankful for. Or at least, that's how I decided to look at it."

At a loss once more, I continued cutting away the damaged parts of Sumie's hair without saying anything further. Soon enough, the once-dyed portions were gone, and all that was left was a fall of thick black hair.

"I'm done."

I slid the scarf from around her, and Sumie jumped to her feet with a quick "Thank you!" Then she turned toward me and pressed her lips to my cheek.

"Is it okay if I come back to the bar?"

"It's a free country."

"Great! Now I just need to find a mirror . . ."

She ran up onto the porch, slipped off her sandals, and went inside. The old man and I watched her retreating back, and then looked at each other.

"If you're lonely, you're welcome to stay here too, Majima-san."

Kagawa smiled as he said this to me. I began to understand what Sumie had meant when she told me to stop treating her like someone who needed to be rescued.

Thirty minutes before opening the next day, my daughter showed up for a surprise visit. She peeped her head in the door, still dressed in her school uniform, and asked nervously, "Can I come in?" I dropped the chicken skin I'd been threading onto some skewers and ran over to her.

"What's going on? Are you okay?"

This was the first time she'd ever set foot in my bar. And now she was here without even a call to warn me, despite having always restricted her visits to once every three months—surely something had happened.

"Did you and your mother have a fight?"

"Not at all. I came for my palm reading."

"Your palm reading?"

"When does that lady usually get here?"

"Are you worried about something? You can tell me, I promise I won't get angry."

My daughter set her school-issued backpack on a counter seat and took off her navy peacoat.

"It's not like that. I just wanted to see you, and besides, I realized I'd never seen your place!"

Her expression was cheerful and open; at least from the outside, she didn't seem to be hiding a thing.

"To tell the truth, I don't know for sure if she's coming tonight."

"That's fine. As long as there's a chance, I'll just wait."

"No! You should go home. I have to work, I don't have time to take you back to your mother's place tonight."

"Is it okay if I stay over at your place, then? Or will that lady not like it?"

She's long gone, I almost said, but I couldn't bring myself to.

"Why wouldn't she like it? But more importantly, did you ask your mother? And don't you have school tomorrow?"

"I'll call in sick!"

My daughter said this with a mischievous glint in her eye. I felt tears coming to my own eyes, so I turned away with feigned gruffness, saying, "Do what you like, then!" as I went back behind the counter.

I set out some yakitori, rice balls, and miso soup for my daughter, and then, after going back and forth for a bit, I called up Takurō, telling him how to get to Kagawa's house and then asking him to stop by on the way to work to try to convince Sumie to come with him. I didn't love the thought of my daughter sitting at the counter all night surrounded by drunk old men, so I wanted Sumie to come read her palm sooner rather than later if at all possible.

Not even twenty minutes went by before Takurō and Sumie walked in. My daughter had only ever met Sumie once, but they waved at each other like old friends. Sumie guided her to the back of the counter right away, taking my daughter's tiny hand in hers.

"Wow, what a prosperous palm!"

"What are you saying to her? Remember, she's just a kid."

"Butt out, Papa!" retorted Sumie, merrily.

They huddled together then, their voices low so I wouldn't hear them. What did my daughter want to talk about so urgently? Had she met a boy? I couldn't help but worry.

Takurō ate his family meal, then washed his hands and threw on his happi coat. He stood in front of the grill and lit the charcoal.

"Your daughter looks like you."

He wasn't a man prone to pleasantries—was this something he really thought?

"Is that so?"

"She's going to be a real beauty when she grows up."

"Good thing you're gay, then."

A thoughtful look came over Takurō's face, and then he spoke again.

"I didn't say this at first because I thought it would just confuse you, but the truth is, I'm really bi. Though if I had to choose, I'd say I like men better."

Huh? I was about to ask what he meant by that, but Takurō had already stubbed his cigarette out in the ashtray and was walking over to where Sumie and my daughter were sitting. Smiling, he struck up a conversation with my daughter. I walked behind the counter in that direction as well, feigning casualness as I listened in with my back turned.

"You're in a band?"

My daughter pointed to the guitar case sitting on the seat next to where she'd put her backpack down.

"I am. You're into music?"

My daughter thought for a moment, then answered.

"Everyone says I'm weird, but lately I've been really into prog rock. It began when I was looking through my mom's CDs and found one by King Crimson."

"Wow—a kid who's into Crimson!" exclaimed Sumie.

"That is weird. Weird is good, you know. Why don't you come see me play one night?"

"Takurō! How dare you! You've never invited me to hear you even once!"

What was going on? My daughter seemed to get along well with this gang of misfits. As I was trying to come to grips with this, the door opened and Kagawa came in, stopping by as usual on his way back from his bath.

"Am I early? The noren's not up."

"Not at all, come on in!"

I hurried out to hang up the noren and light the lantern, and then came back to find that Kagawa had been added to the little group.

"So she's yours? How lucky, to have such a lovely girl as a daughter."

Takurō chimed in, saying, "This girl's destined to leave her mark on the world, I know it." My daughter blushed, looking bashfully up at Takurō as he talked.

I was lucky. Lucky to have a daughter so clever, so beautiful, so kind. Of course the world was hers. She was my pride and joy. I started to say this aloud, but no words came out. I was still facing away from the door, and behind my trembling back, I heard the sound of the door opening again. Two customers came in. My head still bowed, I finally managed to make myself say something. "Welcome!"

I realized Sumie had come over at some point to stand next to me. She reached over to rub the back of my head.

"There, there," she said. "It's gonna be okay."

A Note from the Translator

I was living in Yokohama when Fumio Yamamoto was awarded the 2001 Naoki Prize in literature for the book you are currently reading. She was a cowinner with Kiyoshi Shigematsu, the author of another collection of short works, *Vitamin F*; these two prize-winning collections, one by a woman writer and concerned with the lives and struggles of women, and the other by a male writer and concerned with the lives and struggles of men, were presented in the press as a kind of diptych portrait of gendered social anxiety in contemporary Japan. I bought both. Reading them together indeed offered a glimpse of the zeitgeist and of how the recession that had begun at the start of the 1990s continued to take its toll on the twinned spheres of family and work. However, it was Yamamoto's book that really grabbed my attention—and I was not alone.

The Dilemmas of Working Women—originally titled *Planarian*, after the novella that came first in the Japanese edition of the collection—was more than a book that won a big prize; it was a phenomenon, selling hundreds of thousands of copies and representing the culmination of Yamamoto's burgeoning career, one that began in the late 1980s when, by her own telling, she entered a contest to write formulaic romance novels for young women while working as an "office lady" in a small securities company. In later interviews, Yamamoto talks about how writing these books, with their rigidly set narrative structures and titles she had no power to choose, was like a crash course in fiction writing, an endeavor she initially saw as just another job and only later as a form of art. Eventually, she began to chafe against the rules of this genre and yearned, as she put it, not to have to write another happy ending.

So, she began to write for a general audience, still prolific but now finding her own voice, experimenting with genre and approach throughout the 1990s. Much of her work was still marketed as "romance," but her deep knowledge of the genre's conventions led her to play with and subvert them. She became known for her "difficult" heroines and her ambiguous endings, and her interest in the emotional contours of women's everyday lives. Eventually, in 1998, she put out *Loveaholic*, a novel about love, work, and obsession that turns readers' sympathies on their head with a series of revelations near the end about its heroine. It became a bestseller and won the 1999 Eiji Yoshikawa Prize for New Writers—her first major literary award. Around that time, she also began publishing the novellas that would become *Dilemmas*; these stories captured the millennial mood of work- and home-related anxiety gripping the nation at the time with a beguilingly light touch, their self-deprecating heroines (and hero) facing the same dilemmas faced by millions across Japan as the effects of a long-lasting recession set in for good.

But there is more to Yamamoto's writing than its timeliness. To be sure, the stories in *Dilemmas* are studded with contemporary references and allusions—the specter of corporate "restructuring," the English loanword becoming ubiquitous in the media as the lifetime employment system fell apart; the rise of winner/loser discourse expressed through canine metaphors, with the losers called make-inu, or "loser dogs"; the largely media-generated moral panic around out-of-control, violent young boys that became a staple of news coverage at the time; the much-publicized scandals about aging celebrities like Dewi Sukarno, a.k.a. "Madame Dewi," who was the ex-wife of the first president of Indonesia before becoming a Japanese television personality, and singer and actress Rumiko Koyanagi, whose divorce from her younger husband Kenya made headlines. These references add more than just familiar texture to the stories—they show how the characters' lives are mediated through the popular culture around them, providing ways for them to understand (and misunderstand) themselves as they navigate their individual struggles. They also create a sense of intimacy between character and reader, as the passive consumption of these ambient media narratives are revealed to be shared, crossing the boundary between the fictions of literature and the fictions of real life.

For example, in "Here, Which Is Nowhere," the protagonist recognizes that her mother is consuming the stories she tells her about her life the same way she follows celebrity scandals on television, and she bridles at the superficial impersonality of it, deciding not to ask for financial help to avoid having her life become another salacious scandal for her mother to consume. It's a paradigmatic Yamamoto moment, her heroine choosing to do something that initially seems self-destructive—refusing to seek financial help that she clearly needs—so as to preserve a sense of self and agency. The women in these stories frequently exasperate both themselves and the people around them with their obstinate refusal to go along with things; they describe their own personalities and decisions with words like "perverse," "twisted," and "warped." In "Dilemmas of Working Women," the narrator recognizes that she's in a type of Prisoner's Dilemma with her boyfriend, but in an inverted sense—they're both trying to give away the upper hand to the other, not gain it. The narrator of "Planarian" states outright that she's "unfit for society," while the protagonist of "Naked" is shocked by the extent of her own apathy in the face of an opportunity to resume her former career.

Yamamoto aims less to make a statement about the pressures on working women than to capture a particular feeling, one of disassociation and detachment that's also an attachment—a clinging to drifting away that seems preferable to the alternatives, at least for the moment. This clinging is a form of strength even as it leads to seeming ruin, a mode of lying to oneself that ultimately reveals a larger truth. It seems telling that the happiest, least conflicted woman in the collection—Sumie, in "A Tomorrow Full of Love"—is also the most precarious. It's also telling that she's not the narrator of the story she appears in—rather, the novella's trajectory shows the male narrator, Majima, learning how to come to terms with his altered station in life by letting go of his old-fashioned, masculine expectations of both her and himself and embrace the way his life is now, in all its makeshift loveliness. Sumie's seemingly self-destructive refusal to accept what he offers her—a job, a marriage—stems from what she calls her "brain problem": her incapacity to long for what she cannot have. But it's a "problem" that's a type of solution; Majima must accept the love, and life, he's been given, rather than reject them for not taking the form he expected. Like the Hermès scarf he ends up using as a barber's cape, these things are too precious *not* to use while he has them.

Following the overwhelming success of this book, Yamamoto succumbed to the depression she had been fighting all her life, and she stopped writing for nearly six years, spending this time supported by her second husband and moving between institutional and home care. Then, in 2007, she returned to writing, publishing a diary of these years spent dealing with mental illness. Indeed, Yamamoto had published diaristic writing before this as well, in women's magazines and on her own home page; as this collection attests, there is something a bit diaristic about the first-person narration she tends to employ in her fiction as well. After the success of this chronicle of her depression, she returned to writing fiction, which culminated in the 2020 publication of the novel *Rotating while Revolving*, an expansive portrait of a woman's self-discovery that became one of her most acclaimed works, winning the 2021 Chūō Kōron Prize and Shimase Romantic Literature Prize, as well as being nominated for the Japan Booksellers' Award. In a cruel irony, though, during the same year she was receiving some of the greatest acclaim and recognition of her career, she was diagnosed with stage 4 pancreatic cancer. Upon her diagnosis, she decided to keep a diary of her life with this disease, a chronicle that, in the end, includes entries up to nine days before her untimely death in November of 2021 at the age of fifty-eight. Published posthumously the next year under the title *A Deserted Island for Two: A Diary of Having to Make Myself Live 120 Days More*, this final testament to her commitment to giving clear-eyed, witty voice to even the most difficult aspects of life has gone on to become one of her most beloved works.

In an interview given in 2000, right after she won the Eiji Yoshikawa Prize and just before winning the Naoki, Yamamoto describes the trajectory of her success as a series of choices to run away:

> "I've spent my life running away from whatever I don't like. I realized I could only stand being the 'good girl' society wanted me to be for about four days a week, so I ran away from my life as an office lady; I got married but realized that

wasn't the life for me, so ran away from that; I realized I disliked working within the rigid framework of the 'girls' novel,' and so I ran away from that too. I've kept running and running and ended up here, which makes me think, well, maybe it's better not to put up with things—that it's best just to run away" (*éf magazine*, September 2000).

As the interviewer points out, looked at another way, this is a tale of strength, of Yamamoto choosing not to compromise in how she wishes to live her life, of her standing on her own two feet on her own terms. It's hard to read Yamamoto's self-deprecating descriptions of her life choices and not be reminded of the women she writes about in her fiction, who tend to describe themselves as twisted or perverse even as readers can clearly see their resilience and strength. Yamamoto's sly, perspicacious voice beguiles us into total sympathy with her characters even as she allows us to view them critically as well; in this way, her fiction speaks beyond the specifics of its time to resonate even now, over twenty years later. It helps that ongoing economic precarity has become a worldwide, rather than Japan-specific, condition, which lends immediacy to her characters' predicaments. But it is in her emotional acuity—the way her writing allows us to access and recognize complex emotions that usually remain nameless in our everyday lives and even in most fiction—that her writing achieves the timelessness necessary to speak to us beyond the time and place of its initial creation and reach us where we live, right here and right now.

—Brian Bergstrom
July 2024, Montréal, Canada

Here ends Fumio Yamamoto's
The Dilemmas of Working Women.

The first edition of this book was printed
and bound at Lakeside Book Company
in Harrisonburg, Virginia, in July 2025.

A NOTE ON THE TYPE

The text of this novel was set in Chaparral Pro, a typeface designed by Carol Twombly that combines the legibility of nineteenth-century slab serif designs with sixteenth-century roman book lettering. Its versatile, hybrid design allows accessibility and clarity in all text settings. Chaparral Pro remains true to its sixteenth-century print origins and has since become a popular standard for many print applications.

HarperVia

An imprint dedicated to publishing international voices,
offering readers a chance to encounter other lives and other
points of view via the language of the imagination.